Praise for the Nick and Nora Mystery Series

"This mystery is rock star exciting—Nick and Nora are a hoot. I was hooked from start to finish!"
—Laura Childs, *New York Times* Bestselling author

"Nick and Nora are a winning team"
—Rebecca Hale, *New York Times* Bestselling author

"A fast-paced cozy mystery spiced with a dash of romance and topped with a big slice of 'cat-titude.'"
—Ali Brandon, *New York Times* Bestselling author

"Nick and Nora are the purr-fect sleuth duo!"
—Victoria Laurie, *New York Times* Bestselling author

"Excellently plotted and executed—five paws and a tail up for this tale."
—*Open Book Society*

"Nick brims with street smarts and feline charisma, you'd think he was human . . . an exciting new series."
—Carole Nelson Douglas, *New York Times* notable author of the Midnight Louie mysteries

"I love this series and each new story quickly becomes my favorite. Cannot wait for the next!"
—*Escape With Dollycas Into a Good Book*

"I totally loved this lighthearted and engagingly entertaining whodunit featuring new amateur sleuth Nora Charles and Nick, her feline companion."
—*Dru's Cozy Report*

Books by T. C. LoTempio

Nick and Nora Mysteries

Meow If It's Murder
Claws for Alarm
Crime and Catnip
Hiss H for Homicide
Murder Faux Paws
A Purr Before Dying
Bell, Book and Corpses

Urban Tails Pet Shop Mysteries

The Time for Murder is Meow
Killers of a Feather
Death Steals the Spotlight
Cats, Carats and Killers

Cat Rescue Mysteries

Purr M for Murder
Death by a Whisker

Bell, Book and Corpses

A Nick and Nora Mystery

T. C. LoTempio

Acknowledgments

Many thanks, as always, to my agent, Josh Getzler, and his assistant, Jon Cobb. I am also extremely thankful to have Bill Harris as the editor for Nick and Nora. Sometimes I think he loves them more than I do!

And, as always, many thanks to all the fans who support and buy the Nick and Nora series. It couldn't continue without your support, and I value each and every one of you!

To Mary Kennedy—a superb writer and an even better friend!

<u>Prologue</u>

Manny didn't believe in ghosts, or the supernatural—although in retrospect, he probably should have.

After all, he'd been born in Salem, Massachusetts. Everyone there was practically weaned on tales of witchcraft and the like. Fortunately for him, his family had moved to California when he was six, and his father had always been a scientific sort of fellow—more interested in what he could see, feel and touch, not in something that was, for the most part, figments of someone's fertile imagination. *Thank God I took after you, Dad,* Manny thought. To his mind, people these days read too much Stephen King and not enough Isaac Asimov.

There were no such things as ghosts, or witches, or . . . even worse, vampires. He gave a soft chuckle. What was the fascination with the living dead, anyway? People had been carrying on a love affair with them ever since Bram Stoker wrote *Dracula.* Although, he had to admit, he'd found the Christopher Lee movies quite amusing. But the thought of anyone sustaining life by actually drinking someone else's blood made him want to puke.

He paused at the crest of the hill and glanced at the mansion silhouetted against the full moon. He had to admit, Waincroft Manor certainly looked like the kind of place a chap like Dracula would call home. With its sloping roof, wide gables, rounded windows and black shutters, the ancient mansion looked like the perfect place to film a horror movie—or hold a Halloween Festival, like he'd heard that real estate woman talking about at the Poker Face night before last. According to her, the deal was sealed. People were supposed to be coming tomorrow to look the place over, see how much cleaning had to be done to get it in shape.

That's why he couldn't put it off any longer. He had to get in there *now.*

He jumped as he felt a slight vibration at his hip, grinned sheepishly when he realized it was his cell phone. He'd left it on vibrate. He pulled it out, glanced at the number before hitting the answer button. "Thanks for calling back," he said, fighting a sudden urge to whisper. "I'll meet you in an hour at the usual spot. No, I'm not playing any games. You won't be disappointed, I promise."

He rang off, slid the phone back into his pocket, and then paused. For a minute he thought he heard the sound of someone cackling, far off in the distance. He passed a hand over his eyes and shook his head; as he did so, a giant crow flew right over him—a huge beast, with a giant wingspan, almost as big as an eagle's. The crow circled, then lit on the branch of a nearby tree and sat, its black beady eyes fixed right on him.

"Caw. Caw."

"Yeah, yeah." Manny let out a long sigh and swore softly under his breath. "You and me both."

• • •

He had the back door open in less than three minutes. The years hadn't diminished his talent for picking locks, and the ancient ones in these doors were child's play for him. He let himself in, pausing for a moment to let his eyes adjust to the abject blackness, then made his way toward the parlor. Just as he got to the double doors he froze in his tracks.

Out of the corner of his eye, he saw something move in the dark shadows that surrounded the circular staircase off to his left. It had been swift, a blur of movement, but it had definitely been something. Gathering all his courage, he called out in a raspy tone, "Who's there?"

Silence.

He laid his hand on the handle of the parlor door and felt a tingle go up his spine, like an electric shock. He sensed, rather than felt, the presence of someone behind him.

Or was it some*thing*?

He whirled, ducking as something dark and slimy flew past him. He peered upward and made out the outline of a pair of wings, two beady eyes.

Manny started to laugh. "A bat! That's all it was. Just a bat."

Still, he wasn't taking any chances. He whipped the parchment from his jacket pocket, ripped it down the middle. He tiptoed back into the tiny room just beyond the alcove and walked directly to a square of the wood floor he knew was loose. Prying it open, he shoved half of his prize into the dark cavity, then replaced the square and made his way back to the parlor. He'd barely stepped inside when that feeling of being watched swept over him again.

"Give it to me," said a gruff voice behind him.

Manny whirled and found himself looking into what he could only describe as a grinning skull. Moonlight streaming in through the large picture window reflected off the shiny bald pate, bathing the newcomer in a sinister light. "Give it to me," the figure repeated.

Manny took an involuntary step backward. "Give what to you? I don't know what you mean?"

"Oh, yes, you do. I know you found it, I saw you. Give it to me."

Manny turned and started to run, but then another dark-caped figure emerged out of the shadows, blocking his way. The second figure raised its arm and Manny saw it held a dripping syringe.

"What the heck?"

The first figure spun Manny around, roughly pulled his jacket off. His fingers closed over the map, and his face twisted into an ugly sneer when he saw there was only half there. "What did you do with the other half?"

"I ate it," Manny shot back. "You'll never get it."

"That's a shame," the figure said softly. "It seems you leave me no choice."

Manny shrugged free of his grasp and darted around the other figure out of the parlor and into the hall. Behind him he heard the gentle pad of footsteps. No time to escape out the back, he reasoned, and careened down the hallway toward the front door. He lunged for the door handle, twisted it—and nothing happened. Frantic, he pulled harder.

The door was stuck.

His breath came faster, and the pounding in his chest was so hard he felt sure people in Cruz could hear it. He tugged harder on the handle. Behind him, he could hear the soft pad of footsteps. Someone . . . or something . . . coming closer . . . closer . . .

His breath wheezing out in short, uneven gasps, he pulled down hard on the handle and the door suddenly swung inward, almost smacking him in the face. He thought, for a brief instant, of glancing over his shoulder, but then quickly abandoned that idea and launched himself onto the front porch, letting the door slam shut behind him with a resounding *thud!* He leaned against the railing, huffing and puffing. He knew they wouldn't be pleased that he had nothing to give them, but maybe he could put them off a day or two, get someone to come back out here with him, maybe in the daylight . . .

A shadow slipped out of the darkness of the porch. Manny saw the hand raise out of the corner of his eye, felt a sharp *thwack!* at the base of his skull and then . . .

Darkness.

Chapter One

"Here we are. What do you think?"

I eyed the enormous mansion and bit back a shudder. A vision of every old Hammer horror flick I'd ever watched on late-night TV flashed through my mind and I shot my BFF, Chantal Gillard, a dubious look. "Wow, do you think Gomez and Morticia are at home?"

Chantal barked out a laugh. "Actually, I think this place might have given Charles Addams a few nightmares," she said, with a cautious glance toward the crumbling edifice.

"Why would anyone want to host a charity event here?" I murmured. "It's like they want to scare everyone into being generous."

"Well, Kay Trilby got it into her head it was the perfect place to hold a Halloween gala, and you know Kay."

I certainly did. When it came to wealth and influence, Kay Trilby was right up there with Violet Crenshaw. A widow who'd inherited millions from her deceased husband number two, she was very active in community affairs. I'd catered several fundraisers for her over the past year, everything from a casual cookout to elegant sit-down dinners. Kay had recently decided to make the Cruz Youth Club one of her pet charities and had been working tirelessly to ensure its success. The club had always been funded through the town budget, helped along by generous donations from wealthy patrons, but the last few years had seen some of the patrons die off and its budget had suffered some severe cuts. Actually, I was glad Kay decided to get involved. The charity would surely flourish under her wing.

Chantal chuckled. "Kay certainly worked her magic on you. Free catering for the gala, plus help with the cleanup."

"I'm glad to do it," I said. "Although if the inside's as bad as the outside, I hope we can get the place ready in time. The gala's only three weeks away."

"Joannie said she doesn't think the inside is too bad. She came here the other day for a quick look-see. Said it just looked deserted and dusty. Lots of white-sheeted furniture."

"Um, well, I guess that's to be expected. No one's lived here in what? Fifty, sixty years?"

"More like a hundred," my friend answered. She lowered her tone to a mere whisper. "All because of the curse of Waincroft Manor. You remember that story, *chérie?*"

"Vaguely. Things like that don't interest me the way they do you." My friend has psychic abilities, and she's a big believer in things that go bump in the night.

Chantal tossed me a sly glance. "Hm, what does interest you lately, Nora?"

"I've been experimenting with some smoothie recipes," I said. I'd recently purchased a used smoothie machine with the proceeds from Nick's television debut on a popular daytime drama. Even though his scenes had been cut, he'd still been paid, and I had an idea it was because he—and I—had been instrumental in solving a cold case and bringing the killer to justice. "A lot of them call for coconut water, so I put an order in at the farmer's market for a case. There's one in particular I'm anxious to try. They call it Coconut-Banana Delight."

Chantal waved her hand. "All well and good, but I was thinking more along the lines of a certain dark-haired former head of Homicide turned FBI agent?" Her lips curved upward in a cat-ate-the-canary grin, and I knew why.

A few weeks ago I'd made the decision to start dating FBI agent Leroy Samms. Samms and I had shared a brief, intimate moment back in college and neither of us could deny there was a certain amount of chemistry between us. My sister and Chantal had been urging me to give the guy a break for months, and now that the man I'd currently been dating, FBI agent Daniel Corleone, had accepted a top secret assignment in London with no visible end date, I'd run out of excuses.

"You know, chérie," Chantal said, "I am not one to say I told you so, but . . . things are going well, are they not?"

"They are considering Samms's schedule is even worse than Daniel's was, especially now that they're short-handed. But we did manage to get to the multiplex at Branson to see the new Robert Downey Jr. movie last week, and the week before that we tried out the new seafood place in Monterey." I let out a small sigh. "I do enjoy his company, and we have fun. Still . . ."

"There is a part of you that misses Daniel," Chantal finished as I grew silent.

"It's more like feeling guilty," I admitted, "even though he practically gave me his blessing to date. Lacey thinks I'm nuts. She has no problem dating both Hal Frey and Peter Dobbs."

Chantal raised an eyebrow. "Peter is back in the picture?"

I nodded. "She was out with one of her friends and ran into him. Apparently time heals all wounds and they kissed and made up. Literally."

"Hm," Chantal muttered. "How do the men in question feel about it?"

"Lacey made it very clear to both of them that they're not exclusive, and there are no strings attached. Apparently both of them like her well enough to accept it."

"Well, you and your sister are two distinct temperaments. Lacey's specialty is playing the field, but you, Nora Charles, are definitely a one-man woman. Your problem is deciding which man."

"True. Unless, as you said, the Universe has already made that decision for me."

"That sounds rather ominous." Chantal raised a brow. "You think Daniel gave you permission to date because he thought he might not return from this mission?"

"He didn't come out and say that, but he did say it was a dangerous mission." I felt a bit uncomfortable discussing this, so I stole a quick glance at my watch. "It's getting late. Should we wait for Joannie or take a look inside ourselves?"

"Owrrr?"

We both glanced toward the backseat of Chantal's convertible, where the large black and white cat who'd been asleep there now raised his head and opened one golden eye to stare at us. The cat formerly known as Sherlock had belonged to a now MIA private eye, but when I'd adopted him (or rather, when *he'd* adopted *me*) Chantal had christened him Nick, after my favorite fictional detective (a no-brainer, since my name is Nora Charles). Nick has a definite talent for detection, and his abilities can be downright spooky at times, particularly his penchant for spelling out a pertinent clue with his favorite toy, Scrabble tiles. Together we've managed to solve a few mysteries, with the exception of the one I considered the most puzzling of all: the whereabouts of his former human, PI (and possibly spy?) Nick Atkins.

Chantal leaned into the backseat. "What's the matter, Nicky," she crooned. "Did we disturb your beauty sleep?"

"Owrrr," Nick said again, and this time closed his eye and put his paw across his face.

I laughed outright. "I think he wants us to hurry up and get this over with so we can get home. He prefers to take his naps in front of my refrigerator."

Chantal reached over to give Nick a pat on the white streak behind his ear. "He is probably impatient to get home. He must sense that I have some new collars I want him to model later."

Another *grr* from the backseat and I sighed. "Remind me again why I brought him along."

"You didn't," Chantal said and giggled. "He snuck in the backseat, remember?"

"Ah, yes." I cocked an eyebrow at my cat, who now lay on his back, all four paws in the air. "You have a distinct talent for that, don't you, Nick?"

One paw wriggled as Nick winked an eye open. *"Grrr."*

I laughed. "And that is that. Nick apparently doesn't want to be disturbed, so what do you think? Wait for Joannie or brave the mansion alone?"

A horn honked just then and a silver Cadillac pulled abreast of us. A trim woman wearing a black and white houndstooth jacket, frilly white blouse and black slim skirt alighted from the driver's seat with a jaunty wave. "Sorry to be late," Joannie Adams sang out. "I got a bit hung up at the office."

We exited the convertible and Chantal gave me a swift poke in the ribs. "Oh? Were you showing Ethan Howell another house?"

Joannie's cheeks flushed a bright pink. Ethan Howell was one of Cruz's newer residents. He'd moved here a few weeks ago and rented a shopfront on Main Street, where he sold musical instruments and offered guitar lessons. Joannie had brought him into Hot Bread for lunch one afternoon after showing him some houses, and he'd seemed pleasant enough, if not a tad condescending. I remembered Joannie fawning all over him, and I was pretty certain a fat commission wasn't the only reason behind her coquettish behavior. He wasn't particularly good-looking, but as Chantal put it later, Ethan fit Joannie's stringent requirements for a man: eligible and breathing. We were also convinced that Joannie's volunteering to head the decorating committee stemmed from the fact that Ethan had also volunteered to be on that committee. Yep, she was out to impress, all right, but as far as we could tell, so far she hadn't succeeded. Ethan hadn't asked her out as far as we knew.

Pink cheeks notwithstanding, the corners of Joannie's lips pulled down and she gave her head a quick shake. "Oh, no, I've had it with that man. It seems like he's perfectly satisfied to stay at the Cruz Inn forever."

"And why not," Chantal remarked with a chuckle. "Think about it. He doesn't have to worry about housekeeping, they offer a complimentary continental breakfast, they have free appetizers every evening in the bar area that one could make a meal out of. It seems pretty ideal for a single guy."

"Too ideal," Joannie sniffed. "Anyway, he doesn't act like a guy who wants to put down roots, but I could be wrong. It's just a gut feeling." She tapped at her stomach.

Chantal and I exchanged a quick look and I flashed the realtor a smile. "Yeah, I get those too. They can be amazingly accurate." I swept my arm in the direction of the house. "I guess we should go inside and see what sort of cleanup job awaits us?"

As we made our way toward the house, Chantal remarked, "I'm a bit surprised Enola agreed to put the family house on display. She was always a private sort of person." Enola Waincroft had been in our graduating class at Cruz High. She'd always been considered one of the "odd ones," showing up for class in her signature black cape, her dark eyes ringed with kohl eyeliner. "I always liked her though."

"I did too. I thought that moving in with her aunt in San Francisco after her parents died might have made her a bit more outgoing, but . . ." Joannie shrugged. "She still seems as reclusive as ever, although when Kay contacted her about renting out the mansion, she didn't put up a fuss. As a matter of fact, she donated its use for free."

"She did? That was pretty generous," Chantal remarked.

"More like clever," Joannie said with a wise nod. "She knew darn well the place would have to be cleaned top to bottom before Kay would host a fundraiser here. It was a golden opportunity for her. After all, she's going to have to sell it someday. The taxes on it must take up a good chunk of her income. A good cleaning might make it more attractive to a prospective buyer, if they can get past the house's history." Joannie's nose wrinkled as she added, "Even though it's obscure, people know enough to be leery of it. And that," she finished with a light laugh, "is the trouble with old houses and small towns."

As we approached the mansion, it was evident years of neglect had taken a definite toll. Heat and rain had pummeled the mansion's wooden exterior, stripping away the paint and rendering it a dull-looking prison gray. The front veranda tilted at a dangerous angle, and the steps were old and rickety. A tangle of weeds spoiled what must have once been a perfectly manicured lawn. Thick patches of ivy and moss ran up one entire side of the building.

And this was only the outside.

We all paused before the steps and Joannie looked around, shielding her eyes from the harsh midafternoon sun with her hand. "Eddie McGee said he'd take care of some light landscaping so the grounds would be presentable. Boy, is he in for a surprise." Joannie chuckled. "He's got his work cut out for him."

"Well, what can you expect from a place that's been deserted for centuries?" I said.

"Touché. Guess we might as well bite the bullet and see what the inside looks like. Ah, I see you brought your bodyguard along, eh, Nora? He might come in handy, especially if there's a rat or two lurking about in there."

I followed the direction of Joannie's gaze and saw Nick just off to my left, his tail curling behind him in the air like a large question mark. Chantal let out a squeal. "Nicky! How did you get out? The car was locked."

"Little things like a locked car never stop Nick from getting where he wants to go," I said. The cat in question tipped up his lips and blinked at me, and I bent over and scooped him up. No easy feat, since my tubby tuxedo weighs well over twenty-two pounds. I looked him straight in the eye. "You rascal. I thought you were sleeping, but you weren't. Playing possum, huh?"

Nick ducked his head and started to purr.

I carried him up the steps but set him down immediately once we were on the porch. We all went over to peer in the giant picture window. The room beyond appeared to be anything but empty. Tables, chairs, even pictures seemed to peer out from behind white coverings. "Looks like a lot of stuff is in there," I observed. "Most of it will have to be cleared out."

"The interior doesn't appear to be too bad, though," said Chantal, pressing her nose to the glass. "It just looks like all it might need is a good dusting."

Joannie let out a loud grunt. "Dammit," she grumbled. "I can't find the key, and I was certain I put it in here."

"Maybe you don't need it." I inclined my head toward the front door, which appeared to be slightly ajar. I walked over and was about to press my fingertips against the wood when suddenly the door burst open and a young boy stood on the threshold. I judged him to be in his early teens—thirteen, no more than fifteen. His hair was mussed, his pumpkin-colored jacket dirty and torn, and his eyes held a wild gleam. He started to barrel past me but I caught his arm and swung him around.

"Hey, who are you? What were you doing in there?"

He looked at me, eyes wide, and tried to jerk away, but I held on fast. "What's wrong with you? What were you doing in that house?" I asked again.

"Yeah," chimed in Joannie. "It's private property. We have permission to be here."

His eyes darted nervously around and he mumbled something under his breath. I wasn't quite sure what I'd heard, but before I could ask him to repeat it, he reached out, gave me a push, and went flying down the steps and across the lawn.

"*Mon Dieu,*" cried Chantal as she helped me to my feet. "Are you all right?"

I nodded. "I'm fine. Did you see where that boy went? Something spooked him."

"I think he cut through the woods," Chantal answered. "Should we go after him? He's got a pretty good head start."

I was about to answer in the affirmative when I caught a flash of black slip through the doorway and into the house. "Oh, swell. I think Nick just went inside."

I turned toward the door but Joannie grabbed my arm. "You're not going in there," she whispered.

"Joannie has a point," Chantal piped up. "That boy was pretty scared. Who knows what he found."

I set my jaw. "Don't worry, I'll be careful. I just don't want Nick to get lost." I slipped inside before either of them could protest and stood for a minute in the entryway, letting my eyes adjust to the darkness. "Nick," I called. "Hey, Nick. Where are you, buddy?"

A soft meow came from the darkness beyond.

I moved carefully down the dark corridor in that direction, wishing I had a flashlight. I turned a corner and jumped as I came face-to-face with a white-faced object, then let out a sigh of relief as I saw it was a statue underneath a white cover to keep off the dust. Nick was nowhere to be seen. I called his name out several times, but no answering meow came forth.

"This is no time to play hide and seek, Nick," I muttered. By now I'd come to the end of the corridor, which branched out in three directions. I did a quick eeny, meeny, miney, moe and started down the corridor to my right. I'd only taken a few steps when the corridor opened into a large dark room. As my eyes grew accustomed to the dark interior, I could make out a large lump on the floor in front of us. A long, angular lump with a rounded top and big brass handles.

A coffin.

"Good Lord," I murmured. "Who puts a coffin in a living room?"

I frowned. Obviously this was someone's idea of a joke, and no doubt what had scared that boy. Kids and their practical jokes. I walked over and grasped the coffin lid. As my fingers curled around the brass handle, Nick suddenly leapt out of the shadows and hurled himself on top of the coffin. He stood there, a true caricature of a Halloween cat, his back arched, tail fanned and spread out, every hair visible. His golden eyes gleamed and his lips drew back in a snarl. He let out a loud hiss.

"Nick!" I reached out, grabbed Nick and lifted him off the coffin. His tail returned to normal size, but his eyes remained slitted and there was no mistaking the growl that rose, deep in his throat. I spoke in a soothing tone. "Nick, calm down. There's nothing in here, see . . . oh!"

I'd raised the lid as I was speaking, and now I let it fall back with a loud crash. Dead silence prevailed as I stared at the coffin's contents: a man who looked like a vagrant, curled on his side, face a sickly white, his lips bloodless. But that wasn't what captured my attention.

It was the two red-tinged holes on his neck.

Chapter Two

Blue and red strobes from the police cruiser played across the porch. The Cruz PD had responded in record time to my 911 call. Two officers got out and hurried over to us. One looked as if he'd just graduated high school. He sported sandy hair with a stubborn cowlick, slightly mottled skin that spoke of a teenaged bout with acne, and a firm, prominent jaw. His name tag read *Officer Bolton*. The other I recognized at once from his frequent coffee runs to Hot Bread; Milton Fielding, mid-fifties, paunchy and balding. The two of them listened as I explained what had happened, but when I got to the part about the body in the coffin the two of them exchanged a wary glance.

"A . . . coffin, you say?" Milton's tone held a note of incredulity and the two officers exchanged a glance that said, plainer than words, *is she crazy*? "What was it, one of the decorations for that gala? Or someone's idea of a joke?"

"The latter was my first thought," I said dryly, "until I saw the contents."

"If that don't beat all. A coffin in a house," Milton muttered as he scribbled in his notebook. "Guess I shouldn't be too surprised though, considering where we are." He motioned to Officer Bolton. "We'll have a look. Can you show us where it is?"

I nodded. "Yes, but first there's something else you should know. There was a young boy in the house when we got here. He came barreling out like his pants were on fire, knocked me over, and took off across that field."

The officers looked at each other, then at me. "A trespasser, eh." Fielding shook his head. "What is it about Halloween that brings out the worst in kids? They're always sneaking into one deserted house or another around this time; although they usually stay away from this place."

"You didn't see his face when he came barreling out of the house. He looked positively terrified."

"Well, sure. Young boy, nosing around a creepy mansion. He probably found the coffin and opened it too." Fielding reached up to scratch at his forehead. "Did you see which way he went?"

I pointed toward the thick expanse of woods that spanned the left side of the hill. "He cut across the field and went into the woods, oh, it must be a half hour at least."

"Hm, he's got a good head start. No telling where he might be." He jabbed a porky finger in Bolton's direction. "Larry, get in the patrol car and see if you can find any trace of that kid." He turned back to me. "What's he look like?"

"Around thirteen, on the slender side. Dark hair, an olive complexion and dark eyes. He had on faded blue jeans and an orange windbreaker that looked as if it had seen better days."

Bolton shot me a grudging look. "Pretty good description," he muttered. He turned his head slightly and called over his shoulder, "Got that, Larry?"

Larry looked up from his notebook. "Yep. Thirteen, worn jeans, dirty orange windbreaker, brunette hair and complexion." He snapped the notebook shut and with another wary glance my way hurried down the steps, got into the patrol car and whizzed off, siren blaring.

I shook my head and glanced at Milton. "That siren's likely to do more harm than good. It'll probably frighten him more than he already is if he thinks the police are after him for trespassing."

Milton shot me a hard look then pulled out his cell and dialed a number. "Larry, cut the siren. It might scare the boy." He hung up, and a few seconds later we heard the siren shut off. He slid the phone back into his pocket and motioned to me. "Now then, want to show me where that body is?"

• • •

A half hour later Joannie, Chantal and I were all sitting on the porch steps. After I'd shown Milton the body, and he'd exclaimed "Oh my goodness" about a dozen times, he'd made some more phone calls and asked us to stay put for a while. Two more cruisers arrived, with more officers I didn't recognize, two of whom took statements from Joannie and Chantal. There was still no sign of Larry Bolton or of the teenaged boy who'd taken off like a bat out of hell. Nick sat next to me, his head and front paws in my lap, snoring peacefully. I stroked him on the white streak behind his ear. "I'm glad this is all a walk in the park to you," I said. Nick winked one eye open, blinked, and resumed snoring.

The coroner's wagon arrived, and two EMTs hurried up the steps and inside, dragging their equipment with them. Another police cruiser pulled up and a trim figure alighted. Dale Anderson, the current head of Cruz Homicide, glanced over, saw us all sitting on the porch, and her lips

13

thinned. She walked over to one of the patrol cars and leaned inside to talk to the officer who sat there. They conversed for a few minutes, then Dale shook her head and made a beeline for where we were sitting.

"Well, well, Nora Charles," Dale said. Her gaze raked over me, then moved to Nick. "And your cat too. I see you've found another body. What else is new, other than this time you've added to your entourage?" She glanced over at Chantal and Joannie, then reached into her jacket pocket and whipped out a pad and pen. "I'd like to hear your account of what happened, please."

I repeated the afternoon's events just as they had happened. Dale listened intently to what I said, pausing to scribble something down on her pad every now and then. When I finished, she waved at Chantal and Joannie. "How about you two? Have you anything to add to Ms. Charles's account?"

Chantal shook her head, and Joannie said, "Not a thing. Nora covered it very well. Listen, Detective Anderson, would it be possible for me to leave? We weren't supposed to be here this long and"—she tapped at her watch face—"I have an urgent appointment that I'll just about make."

Dale's eyes swept over Joannie. "I'm afraid I'll have to ask you to postpone your appointment, Ms. Adams. This is a potential murder investigation."

Joannie's shoulders shot back. "I could of course but the appointment is with one of the gala sponsors. Kay Trilby, to be precise. Like I said before, Nora's covered it all. I really can't add anything to what's already been said."

Anderson's well-shaped brows drew together, and I could tell she was torn between duty and politics. Kay's late husband number one had been a sergeant on the Cruz police force, and she'd always been a heavy contributor to the Policeman's Retirement Fund in his memory. Investigation or not, Anderson knew what side of the bread the butter was on. Bottom line: it was best not to irritate Kay Trilby. After a few moments her slim shoulders lifted in a shrug and she bit out a sigh. "All right, you can go, but stay available. I'll need a more formal statement so I'll either need you to come to the station later or else I'll send an officer to take it."

Joannie held up her cell. "I'll be available, I promise." She turned to us, mouthed "sorry" and then took off down the steps and over to her car. A few seconds later she pealed out of the drive like her tires were on fire.

"Kay Trilby my ass," whispered Chantal.

I looked at my friend. "You think Joannie lied about meeting Kay?"

"Probably not, but it wouldn't surprise me if she's got something lined up with Ethan for right after."

I chuckled. "It wouldn't surprise me either."

Dale shot us a dark look. "What are the two of you whispering about? Never mind, I probably don't want to know." She fastened her gaze on me. "I know how observant you are, Nora. Aced that in your PI class, didn't you?" Without waiting for me to answer, she brandished her pen and asked, "Did you see any noticeable wounds or marks on the victim?"

"Nothing other than some blood around the two red, round holes on his neck."

Dale's eyebrows shot up. "Excuse me? Did you say two holes on his *neck*?"

"Yep. The way he was positioned inside the coffin they were very noticeable."

Her hand stilled, poised over the paper. "Inside the . . . what did you say?"

"Coffin. Didn't Fielding tell you?"

"He just said a body was found inside the mansion. No one mentioned that it was *in a coffin*." She muttered something else under her breath and scribbled furiously in her notebook. "Okay, so you opened the coffin. You didn't touch anything else, right?"

"Heck, no. I just grabbed Nick and we got out of there. I called 911 and Officers Fielding and Bolton were outside pronto."

Dale muttered something under her breath and snapped her notebook shut. "Did either one of you see anyone other than this boy lurking around?"

Both Chantal and I shook our heads.

"Okay, well . . ." She slid the notebook into her pocket. "Thanks for your time. You're free to go, but stay available too, in case I have more questions."

"I have one," Chantal piped up. "What will this do to the plans for the gala?"

"A good question," Dale said. She swiped at her brow with the tips of her fingers before answering. "As of right now, Waincroft Manor is a crime scene. We have to collect all pertinent data and process it before I can release anything, so I'm afraid you'll have to put any decorating plans on hold for now. I'm sure that decision won't be a popular one, but it's procedure." With another sharp look, she turned on her heel and walked back down the steps and over to one of the cruisers.

Chantal's lips twisted into a wry smile. "That does not sound encouraging. I would suggest the committee look for another venue, like the Cruz Museum, but I am ninety-nine percent sure Kay Trilby wouldn't go for it. Dead body or not, she's got her heart set on having it here. And Kay hates to be disappointed."

We'd reached the bottom of the steps just as a dark sedan came careening down the hill, screeching to a stop just behind Dale's police cruiser. I watched, my breath caught in the back of my throat, as Leroy Samms climbed from the driver's side of the vehicle. His blue-black hair was combed straight off his high forehead and his muscled body was encased in tight blue jeans and a tan windbreaker. His dark eyes scanned the scene, and when his gaze fell on me he immediately walked over to where we stood. "I should have known you'd be here, once I heard about the body," he said with a smile.

I made a face at him. "Very funny. What are you doing here? This isn't an FBI matter—is it?"

He shrugged. "Dale called me and asked me to come out. Probably wants to consult on something."

"Uh-huh." I frowned. Even though Samms insisted there was nothing between him and the pretty lieutenant except friendship, I got a distinctly different vibe. Almost as if to prove my point, Anderson appeared at that moment. She walked right up to Samms and laid her hand possessively on his arm.

"Thanks for getting here so quickly, Lee," she said. "There's something here I think you'll be very interested in."

"Okay then, Dale. Lead the way." Samms looked over at me. "I'll give you a call later tonight, okay?" Without waiting for me to answer, he turned to follow Dale up the steps of the mansion. I stood watching them for a moment. They paused on the steps, Anderson practically attached to his hip, talking earnestly. Samms stood, head cocked, listening, but I saw his gaze stray more than once in my direction.

I jumped as Chantal nudged me with her elbow. "He cannot keep his eyes off of you. That is a good sign, chérie." Her gaze shifted to the policewoman. "I think you are right, though. I get the distinct impression Dale's feelings for Samms are more than just professional."

"Which explains why I never get that warm and fuzzy feeling around her." I sighed. "It's too bad. In a Samms-less world, I think Dale and I might have become good friends. I've always admired her work ethic."

Chantal rolled her eyes. "Uh-huh."

We walked over to Chantal's convertible, and I was just about to step in when memory kicked in. I slapped my forehead with my palm. "I just remembered something I should tell Anderson. Wait here with Nick. I'll only be a minute."

I hurried back to where Dale and Samms stood, their backs to me, their heads bent close together. Out of the corner of my eye I saw two more EMTs head up the steps, dragging a gurney. As I approached, I heard Dale's voice distinctly.

"Once my man radioed in the description I knew you'd be interested. Never in a million years did I expect a coffin . . ." Her voice trailed off as she caught sight of me, and her lips arranged themselves into a hard, thin line. "Yes, Nora? Did you need something?"

I moved forward. "I'm sorry to interrupt, but there's something I neglected to tell you." As Dale's eyebrow rose I added, "It might be important."

Dale hesitated, and Samms said, "Go on, Dale, see what Nora has to say. I'll wait for you to go in." He flashed me a quick smile, then turned and hurried up the rest of the steps. Dale let out a long sigh and turned to me, hands on hips. She cleared her throat. Loudly. "So? What is this something important you want to tell me?"

"It's about the boy who ran out of the mansion. He muttered something under his breath right before he took off. I'm not entirely certain, but it sounded like 'before he gets us.'"

Anderson frowned. "You think he might have witnessed the murder?"

"Either that, or he saw the person responsible. And if that person has any idea he's been seen, that boy could be in real danger."

"I'll make sure my men are on it. Thanks for all your help." Dale nodded curtly, then turned and walked up the mansion steps. She joined Samms and then the two of them went inside. I walked back to Chantal's convertible and slid into the passenger seat. Chantal leaned over and peered at me.

"Well, you appear to be unscathed," she said.

I tossed her a rueful grin. "For now. Anderson didn't seem very interested in what I had to say, but . . ."

"*Er-ooo.*"

We turned around. Nick stood up in the backseat, his back arched, tail sticking straight up, every hair standing on end.

"Nick, what's the matter?" I cried. "Why are you howling?"

He let out another mournful yowl just as two EMTs emerged from the house, wheeling the gurney, which now had a black sack on it. *"Er-ooo,"* he wailed again.

I reached over and stroked his head, murmuring softly to him. Finally he stretched back out on the seat, head on paws, and shut his eyes. A few minutes later he started to purr.

Chantal started up the car and pulled out of the driveway. "Goodness, I'm glad you calmed him down. What got him so upset, I wonder?"

"They say animals have psychic senses, right? Well, apparently Nick can sense there's something off about all this—really off."

Chantal frowned. "Chérie, what do you mean?"

"Truthfully? My first thought when I saw that body was that the whole tableaux had been staged."

Nick winked one eye open, then lifted his head. *"Er-ooo,"* he wailed.

My cat apparently agreed with my deduction. But who would want to stage such a macabre scene? And why?

Chapter Three

It was a little after nine a.m. the next morning. My usual breakfast rush had dissipated somewhat after I'd taken care of all the people eager to try my new special, the Chris Evans Hotcake Sandwich: a sunny-side-up egg, slab of ham and slice of bacon between two pancakes. Of course, my busiest morning would naturally be the one when I had to go it alone: Chantal had to help Remy with a big order, my sister Lacey was nursing a bad cold (or so she said—I suspected she just wanted to lay in bed and watch the Johnny Depp marathon on cable all day), and Mollie Travis, the high school senior who helped me out most mornings, was on a field trip with her botany class. I'd just served my last customer and was looking forward to a hot cup of java and some quality alone time when the bell above my shop door tinkled. I sighed and turned back to the counter, prepared to offer my spiel, and then stopped as I saw the smiling countenance of the man who stood there.

I first met Oliver J. Sampson, aka Ollie, when I was trying to track down Nick's original owner. Ollie was Nick Atkins's partner, and it wasn't long before the two of us struck up a friendship. Ollie has the utmost respect for my sleuthing abilities, and supported me all through my PI course. He'd like nothing better than for me to give up making sandwiches and work with him full-time. He's a large man of color, with springy gray hair and eyes to match, and he laughs like a hyena when he's nervous. I don't know too much about Ollie's background, other than that he had a drinking problem at one point caused by family issues, and that he has a son that he's been estranged from for quite a while. However, he's proven himself a dependable and loyal friend and that's all that really matters.

Ollie raised one stubby finger and pointed to the sign above my counter that listed the specials of the day. "Am I dreaming, or is that Chris Evans item a real, honest-to-goodness hotcake breakfast sandwich?"

"It is," I said with a large grin. "Can you believe it, most of my customers thought the hotcakes were in a roll, or large slices of sourdough bread?"

"Oh, I believe it." Ollie walked around the counter into the kitchen and ambled over to my back table. He paused to kneel before the refrigerator and scratch Nick behind the ears before easing his frame onto one of my high-backed chairs. "I haven't had one of those in ages. My mother used to make them."

"Yeah? Well, I can't promise mine will be as good as your mother's. You know nothing beats a mother's home cooking," I said, eyes twinkling.

"True, but I bet you'll come close. I'll have mine with scrambled Egg Beaters, though, if you don't mind. And no cheese." He patted his bulging stomach.

I poured egg-beater mixture into a bowl. "Watching your weight?"

"Sadly, no. My cholesterol. It was up forty points from my last doctor visit." He shot me a lopsided grin. "I can't be dying just yet, at least not until I convince you to go into business with me."

I added milk and started whipping the eggs. "Nick Atkins will probably return before that happens," I said. I added salt and pepper to the mixture and dumped it into the frying pan. "Any more postcards?"

He shook his head. "Not for a long time. You?"

"Nope."

For a while Ollie had been receiving postcards signed "N," all with odd messages that we'd finally figured out were in code. The last one I'd received had read simply: *Good job. N.* The card had depicted the *Queen Mary* and been postmarked from Southern California, but that had been months ago, and neither Ollie nor I had heard anything from the elusive Atkins since.

Ollie leaned back in his chair and laced his hands behind his neck. "They say no news is good news, but in this case I'm not so sure." He glanced around the shop. "You certainly went all out on your Halloween decorations," he said.

I smiled. Orange and black streamers hung from the ceiling, paper bats suspended from them. Off to one corner a life-sized dummy dressed as a wicked witch stirred a cauldron, while a stuffed black cat watched. Near the picture window was a potted tree. On top of the tree was a Halloween lantern in the shape of a goblin's head. Farther down was a nest with paper owls. Their eyes reflected the light from the lantern. A skeleton wearing a gray wig and an apron posed behind the counter, while an assortment of Halloween masks that included a clown, a pirate and a wolf were hung up above the bulletin board. "The masks and streamers were in a box in the garage," I said. "The tree and those decorations were Chantal's contribution. If you like these you should see what she and Remy have done with Poppies' window—especially if you're a Hitchcock fan like Remy."

"I do like Hitch," said Ollie. "I just may have to stop by."

I flipped the hotcakes on the griddle, transferred them to a plate, put the finished scrambled eggs, a slice of ham and a slice of bacon on top and covered it with the other hotcake. I carried the plate over and set it in front of Ollie. As he picked up his fork I said, "Getting back to the subject of Nick Atkins, if Alexa Martin was right and Atkins really is a special agent on a mission, we might not hear from him for a long while."

Ollie waved his fork in the air. "That's true, but . . . you don't know Nick. He was one resourceful fellow. He'd find a way. Look what he did with those postcards."

"Yes, but we don't know what he might be mixed up in now. It might be more dangerous. He might not have an opportunity to send you cryptic messages." I bit down hard on my lower lip. "For example, I haven't heard from Daniel since he left on his mission."

"I wondered if you'd heard from him, but I didn't want to pry."

I shot him a teasing glance. "Since when?"

"Since about five minutes ago." He leaned toward me and said, "For what it's worth, I think you made the right decision to date Samms. He's a good guy, and you really don't know when, or if, Daniel might ever come back."

"I suppose that's true," I said. I hesitated and then said, "About that other matter I asked you to look into . . ."

"Oh, yes, the magic shop," Ollie said. "I didn't find any more notes, but I did some digging. Apparently the stakeout was on a sporting goods store next to Castorelli's shop. Turns out the proprietor was operating an illegal gambling ring. The next day Castorelli's House of Magic never opened. Some customers came over, looking for promised items, but . . . the shop remained dark. Police investigated, and it turned out that Castorelli was pretty heavy into debt from gambling. Apparently he owed a good deal of money to some pretty unscrupulous characters."

"Unscrupulous, huh? Like the Mob?"

"Mob ties were mentioned as a possibility," Ollie admitted. "Anyway, the police followed up on a few leads, but none panned out. After a few months they dropped the investigation. The general consensus was that Castorelli didn't want to be found." Ollie paused. "I understand the store's since been reopened, under new management. It's been run by a woman named Glenda Goodrich the past three years."

I raised an eyebrow. "If all that's true about the gambling, I can understand why he'd want to disappear," I said.

Ollie raised and eyebrow. "You have doubts?"

I sighed. "I don't know enough about the case to feel one way or the other, but . . . it just seems like a pat explanation. Too pat."

"It's possible Castorelli could have been involved in something else that necessitated the sudden vanishing act," said Ollie thoughtfully. "Another type of illegal activity, perhaps?"

"Perhaps, but . . ." I let out a long breath, then folded my hands in front of me and looked Ollie straight in the eye. "I want you to stop looking into this."

Ollie's jaw dropped. "What! Stop looking, are you sure?"

I hesitated, then nodded. "Yes. I don't think tracking down Philip Castorelli is a good idea. After all, we have no idea what sort of Pandora's Box finding him might open—especially if he did have mob ties."

Ollie arched a brow. "You've never shied away from anything to do with the mob before," he observed. He reached out to cover my hand with his. "You can't fool me, Nora Charles. You're afraid to find Castorelli, because you think he might want little Nick back, am I right?"

"That's part of it," I agreed. "I always said that if Nick Atkins came back, I'd fight him for feline Nick, and I don't relish the thought of another possible owner throwing himself into the mix."

"Aren't you getting a bit ahead of yourself, Nora?" Ollie asked gently. "You have no idea if Castorelli would want little Nick back or not. Heck, we don't even know for sure that he owned him. Little Nick could have just been a stray kitten who wound up in that alley." He waited a beat and then asked, "You said that was part of it. What's the rest?"

I expelled a breath. "Call me crazy but . . . what if it should turn out that Nick is . . . more than just an ordinary cat?"

"More than ordinary?" Ollie's eyes widened. "You mean . . . you think Nick has magical powers?"

I looked at Nick, sitting serenely in front of the refrigerator. "You have to admit that at times he does things that are . . . extraordinary."

Ollie reached up to scratch behind one ear. "I'll admit that at times it does appear that way, but—good gosh, Nora, you can't really believe that."

"The sensible part of me says no. But there's another part of me that wonders. And if it should turn out that he is . . . extraordinary . . . I just don't know." I looked at Ollie. "I think that it might be best if Nick's past remains in the past . . . at least for now."

Ollie hesitated, then nodded. "Okay, Nora. I'll drop it. But if you change your mind, just say the word. I confess, I have a certain amount of curiosity about little Nick as well." He spooned a large helping of hotcakes into his mouth. "Um-um, good," he mumbled. He wiped at his lips with his napkin and then said, "As talented as you are at cooking, Nora, you're even more so at unraveling clues and following up leads. One day you'll realize it's only a matter of time before you hand the management of the sandwich shop over to Lacey and come into business with me."

"I might be tempted to pursue PI work full-time in the future, but that's a long way off. Besides, If I were to hand the business over to my sister, I might as well put an *Out of Business* sign on the door now, and then my mother would surely come back to haunt me," I remarked. "In case you haven't noticed, Lacey doesn't exactly have a head for business."

"She might not have a head for business, but she can draw up a storm. Too bad they laid her off at St. Leo. She liked being a sketch artist."

"That she did. I'd thought about asking Anderson if they could use another one on the Cruz force, but seeing as she and I don't exactly have a good rapport, I guess I'll leave well enough alone."

Ollie took another bite and said, "You know, if you don't feel you can broach the subject to Anderson, maybe you could get Samms to do it. After all, he recommended Lacey for the job on the St. Leo force."

I snapped my fingers. "That's a great idea, Ollie. I'll ask him if he'd mind putting in a good word for Lacey. Anderson would probably put more weight behind the request if it came from Samms."

He chuckled. "You still think Anderson's got it bad for Samms, don't you?"

"I don't think. I know. You should have seen her making goo-goo eyes at him at the mansion yesterday—say, what's so funny?" I demanded as Ollie let out a low chuckle.

"Just the thought of Anderson making goo-goo eyes at anyone. Anyhow, what do you care, so long as he doesn't make them back at her?"

"True." I filled two mugs with coffee and brought them over to the table. "The thing that bothered me the most about the whole incident was that boy. The look on his face, and the way he took off, tells me he saw something. I just hope it doesn't put him in danger."

"Teenagers can be remarkably adept at disappearing when they want to," Ollie said. "Of course, there's always the possibility he just wanted to make a quick getaway."

"Maybe, but I don't think it was a ploy." I leaned forward and cupped my chin in my palm. "Who would want to put a body in a coffin? And those marks on the neck, why it's almost as if someone wanted everyone to think a vampire was responsible."

Nick, lounging in front of my refrigerator, all four paws in the air, wriggled around as soon as I said the word *vampire*. He opened one golden eye, then inclined his head in an almost imperceptible nod before closing said eye and flipping over on his side.

Ollie laughed. "It certainly looks like Nick's open to that possibility." He picked up the mug and took a sip of the coffee. "This coffee is great, by the way. New flavor?"

"No, I just added some extra chicory. I tried googling Waincroft Manor's history last night before I went to bed, but I came up empty-handed. I thought maybe there might be some sort of clue there."

Ollie scratched thoughtfully behind his ear. "Has the John Doe been identified yet? Maybe once you know who he was, the rest will fall into place."

"Good point." I got up, walked over to the back counter, pulled open the drawer and whipped out my cell phone.

"Who are you calling? Anderson?"

"Heck, no. She'd never tell me. But Al Bennett over at the coroner's office owes me a favor. He forgot to order sandwiches for his wife's canasta party two weeks ago and I made them up with an hour's notice. Or, as he charmingly put it, I 'saved his bacon.' Apparently Mrs. Bennett has a short fuse when hubby forgets to do chores."

Ollie's brow furrowed. "You said Al Bennett? I know most of the guys over there, and that name isn't familiar."

"He's fairly new. He works in the office. His brother-in-law got him the job."

"Yeah? His brother-in-law must have some pull, because those jobs are tough to get."

I chuckled. "He's got a little pull. His name is Harvey Fishbein."

Ollie's eyes popped. "As in Assistant County Coroner Harvey Fishbein?"

"The very same."

The operator answered, and I asked for Al. A few minutes later a reedy voice came over the line. "Bennett."

"Hey, Al, it's Nora Charles."

"Ah, I was wondering when you'd get around to calling," Al said. "Particularly since I understand you found the body."

"It wasn't exactly the highlight of my day. I was wondering if they've identified him yet."

"Not yet. There was no identification of any kind on the body. We ran a dental check through the missing persons database but no match."

"What about his fingerprints? You ran them through IAFIS, right?" IAFIS is the FBI's Integrated Automated Fingerprint Identification System, the largest database in the world.

"We tried, but some of the guy's fingers had been burned at one time, obliterating the prints, so we can't get a definitive match."

That was interesting. Successful fingerprint matching by IAFIS relied on clear, legible prints of all ten digits—IAFIS couldn't identify altered prints. Al continued, "We took some DNA samples, but with no leads and nothing to compare it to, it will take time to get any sort of result, which may or may not be accurate."

"Any definitive word on the cause of death?"

There was a slight hesitation and then Al said, "No. There were some mitigating circumstances that make drawing a conclusion . . . difficult."

"Mitigating circumstances? What does that mean exactly?"

Another hesitation and then he grumbled, "I'm not at liberty to say."

"Oh, come on, Al."

Al hesitated and then said, "Look, if Harvey finds out I'm blabbing about this, he'll have my head. The whole thing is being kept very hush-hush. He only confided in me in the first place because Head Coroner Parks wasn't around and he had to tell *someone*."

"Well, now you've really got my curiosity piqued. No one will find out from me, I promise." When he remained silent I added, "I can make it worth your while."

There was no mistaking the interest in his tone as he replied, "Yeah? How much worth my while?"

Ah, I'd hit Al right in his weak spot—his wallet. "How about free lunch for a week."

"Really?" I could practically see him salivate at the other end of the phone. "Anything on the menu?"

I mentally counted to ten and then said through clenched teeth, "Anything."

"Drink included? Like one of those new smoothies?"

"Sure."

He paused. "You know, I could get in a lot of trouble for this."

I bit back a sigh. "Fine. Two weeks. Sandwich, smoothie, anything you want." When Al remained silent I said, "Okay, a month. But that's my final offer."

"Okay, then." He let out a sharp breath. "He was all upset because he couldn't run his usual tests. He said he didn't have any blood to run a complete panel."

I frowned. "You mean *enough* blood."

"No," he said slowly. "I mean *any*. None, nada—zippo." He lowered his voice to a mere whisper. "The body was drained of blood. And, considering how and where it was found . . . well, he's loath to draw any conclusions . . . yet."

I gripped my phone tighter. "Are you sure?"

"Well, of course I'm not one hundred percent sure. I wasn't in on the actual autopsy, and I guess it's possible I might have misunderstood Harvey. He talks fast when he's excited. Look, he's coming over to my house for dinner tonight. Jennie's making his favorite pot roast, so I'll pump him some more, maybe after he has a couple glasses of white wine. He always talks slower after a few drinks."

Al rang off and I stood for a minute, tapping the phone against my palm.

"Something wrong?" Ollie asked finally.

I turned to face him. "I'm not sure. According to Al, the body was drained of blood."

Nick lifted his head and opened both eyes. *"Er-ooo."*

Ollie jerked his thumb in Nick's direction. "What's up with him?"

Nick looked straight at me, then got up and vanished underneath the table. A few seconds later we heard a scraping sound and then a Scrabble tile came flying out, followed by two more. I picked them up and laid them down in front of me. A *t*, an *a* and a *b*.

Ollie frowned at the tiles. "Tab?"

I switched the *b* and the *t* and then looked up at the black bats floating from the ceiling. "How about bat?"

Nick let out a loud meow.

Ollie let out a low laugh. "You know, little Nick's intuition is usually right on the money. And in light of what Al Bennett just told you, maybe you shouldn't be too hasty to cross a vampire off your list of possible suspects."

Chapter Four

Shortly after Ollie left, I heard the door to my upstairs apartment bang and I knew my sister was about to grace me with her presence. Sure enough, a few seconds later she shuffled into the kitchen. She had a fluffy terry-cloth robe wrapped around her and I could see the tips of a pair of blue flannel pj's peeping out from underneath. Her blonde hair was caught up in a messy ponytail, and her eyes and nose were red. She pulled a Kleenex out of the robe's pocket and blew her nose loudly.

"Feeling any better?" I asked.

She gave another good blow into her Kleenex. "A little. This will teach me not to skip those vitamin C pills."

I walked over to the stove and put the kettle on, then reached up into the cupboard for the box of herbal teas, which I held out to her. She frowned, studying them, selected a peppermint bag and passed the box back to me. As I shoved it back in the cupboard I asked, "So, how's the Johnny Depp marathon?"

"Great! They're showing all the creepy ones since it's almost Halloween. *Edward Scissorhands* just finished, and before that it was *Sweeney Todd*. Man, can Johnny sing! *Dark Shadows* is next, but I'm not crazy about that one, so I thought I'd come down here and grab something to eat." At my look she said plaintively, "You need to go shopping for us. The fridge's pretty empty up there."

I sighed. Yes, I did need to go shopping, but fool that I am, I thought that perhaps Lacey might take care of it, seeing as she consumed most of the food kept in the upstairs apartment. "I'll try and go after I close. I'll make you something now. What do you feel like?"

She sat down on one of the high-backed chairs, tucked one leg under her and said wistfully, "Mama always used to make us grilled cheese when we were sick. Remember?"

I remembered many times, lying on our threadbare living room sofa, sniffling and achy, and my mother bringing me one of her delicious grilled cheese and tomato sandwiches and a nice cup of hot tea with lemon. It had always hit the spot back then. I pulled out the loaf of white bread, selected two slices, and started to butter them. "Yellow American?"

She blew her nose loudly before responding. "Cheddar." She pointed to the bread. "And could I have whole wheat instead? Please?"

I set the white bread off to one side, pulled out two slices of whole wheat, then got the cheddar out of the case. I cut off several slices, then arranged them on top of the bread. I added a slice of fresh tomato, capped it with a slice of bread, and put it in the frying pan on top of the stove.

"Mm." Lacey sniffed the air. "I can taste it already." She was silent for a few seconds and then said, "I heard on the news about the body at Waincroft. You were there, right?"

The kettle whistled. I poured hot water into a mug and carried it over to her. "Not only was I there, but Nick and I found the body." I wrinkled my nose. "In a coffin, no less."

Lacey made a face. "A coffin, ugh. I get chills just thinking about it." She paused dunking her teabag and shot me a look. "Let's talk about something more pleasant. How are things going with you and Lee? Has he kissed you yet?"

I made a face right back at her. "Yes, we've kissed. And yes, he's a fabulous kisser. I've already had this discussion with Chantal, so if you want more details, ask her."

Both her hands shot up. "Okay, okay. I'm just glad you finally broke down and decided to give the guy a chance. He really, really likes you, Nors."

"I like him too."

She raised the mug to her lips. "But you like Daniel more?"

"Right now I wouldn't say I liked one more than the other. The two of them are very different."

My sister rolled her eyes. "That's for sure. Lee's sexy, and dangerous, and Daniel's steady and dependable."

I arched a brow. "You don't think Daniel's sexy?"

She ran her finger around the rim of her mug. "Daniel's more of a boxer type of guy, while Lee's briefs all the way. Maybe even a jockstrap."

"Lacey!" I put my hand up to my face. I could feel the flushes of red heat coloring my cheeks. "How on earth do you know what kind of underwear Samms wears?"

She grinned at me wickedly. "I don't. I'm just making an educated guess. Anyway, it doesn't matter what I think, Nors. It matters what *you* think. What type do you prefer, boxers or briefs?"

This conversation was definitely making me uncomfortable, so I whipped out a pad and pen from my middle utility drawer and set them in front of her. She eyed them suspiciously. "What's this?"

"I remember you saying how much you missed working at Saint Leo," I said innocently. "I've thought of a way for you to practice your sketch artist skills." I explained about the boy who'd run away from the crime scene. "I think he might have seen whoever put that body in the coffin," I finished. "And if he did . . . let's just say it's in his best interests for the police to find him."

"Oh, wow!" Lacey's eyes were as round as saucers. "Sure, I'll help any way I can. Are you sure the police haven't found him yet?"

"I called the station early this morning, and Officer Bolton said there was no trace of him anywhere, but they're still looking."

Lacey frowned. "Officer Bolton? Larry Bolton?"

I stared at her. "Yes. You know him?"

"I met him a few months ago when Carissa and I went to the Hog's Breath Inn. Remember, I asked you to go but you had a headache? It was Karaoke Night, and LB brought down the house with his rendition of 'Uptown Girl.'" Lacey smiled, reminiscing. "He sounded really good but of course we were all drunk. Even you would have sounded good, Nors."

I doubted that, since I was tone-deaf. "Gee, thanks."

"He'd just graduated," my sister continued. "He'd gone on his very first interview that afternoon with guess who?"

I put my hand to my forehead and closed my eyes. "Dale Anderson."

"Right. He didn't think he'd gotten the job. He said Dale was like a grizzly bear." She giggled. "He was pretty down too. Said that if he didn't make it as a cop, then he'd have to go work with some cousin, and he didn't seem thrilled at all with that prospect. Apparently the cousin is a bit—you know." She made a motion of wheels whirling next to her temple. "Man, was he relieved when she hired him."

"Wow, you're pretty well informed about this guy." I noted the flush creeping up my sister's neck and leaned forward. "You're dating him, aren't you?"

The flush deepened and Lacey made a big show of inspecting her nails. "I wouldn't call it dating, exactly. We've been out a few times. He's a fun guy, believe it or not. And before you ask, yes, Hal and Peter know."

"And they're fine with that?"

She barked out a laugh. "Of course they're not fine with it. They're not even fine with me dating both of them, but . . ." She waggled the ring finger on her left hand. "I'm not tied down to either of them, same as you're not tied to either Daniel or Lee. You're well within your rights as a free agent to date both, and there's not a darn thing they can say about it . . . unless, of course, one or both of them want to get more serious." She waggled her ring finger again.

"Speaking of serious . . . I don't suppose LB talks about work on any of these dates, does he?"

"Talk about a segue . . ." Lacey's eyes narrowed and she clasped her hands in front of her. "Okay, Nors, spill it. You want me to see if I can get some information out of LB, right?"

I widened my eyes. "Did I say that?"

"You didn't have to. I know you."

"Okay, fine. If you could pick his brain, find out just where they stand on the John Doe case—if they've ascertained his identity, the cause of death . . ."

"Is that all? Are you sure you don't want me to ask him to see if he can get his hands on Anderson's case notes for you?"

"Nah, that would be asking too much."

She arched a brow. "You do realize this is going to cost you?"

I groaned inwardly. My sister's rewards didn't come cheap, either. "Fine." I hesitated, then added, "While you're at it, would you mind doing a sketch of John Doe? I can give you a pretty good description."

"Sure. I'll just add it to the bill." She rubbed her hands together, then suddenly sniffed at the air. "I think you'd better hightail it over to the stove. I think my grilled cheese is burning."

• • •

An hour later my sister was back upstairs, well-fed and ready to continue her Johnny Depp marathon, and I had two very nice sketches, one of John Doe, the other of the teenaged boy. Both were so real-looking I almost thought they'd come off the page and speak to me. I'd forgotten just how talented an artist my sister was. I figured I'd show the sketch of the boy around at lunchtime, see if he looked familiar to any of my customers. If that didn't produce a lead, my next step was to walk over to Cruz High and show it around there. Even if the boy wasn't local, maybe he had friends who were. I only hoped this wouldn't be a case of too little too late. And if none of that produced results . . . well, I'd cross that bridge when I got to it. As for the sketch of John Doe, I'd show that to my customers as well. Maybe I'd get lucky and someone would recognize him.

As I slid the frying pan into the sink, I happened to glance down. Nick was lying at my feet, his claws wrapped around a bit of paper. He saw me looking at him and he flopped over on his back, the paper between his front paws.

"What have you found now?" I asked him as I squirted dish liquid into the pan and ran water into it.

"Merow."

When I looked down again Nick had the paper clamped between his teeth. He reared up on his hind legs and pawed at my apron.

"Are you trying to tell me you want me to have that paper? Okay, just a minute."

I wiped my hands on a nearby towel, bent down and pulled at the bit of paper. Nick released it almost immediately, sitting back on his haunches with an almost pleased expression on his furry face. "Merow," he said again.

"Okay, okay, I'm looking at it." I smoothed out the wrinkled bit of paper and frowned at the cramped handwriting.

Obscurelegends.com

I shifted my gaze to the cat. "Where did you get this, Nick?"

"Merow," said Nick. His eyes flashed. He raised a paw and I could swear he pointed it directly at the back door before trotting back to his favorite spot in front of the refrigerator. He shot me one of those inscrutable cat looks before lowering his head to his paws and closing both eyes. *Translation: I'm trying to help you. Does it matter where I found it? Stop asking questions and fire up that laptop!* I glanced at the clock—I had about half an hour before the lunch crowd started to pile in. I got my laptop out, booted it up, and typed in the website. A few seconds later a message popped up: *You are being redirected to our new site: Obscure Urban Legends. If you are not redirected within twenty seconds, click HERE.* A few seconds later a drawing of the United States filled the screen, with the caption below:

Obscure Urban Legends from Around the USA—click on a state.

I clicked on California and a list of over a hundred urban legends popped up. Gosh, who knew there were so many? I scrolled quickly down the list and finally, #97 popped out at me.

The Waincroft Curse—Cruz, CA

I leaned forward to read the accompanying article:

Cruz, CA circa 1897: A young woman named Robyn Waincroft was ostracized by the townspeople of this little burg because it was thought she practiced witchcraft. Robyn herself neither affirmed nor denied the rumors, but several townspeople who had arguments with her often ended up with strange blights, illnesses, etc. One family who reportedly burned her corn crop reputedly had a curse placed upon them; however, there is no documented proof of this other than hearsay and the family's own protestations. Robyn fled to Europe for a time, returning with a lover, the darkly handsome Anton Bartescue. Bartescue was rumored to be a vampire because several of the townspeople swore they saw him in the woods at night, drinking the blood of small animals. Bartescue also never appeared during the day, only frequented the town at night. One evening he and Robyn were out and there was a violent rainstorm. A passing vagrant took shelter in the house, falling asleep in a bed in an upstairs bedroom. When Bartescue and Robyn returned home, Bartescue found the vagrant and became livid with rage. He drained the man of blood, stuffed him in his coffin, and then he and Robyn took off in the dead of night, never to be heard from again. Months later, Mortimer Waincroft moved his family into the mansion, but they left when his youngest child came down with scarlet fever and nearly died; two years later, Emily Waincroft moved in, but left after a week, claiming that she saw "strange, pale figures" in the night and could swear she heard wild laughter and crying but no one else was in the house. The Waincrofts believed a curse was on the mansion, and so no one ever inhabited it again; however, that didn't stop Robyn from gaining her revenge on the family that treated her so cruelly: every generation one Waincroft dies in a horrible manner, thus keeping alive the legend of the Waincroft Curse.

"What are you reading?"

I jumped up so fast I knocked the chair over. I glared at Chantal. "Holy cats! Don't do that!"

"Sorry," my friend said. "I said hello when I came in but you were so engrossed you did not hear me. I finished early with Remy, so I figured I'd come over here and lend a hand. The lunch rush will be starting soon, no?" She paused to slip off her jacket, giving a little shiver as she did so, and ran a hand through her unruly mop of curls. *"Mon Dieu!* The wind is really kicking up, and the clouds are getting thicker. I am afraid we are in for one heck of a storm." She stopped as she saw the expression on my face. "What is wrong?"

I hitched my chair back and pointed to the screen. "Have a look."

Chantal pulled up a chair and started to read the article. When she finished she glanced over at me. "Oh my. This explains a lot about poor Enola, wouldn't you say? Growing up in a family like that? It's the Addams Family for real."

"You can say that again. And did you notice the similarities between John Doe's death and the one they blamed Bartescue for? If this gets out, why, some people might think Bartescue himself returned and gave a repeat performance."

"That's exactly what they do think," said a deep voice.

Chantal and I both jumped and whirled around to face Samms, leaning against my counter. We'd both been so engrossed in the website that we hadn't heard the bell above the shop door jangle. I got up and went over to the counter. "What do you mean? Who thinks that?"

Samms brushed an errant black curl from his forehead. "One of those TV shows got wind of what happened at Waincroft Manor and they're convinced it's the work of the supernatural." He drew air quotes around the last word. "They're sending out a team, as they call it, to try and prove that Anton Bartescue has come back and was responsible for that man's death."

Chantal let out a gasp. "Are you serious? That's horrible."

I nodded. "I agree. What makes them think Bartescue's responsible? I thought Dale didn't release any details to the press?"

"She didn't," said Samms. "It had to be someone at the scene who blabbed."

I held up my hand. "Don't look at me. The only person I told was Ollie and he wouldn't repeat it."

Chantal nodded. "And I only told Remy. He also knows better than to repeat it."

The two of us looked at each other. "Joannie," we both said at once. "Who knows how many people she told," I added. "She was pretty upset when she left."

Samms brushed at a curl on his forehead. "Well, what's done is done," he said practically. "We'll just have to deal. And as far as those so-called paranormal investigators go . . ." He grimaced as he made air quotes around *paranormal investigators*. "As far as they go, they'll probably be more of a nuisance than anything else, and nothing Dale can't handle." He gave a soft chuckle. "Trust me. If they try to interfere with her crime scene, they'll be very sorry."

"Unless they somehow manage to get Kay Trilby on their side," Chantal piped up. "She might think it good publicity." She rose and brushed at her pants. "If you two will excuse me, there are some tomatoes in the storeroom that I should bring out." With a significant glance at both of us, she made a beeline for the storeroom door.

Once it closed behind her, I turned to Samms. "Now that we're alone, any other details you can share?"

He shook his head. "Sorry. It's not my case. And even if it were . . ."

I held up both hands. "I know. I know. You can't share details of an ongoing investigation. I know the drill, I heard it enough from Daniel." I hesitated and then asked, "I don't suppose you've heard from him yet?"

He shook his head. "No, and I really don't expect to. I don't know all the details, but I gather the mission they sent him on was pretty dangerous."

"That's the impression I got too."

There was a brief, awkward pause. This was the first time that Samms and I had brought up the subject of Daniel since we'd started dating. Finally I broke the silence by asking, "Did you want something to eat? Your usual Howard Stern breakfast sandwich?"

He gave me a slow smile. "That sounds good, especially since I had to skip breakfast."

"Coming right up." I walked over to the stove and a few minutes later had two eggs sizzling in the frying pan. I removed an everything bagel from the bin, slit it cleanly, and then went over to the glass display case for ham. Samms watched me, then leaned across the counter and pointed at my laptop. "So, what website had you so preoccupied you didn't hear a customer walk in?"

"A very interesting one, Obscure Urban Legends. Believe it or not, it has Waincroft Manor on there with an interesting story about Robyn Waincroft and her lover."

"Ah, yes. Anton Bartescue, the supposed vampire. I've heard a bit about it."

"It was quite interesting reading. I can see where it might interest a ghost buster."

Samms scratched at his ear. "I'll admit finding the body already in the coffin is corny, like something right out of a horror movie. But to think the guy was a vampire's victim is just plain nuts."

I looked at him searchingly. "Not if the point is to make everyone think the guy really was the victim of a vampire."

One shaggy eyebrow dipped. "That's your theory?"

Since I'd promised Al Bennett I wouldn't repeat what he'd told me, I couldn't share more details with Samms, so I just shrugged. "Well, it makes a lot more sense than thinking an actual vampire was responsible, right? Especially since they don't exist."

"There are some people who think they're vampires, though. I've read about such cases. They drink both animal and human blood, although the human type is the preferred. They claim that they need it to make up for a deficiency of proper energy processing within their bodies."

"Yuck. That's disgusting." I slid the egg and ham onto the bagel and then onto a plate. "Is that why Dale thought you'd be interested in the crime scene?"

He frowned. "I'm sorry?"

"I overheard Dale say once she heard the description of John Doe she knew it would interest you."

His eyes narrowed for just a fraction of a second, and then his expression cleared and he made a dismissive gesture. "Heck, who wouldn't be interested? A body found under such macabre circumstances?"

"Considering I'm the one who found the body, I have to agree."

"Yeah, I've been meaning to talk to you about your habit. I can't believe I'm dating a human body magnet." His words were gruff, but there was a twinkle in his navy eyes.

I placed my hands on my hips and thrust out my lower lip in a pout. "I am not."

He leaned across the counter so his nose was level with mine. "You are too, but I have to admit you're the prettiest body magnet I've ever seen."

I caught a whiff of his cologne, of the intoxicating smell of him, and I leaned in closer and lifted my head slightly, anticipating the feather-light kiss he brushed across my lips. He waited a minute and then the kiss deepened. I slid my arms up and around his neck. Who knows where things might have gone at that particular moment in time when suddenly all the lights in my shop went dark. We broke apart almost immediately.

"Swell!" I cried. "A blown fuse right before the lunch crowd!"

"It could be the storm," Samms said, glancing out the picture window. Indeed the sky had gotten much darker, and it was obvious from the leaves and debris whipping by that the wind had definitely increased. "They said it would get worse around eleven thirty."

"Talk about perfect Halloween weather," I muttered. "This is the kind of weather that vampires and witches thrive on."

Beside me, I heard a sharp hiss. I looked down and saw Nick, every hair on his body standing at attention.

"Don't worry, Nick," I reassured him. "There are no ghosts or witches here. Or vampires."

My words had no effect on my tuxedo. He still stood, back arched, eyes gleaming. "Ffft."

"Looks like Nick expects to see one of those creatures any second now," Samms began, but any further comment died as a tremendous gust of wind blew the door of my shop wide open, revealing a figure, clad all in black, standing on the threshold, arm upraised.

Chapter Five

The figure took a tentative step inside and Samms hurried over, grabbed my door and swung it shut with a resounding bang at the same instant the lights all came back on. Well, at least that backup generator I'd spent big bucks on worked. Now I could see that the figure in black was indeed a woman, wearing a long black cape with a hood pulled tightly around her face. She reached up and lowered the hood, shaking free a luxurious mane of long curly hair that was as black as a raven's wing. She reached up and rubbed at her long column of neck, and the gesture struck me as oddly familiar. Suddenly I heard the storeroom door bang, followed by a sharp gasp.

"Oh my gosh, that was scary," breathed Chantal. "Thank God for generators—oh!" She set down the bowl of tomatoes and rushed toward the caped figure. "Enola! Enola Waincroft! It is you, right?"

Enola smiled, revealing two rows of perfect white teeth that looked like wet Chiclets. "Chantal Gillard! Oh my gosh, it's been like, what? Eighteen years since high school, at least. You're still here in Cruz?"

"*Oui*. I manage Poppies, the local florist, along with Remy, and I have my own business too—homemade jewelry and reading the tarot. And, of course, I help Nora out here at Hot Bread."

Enola's gaze whipped over to me and I came around the counter, hand extended. "It's good to see you, Enola. You're looking well."

Enola took my hand and I was surprised by how strong her grip was. When she released my hand I fought back the urge to flex my fingers in front of her. "You too," she murmured. "You both look exactly the same as you did when we graduated."

I took in her trim figure and perfect skin. "So do you. I heard you have a curio shop in San Francisco?"

"*Oddities*. It was my Aunt Pansy's passion. When she passed a few years ago, she left me the shop, as well as the building it's housed in."

Chantal regarded Enola appraisingly. "You seem to have done pretty well for yourself."

Enola lowered her extremely long lashes. "Oh, I can't complain. I make a decent living."

Enola had removed her cape and draped it across the back of a nearby chair, and I took a moment to study her outfit. She wore a simple black sheath dress that I was positive my sister Lacey had salivated over in last month's issue of *Cosmopolitan*. Dior, unless I missed my guess, with a price tag of over five hundred dollars. Her black-nylon-clad legs ended in mammoth five-inch spike heels of the same color that I recognized as Dolce & Gabbana and easily costing the same amount, if not more. The cape, I also noticed, was very supple—silk, most likely. Lord knew what *that* cost.

If that was what Enola regarded as decent, I'd hate to get her definition of extravagant.

Samms cleared his throat, and I smiled at Enola, indicating Samms with a sweep of my arm. "Oh, I'm sorry. I should introduce you to Spec—"

Samms cut me off. "Leroy Samms, ma'am. Nice to meet you."

Enola's gaze swept Samms up and down, and it was evident she liked what she saw—as did most women who set eyes on Samms for the first time. "If this is a sample of what's around Cruz now, things certainly have improved since I left. Do you live here, Mr. Samms?"

"You can call me Lee and no, I don't live here."

"He just likes to hang around Cruz a lot," I cut in. "Samms used to be—"

"A lot more patient with people than I am now, I'm afraid," he said with a disarming smile for Enola. "Yes, I do hang around Cruz a lot, but I only live a few towns over, so it's not that big of a deal."

I tried again. "Samms used to work in St. Leo. As a matter of fact, you can ask my sister about him. He was her ar—"

"Ardent admirer," he interrupted smoothly. "Of Lacey's artwork, that is. She recently graduated art school at the top of her class."

"Yes, I heard." Enola crossed her legs at her shapely ankles, a gesture that did not go unnoticed by Samms. Enola turned back to me and smiled. "Is she around? I'd love to see her."

"She's nursing a cold," I said. "Maybe I can get her to come down later. If you're not afraid of catching whatever it is she has, that is."

Enola laughed. "Oh, that does not bother me. I have a very strong immune system. I rarely catch cold."

"So, what brought you back to Cruz after all this time? Did you come to help get the mansion ready for the gala?" asked Chantal.

"As a matter of fact, that is exactly why I am here," Enola said. "I admit, when I was first approached about using Waincroft Manor for this event I had my reservations, but Mrs. Trilby made an excellent point. After all, the curse is only a legend, right? If no one else is afraid, why should I be." She made a dismissive gesture with her hand. "Surely, after all these years it would be all right to use the mansion for such a worthy cause. Besides, I know a youth club might have been a boon to me when I was growing up. But then after I gave permission and messengered the key to Ms. Genna, I realized the place must be a total mess." She let out a light laugh. "I just couldn't stand by and not help clean it up for the event. So—" She spread her hands. "Here I am. Just got into town today."

"You shouldn't have gone to all that trouble. We're not sure we can u—" Chantal began, but stopped as both Samms and I flashed her a warning look. "We're not sure we should take advantage of you that way," she amended. "After all, it's enough that you donated the use of the house."

"Oh, I'm sure you won't feel that way once you get a look at the inside." Enola laughed. "It must be a total mess."

"Actually we did get a look at it, through the porch window. It seemed in pretty good shape. There was just lots of furniture covered with white sheets."

"That's a relief, then. I arrived about a half hour ago and was going to go right out there, but then the sky got so dark—" She wrinkled her nose and looked through my picture window at the dark clouds rolling in. "It's going to be a lulu of a storm when it hits, which I have a feeling will be very soon. I guess it will have to wait until tomorrow."

"Of course it can," I said. I gestured toward the blackboard, which held my list of today's specials. "Would you like some lunch? My treat."

"I have to get going," Samms said abruptly. He smiled engagingly at Enola. "Nice meeting you, Ms. Waincroft."

Enola held out her hand. "You can call me Enola, Lee," she said, her tone seductive. "And it was nice meeting you, too."

Chantal flopped into the chair beside Enola, and while the two of them discussed the specials of the day, I followed Samms to the door. "I'm guessing no one's notified Enola yet about the corpse found in her house," I said in a low tone.

He gave his head a quick shake. "Not yet. We were waiting for . . . that's not important."

I had an idea what they were waiting for but I wasn't about to tip my hand. "Fine, but what's up with all the interrupting?" I hissed. "Why don't you want her to know you're FBI?"

"What makes you think I don't want her to know that?"

"Oh, I don't know. Maybe the way you cut off my sentences every time

I tried to broach the subject?" I frowned. "You can't possibly think Enola had anything to do with that man's death . . . or can you?"

Samms cast a careful look over his shoulder at the table where Enola and Chantal were engrossed in conversation. "What I think is that we should exercise a bit of caution. After all, that vagrant was found dead in her house and now she shows up, out of the blue. She's been away from Cruz a long time. No telling what she might have been up to, or involved with." He paused. "And we only have her word for it that she just arrived in Cruz. She made a point of telling us that. Twice."

"Enola was always a bit eccentric," I said, "but a murderer?"

"There's no logic to homicide," Samms said. "I learned that a long time ago." He slanted a quick glance in Enola's direction. "I'm sure she'll find out who I am, but I'd rather it be later than sooner. I'll call you later, Red. Maybe we can finish what we started before the lights went out." He touched the tip of my nose with his forefinger. "I thought when we started dating you might learn to call me by my first name."

I grinned at him. "You did, huh? Well, I thought maybe you'd stop calling me Red, but I guess you and I are examples of an old adage."

"What is that?"

"Old habits die hard."

He released my hand, gave a brief wave and let himself out.

Both women looked up as I approached the table. "Everything sounds so good," Enola said, "and I appreciate the offer of lunch, but I really should get over to the Cruz Inn before the storm breaks."

The sound of rain pelting the picture window made us all look up. "Too late," I said. Sure enough, the storm had started. The rain came down in sheets, and off in the distance we could hear the distant rumble of thunder. I gazed out the window at the heavy drops pelting it. "This is going to be a good one," I said. "But as long as the generator holds out, we should be okay." I looked at Enola. "You might as well make yourself comfortable until the storm passes, so what can I get you?"

Enola eased herself back into the chair and squinted at the blackboard. "Hm . . . I'll try the Joe Pesci and a hot tea with lemon, please."

While Chantal prepared the steaming mug, I sliced the fresh mozzarella and tomatoes and then proceeded to chiffonade the basil, which is really just an artsy-fartsy way of saying I cut them into uniform strips. Then I lightly buttered the baguette, laid the tomato down first, then the mozzarella, then a thin slice of prosciutto, and sprinkled the basil over top.

As I set the plate in front of Enola, she sniffed the air and gave a pleased sigh.

"It looks fabulous. I remember your mother always liked to cook, Nora. I see you've inherited her talent."

"Nora is talented at many things. In addition to running Hot Bread, she writes part-time for an online crime magazine and"—Chantal paused dramatically—"she just passed a PI course."

Enola paused, the sandwich midway to her lips, and looked straight at me. "You're a PI?"

"No, I just took a twelve-week course," I admitted. "I wrote a series of articles on it for *Noir*. You could say, though, investigating is sort of a hobby of mine."

Enola shook her head. "Rather an unusual hobby, wouldn't you say?"

Chantal grinned ear to ear. "Our Nora is not most people. Investigating is in her blood, same as cooking. And she and Nicky make quite the investigative team."

Enola pinned me with a sharp look. "Nicky? Who's that, your boyfriend?"

A loud hiss emanated from somewhere just back of the counter, and Enola jumped. "Wh-what was that?"

Another loud hiss, and Nick leapt on the counter and stood, back arched, tail fanned out, every hair on end. His golden eyes gleamed and his mouth fell open, revealing sharp white fangs and his pink tongue. *"Hsssssss."*

"Nick, stop it. Is that any way to greet a guest." I turned toward Enola. "I'm sor—" I began, but the words died on my lips as Enola stretched out a hand toward Nick, then toppled forward in a dead faint.

Chapter Six

Chantal immediately rushed to Enola's side, while I hurried into the kitchen and soaked a rag in cool water. I handed it off to Chantal and then bustled over to my utility drawer, where I kept a small stash of first aid supplies. I found a vial of smelling salts and hurried back, waved it under Enola's nose. After a few moments she started to cough and her eyes fluttered open. "Goodness," she whispered. "What happened?"

Chantal and I helped her to a sitting position. "You fainted," I said. I looked at her closely. "When was the last time you ate something?"

"I'm not sure. Yesterday, maybe? I had some toast." Enola brushed a black curl out of her eyes. "I was concentrating on wrapping things up at the shop so I could come here." She pointed an accusing finger at Nick. "He startled me, the way he just jumped up on that counter."

I slid a glance toward Nick, poised on my counter, his tail still fluffed out like a peacock's fan, his eyes glowing. He peeled back his lips and a loud *grr* emanated from his throat. I stood up and waved my finger at him. "Hey, Nick! Settle down and behave yourself, and stop scaring the customers."

Nick stared at me for a minute, then trained his golden gaze full on Enola. He stretched out his front paws, and his tail returned to its normal size. "Merow," he finally said, and then jumped down from the counter and pranced back into the kitchen, tail held high.

I let out a soft chuckle. "I think that's probably all the apology you're going to get."

Enola frowned. "You called him Nick. Don't tell me the cat is your sleuthing partner?"

"He is," Chantal answered for me. "Nick's former owner was a PI, and apparently he cultivated quite a flair for detection. Why, he even spells out clues for Nora with Scrabble tiles."

Enola shook her head and glanced over the counter at Nick, now stretched full-length in front of the refrigerator. "I never remembered you having a pet, Nora. I didn't even think you liked animals."

"I liked them, I just never had much luck with them until Nick," I admitted. "He's quite . . . extraordinary."

Enola nodded. I noticed her half-eaten sandwich had fallen to the floor, and I reached down and retrieved it. "I'll be happy to make you another," I offered. "If all you've had to eat the last twenty-four hours has been a slice of toast, you must be starving."

Enola gave a shaky laugh and settled back in her chair. She gestured toward the chalkboard above the counter. "If it's all the same to you, I think I'd rather have one of those smoothie specials. They always fill me up and they're good for you. How about the Coconut-Banana Delight?"

"Sure. Coming right up."

I went over to the freezer and pulled out one of the packages I'd made up of frozen peaches, mangoes, bananas and pineapples. I put that into my blender along with a cup of ice cubes and two cups of coconut water. I hit the button on the blender, and five minutes later presented Enola with a large glass of the frothy mixture. She took a sip and licked at her lips. "It's really good. Very fruity." She settled back in the chair and added, "I have been a bit on edge the last few days. It made me too nervous to eat properly. I haven't exactly been looking forward to returning here, or seeing Waincroft Manor, or worse yet, hearing people speculate about that legend."

"You mean Robyn and her vampire lover, Anton Bartescue?" At Enola's startled look I added, "I found a website that specializes in obscure legends. Waincroft Manor was on it."

Her lips twisted into a grimace. "Obscure Legends? I know it well. It's run by a group of people who thrive on sensationalism, not truth."

"So what was written there about Robyn Waincroft and Anton wasn't true?"

She nodded. "My ancestor liked to read the tarot, and she even practiced healing with different crystals and potions, but she was as far from being a witch as Chantal is. As for Bartescue, she met him overseas. He was a displaced member of Romanian nobility. He was most definitely not a vampire. They were very much in love, and the townspeople believed they were not worthy of it. They took every opportunity to make it seem as if he were one of the undead. The last straw was finding the body. They came home late one night and found it in the parlor, in a coffin, no less. After that they realized it was pointless for them to remain in Cruz. Anton would be certain to be tried and convicted for the murder, so they packed up and left in the dead of night to start a new life."

Oddly, I felt a bit disappointed. "And the curse?"

"A rumor, nothing more. It started after an unfortunate run of bad luck for the Waincrofts. Some distant relation convinced everyone that Robyn had put a curse on the house because the family had been so unsupportive of her. The Waincrofts who were living in the house then moved out, and no one has ever lived there since." She leaned in closer to me. "I know you must be wondering how I know all this, because my father would never speak a word about his ancestors. I can thank my aunt Pansy. When I was twenty-one, she gave me Robyn's journals, which had been passed down to her. They explained so much."

"If the information on that website is incorrect, you should advise them," I said. "Why have all those half-truths floating around about your family?"

"I did try. They were not interested. People would much rather believe the sensational stories than the dull truth, Nora." She let out a long sigh. "My family did such an excellent job of keeping details out of the public eye that when those surfaced people immediately snapped them up." She reached out and patted my hand. "It's all right. I'm more or less resigned to it. No one would believe the truth, anyway. It's not glamourous enough."

"I remember in high school you told some of the kids you had supernatural powers."

"I did do that, didn't I?" The ghost of a smile played across her full lips. "It wasn't that difficult. Most of them thought I was pretty strange anyway. They were all curious about the legend, so I used it to my advantage. Why, I remember when I told Jenny Fishbein I had inherited Robyn's powers, she darn near fainted. Cruel, I know, but at the time it seemed just." She set her glass down, scraped her chair back and rose. "Might I use your restroom? I'm sure I look a fright."

I was thinking I should look half as frightening as Enola, but I merely nodded and pointed toward the door marked *Ladies'* over to the left of the counter. Once she'd gone I glanced at the clock. Usually around this time I had a line almost halfway out the door. I grinned at Chantal. "I guess the rain is keeping all our lunch regulars away. Maybe it's for the best."

Chantal turned to look out my large picture window. "It's coming down harder than ever. You can hardly see more than a foot or two . . . oh, wait. I think some people are coming here. They just got out of that car with big umbrellas and yes, chérie! They are headed straight for your door!"

No sooner were the words out of her mouth than the bell jangled insistently, and two people wearing hooded raingear stepped inside. The one in the lead turned and pulled down the hood of her yellow slicker, and I smiled at the familiar face. "Cathy Genna," I said. "What are you doing out in this?"

The petite woman's blue eyes twinkled as she stepped over to the counter. "It's lunchtime," she said and laughed. "Hannah and I were talking about the gala, and since Hot Bread's so close and you and Chantal are on the decorating committee too, we thought we'd come over here for lunch and discuss some gala issues." She cast an approving glance around the store. "I love your decorations, by the way."

I glanced at Cathy Genna's companion. Hannah Berger inclined her head and her thin lips twisted in what I assumed was supposed to be a smile. "Afternoon, Nora," she said. After a moment she added, "Your decorations are very nice."

Chantal came up to stand beside me. She smiled at the two women and then turned to Cathy. "Any word on how the investigation's coming?"

Cathy's face twisted into a grimace. "I spoke with Detective Anderson earlier. It's still considered ongoing, but she said that she was doing her best to try and wrap it up and release the house by the end of the week. She didn't sound very happy, though."

"I'm sure the detective wants to see the gala proceed," put in Chantal.

Cathy barked out a laugh. "I'll bet the phone call Kay Trilby made to the mayor didn't sit too well with Detective Anderson. Oh well. She's got to learn, just like the rest of us have, that what Kay wants, Kay gets. Oh, and speaking of that." Her hand flew to her cross-body bag. She unzipped one of the compartments and pulled out a sheet of paper and handed it to me. "Kay wanted me to pass these along."

I took the paper and unfolded it. "Purple and yellow steamers instead of the traditional orange and black. Some lifelike dummies dressed as famous monsters could be placed at various vantage points in the mansion. Possibly some original artwork depicting scary scenes, or good copies of famous ones, like the *Scream*?"

Cathy plucked the paper from my hand and stuffed it back in her purse. "Sorry, wrong list. Those are decorations. I've got to give those to Joannie." She pulled another paper out of the depths of the small bag, looked at it and then passed it to me. "Here. This is the one."

I unfolded the paper and gave it a quick once-over. "Frankenstein Franks? Devilish Eggs? I have items similar to this on the menu already, but if she wants to give them these names I have no objection."

Cathy waved her hand. "Not necessary. I told her you most likely had that or better on the menu already. Just between you and me, I think someone else made that suggestion for her to pass along."

"I do like her suggestion about the buffet table, though," I said, tapping at the paper. "Black tablecloth, candelabra, spiderwebs . . ."

"I think her friend suggested that too. Thought it would be cool to set up the buffet table like one you'd find in a haunted mansion. You know, the ones you'd see on those old *Munsters* and *Addams Family* TV shows. I think it's appropriate, considering we're having the gala in a haunted house."

"Cursed," cut in Hannah. "Waincroft Manor's cursed, not haunted."

"Six of one," Cathy acquiesced with a wave of her hand. "It really doesn't matter, does it? As long as Detective Anderson releases the place in time for us to fix it up, everything should run smoothly."

"If you overlook the fact a dead body was found there, sure," Hannah said with a scowl. "Makes you wonder, doesn't it. About that old legend, I mean. After all, this body was found in a coffin—two bite marks on its neck."

"Bite marks!" Cathy's eyes grew round. "You're lying."

Hannah jerked her thumb in my direction. "Ask Nora. She found the body, right?"

I frowned at the woman. "How did you find all that out, Hannah? The police didn't release any of those details."

Hannah shrugged. "People talk, I listen. I hear things. The public should be informed there might be a vampire lurking around Cruz."

"Oh, Hannah!" Cathy gave a little shiver. "There are no such things as vampires."

"Yeah? Tell that to that corpse."

Cathy gave her head a brisk shake. "Well, I for one prefer to concentrate on lunch instead of all this spooky stuff. Nora, how about one of your famous Thin Man tuna melts."

Hannah's head bobbed up and down. "That sounds good. I love Nora's tuna melts. She always puts just the right amount of cheese on it."

"Fine," I said. "Two tuna melts and coffee, coming right up."

Cathy and Hannah trooped over to a table at the rear of the shop and a few minutes later I could hear them engaged in a spirited discussion of Halloween decorations. Chantal pulled out the rye bread as I got out the tuna salad and cheddar cheese. "You know," she murmured, "Joannie is good friends with Martha Larter. Her sister Ali works with Hannah."

That, no doubt, solved the mystery of where Hannah had gotten her information. "It looks as if Joannie's had a definite case of loose lips. I wonder how many other people she told? One thing's for sure, Anderson won't be happy."

"Well, she has no one to blame but herself. She did not tell us not to say anything, after all." She cast an anxious eye toward the restroom door, which was still tightly closed. "Enola's been in there a long time," she whispered. "Should I knock, make sure she hasn't fainted again?"

"That might not be a bad idea," I said. I glanced over my shoulder at the two other inhabitants of my shop. "I'm surprised Joannie isn't with them. You would think she would be here. After all, isn't she the head of the decorating committee."

"Maybe she couldn't make it. She's probably working. People still buy houses, even in mammoth thunderstorms." Chantal started to spoon tuna onto the bread then suddenly let out a little cry and set down her spoon.

"What's wrong?" I asked. I looked in the direction my friend was staring and saw what had captured her attention. Hannah Berger was making a beeline straight for the restroom.

"Hannah," I called out. "Someone's in th—"

The rest of my sentence was left unfinished as the restroom door flew open and Enola stepped out. For a second, the two women just stared at each other. Then, Hannah let out a cry and pointed at Enola.

"Enola Waincroft! What ill wind blew you back into Cruz, and what sort of trouble are you planning now?"

Chapter Seven

For a minute you could have heard a pin drop in Hot Bread as the two women stared at each other. Then Enola found her voice.

"Hannah Berger." Her tone dripped disdain and she looked the other woman up and down. "Still as polite as ever, I see. Not that it's any of your business, but I came back to Cruz to help out with the gala."

"Uh-huh. You should have stayed away."

Cathy stepped between the two women and cast a wary eye at them. "Is everything all right here?"

"Fine," Hannah growled, rocking back on her heels. "I just didn't expect to see her here." She indicated Enola with a swift jerk of her thumb.

Cathy looked at Enola curiously and I decided it was time for some introductions. I gave the girl a little push forward and said, "Cathy, this is Enola Waincroft, the owner of the Waincroft mansion."

Cathy's hand slid from Hannah's shoulder and she thrust it toward Enola. "I'm so pleased to finally meet you. That was such a generous gesture, donating the use of your home."

"Hmpf," Hannah snorted. "It's not her home. She hasn't lived in Cruz for years. And now that she's back, well, that surely explains certain things."

Enola wheeled on Hannah, her gaze dark. "What things?"

Hannah's lips peeled back. "Guess."

Enola's hand shot out, narrowly missing the other woman's chin. "You are still nursing that grudge! Whatever happened to 'your family members had nothing to do with any supposed curse.'"

"No? Those accidents were just coincidence, I suppose. And Lawton's illness too?"

"Whatever they were, they were not the result of a curse," Enola snapped.

"And I suppose neither are recent events?"

Enola's brows drew together. "I'm only back here to help out, not to inflict harm or cause trouble."

Hannah's eyes glittered and she waved her finger in front of Enola's face. "Are you sure about that?"

Enola squared her shoulders. "You are still the same mean, spiteful girl who put spiders in my locker and chocolate syrup in my gym shorts. If anyone's a troublemaker, it's you." She took a step closer to Hannah and said in a low tone, "And if you stick that finger in my face again, I-I'll bite it off."

"Ooh," Hannah squealed. "Like biting things, do you?"

"What's that supposed to mean?"

Hannah goggled at her. "In light of recent events I should think that would be obvious."

Enola waved her hand impatiently. "What recent events? What are you talking about?"

Hannah cocked her head and rested both hands on her hips. "Well, I'll be. You don't know, do you? I can't believe it. No one told you about the body?"

I could see Enola's shoulders tense, but her tone was cool as she asked, "Body? What body?"

I gave Hannah a stern look. "This isn't the right time or place for this, Hannah."

Enola turned to me, her eyes wide. "Please, Nora, do you know what she meant? If you do you must tell me. Has something happened at the mansion?"

Hannah let out a snort and threw her arms up in the air. "Oh, gee. Like she doesn't know."

Enola started forward, her fist cocked. "Know what?"

I stepped in between them. "Hannah, please calm down. You too, Enola." I let out a breath. "Hannah's right. A body was found at the mansion."

"Oh!" Enola took a step backward and placed her hand over her heart.

"Yes, a vagrant," Hannah snarled. "Sound familiar?"

Enola ignored Hannah and gave me an imploring look. "Do you know how the man died?"

"He was murdered," Hannah blurted out before I could answer. "Murdered, in your house, and his body stuffed in a coffin."

Enola's cheeks paled. "Murdered! Good Lord."

I laid my hand on Enola's arm. "The jury's still out on that. The exact cause of death hasn't been determined yet. The police are investigating. That's why Waincroft Manor is considered a crime scene."

"If you ask me, there's no need for an investigation," Hannah said. "It's apparent who's responsible," she added with a withering look at Enola.

Enola drew herself up straight. "How dare you insinuate that I had anything to do with it."

Hannah's eyes widened, and she assumed an innocent air. "Did I say you did?"

"You did not have to, but it does not matter. The whole idea is preposterous. I would not murder anyone."

"Then there is only one other possible explanation," Hannah said in a somber tone. "Bartescue has returned, as he always promised."

Enola clenched her hand into a fist so tight the knuckles turned white. "That's ridiculous and you know it. There is no truth to that legend. Bartescue was not a vampire."

Hannah sniffed. "Says who? You? I know dozens of people who would disagree. Why, once word gets out, you'll have more lunatics than you can count around here, trying to prove his existence."

I thought of the ghostbusters but decided this wasn't the time to spring that piece of news on Enola. Instead, I squeezed her arm and said encouragingly, "Don't worry. Most people know vampires are just fiction. They aren't real."

"There are people who think they are real vampires, though," Cathy Genna said in a hushed voice. "I read about it on the Internet. They suffer from some sort of disease. Vampire lifestylers, I think they call them, because they are people who adopt the vampire lifestyle as their own, even to the point of believing they need to drink blood to survive."

Enola shot me a pleading look. "I would like to find out more about this body. Who can I speak to?"

"Oh, I'm sure Detective Dale Anderson will be mighty happy to talk to you," piped up Hannah. "Why don't you give her a call, or better yet, take a trip down to the police station?" Suddenly she lifted her head and sniffed at the air. "Is something burning?"

I slapped my palm against my forehead and cried out, "Oh my gosh, the tuna melts."

I ran back into the kitchen where, sure enough, the tuna melts I'd placed on the grill had charred to a perfect black on one side. I sighed as I started to scrape the remains off the grill. Nick poked his head out from underneath the table and gave me a stern look. "Owrrr," he said. Clearly he thought wasting tuna in such a manner was inexcusable, and he was right.

"Chérie, it is my fault," Chantal wailed. "I should have been watching the food, not listening to Enola and Hannah argue."

"If anyone's to blame it's me," I said as I scraped the last bit of tuna into the garbage pail. "I knew I put the sandwiches on the grill, I should have been watching them." I glanced ruefully at the empty bowl in my sink. "And that was the last of the tuna salad, too. I'll have to get some cans out of the storeroom and make up a fresh bowl."

Cathy Genna leaned across the counter. "Don't worry about it, Nora. We're all to blame. I've got to get back to the bank anyway. How about you make us up two turkey and Swiss on rye with mayo and we'll call it even?"

"Fine," I said. "But the next time you come in for a tuna melt it's on the house."

I made the sandwiches quickly and put them in two brown paper bags. Cathy handed me a twenty for both of them. I made change and handed her one of the bags. As Hannah approached the counter for hers, I leaned over and touched her arm. "Can I ask you something?"

Hannah hesitated, then nodded. "Sure, but make it quick. I've got to get back to the school office." She turned and waved to Cathy. "You go on ahead. I'll talk to you tomorrow."

Cathy left, and I pulled out the sketch of the boy and laid it in front of Hannah. "Have you ever seen him around Cruz High?"

Hannah picked up the sketch and studied it a moment, then passed it back to me with a shake of her head. "Sorry. He doesn't look familiar."

A sharp pang of disappointment arrowed through me. "Are you sure?"

"Well, not one hundred percent," she said. "Why?"

I tapped at the sketch. "He was in the mansion before we got there, and he ran out. He seemed pretty frightened. It's possible he might have seen something."

"Yeah?" She picked up the paper again and peered more closely at it before setting it back on the counter. "Sorry, it doesn't ring any bells. If you want, I can take it with me, show it around the office. Maybe someone there will recognize him."

"That's my only copy. How about if I have another made and drop it off to you?"

She shrugged. "Sure, if you want to."

I whipped my tote out from under the counter and started to stuff the sketch inside. As I tipped the bag forward, the sketch of John Doe fluttered onto the counter. "Oh, wait, here's another drawing," Hannah remarked, snatching it up.

I shook my head. "That's not the same sketch. This one is of the John Doe."

Hannah stared at the paper in her hand. Her eyes widened slightly, and the corners of her lips twitched. She set the paper on the counter and tapped at it. "He's the man you found? The dead man?"

I looked at her curiously. "Yes. Do you know him?"

Hannah swallowed, then shook her head emphatically. "No. I've never seen him before in my life."

I heard a soft scraping sound at my feet and looked down. Nick had pushed four of his Scrabble tiles right next to my shoe. I looked at the letters: L I A R. The hairs on the back of my neck started to tingle.

When Hannah'd looked at the sketch, I'd gotten the distinct impression she'd recognized John Doe. Nick was right. She was lying. But why?

Chapter Eight

Hannah turned on her heel, stomped toward the shop door and whipped it open. Before she could take another step, Joannie Adams rushed through, shaking her umbrella. The force sent Hannah tottering backward. She stumbled, her arms flailing. Joannie reached out a hand to steady Hannah before she toppled to the floor.

"Hannah, I'm so sorry! Are you all right?" Joannie cried. "I was in such a hurry to get in out of the rain, I didn't see you."

Hannah looked at Joannie and her upper lip curled into a snarl. "Obviously," she snapped. "Why don't you watch where you're going?"

The realtor took a step backward. "I said I was sorry."

Ethan Howell's frame suddenly filled the doorway. He looked from Joannie to Hannah curiously. "Is something the matter, ladies?"

Hannah glanced up at Ethan and for a moment I saw her eyes widen just a tad and her face pale. She tore her gaze away quickly and tugged on her jacket. "Nothing," she grumbled. "Just that some people around here have no manners." With that, she grabbed her umbrella out of the stand and, with another quick glance at Ethan, pushed past him into the street.

Joannie stared after Hannah's retreating figure. "Well, of all the nerve," she said.

Ethan took Joannie's arm. "Are you okay?"

She nodded. "Yes, yes, I'm fine. It was my fault. I wasn't looking where I was going, but . . ." She lifted her shoulders in a noncommittal shrug.

As they approached my counter I looked at Ethan. "Do you know Hannah?" I asked.

His smooth forehead creased in a frown. "Hannah? Oh, do you mean that woman who just left?" At my nod, he shook his head. "Sorry, I've never had the pleasure."

"If you could call it that," Joannie sniffed. "If anyone needs to learn manners, it's her. Such an unpleasant creature."

"Tell me about it." Enola rose from the table where she'd been sitting and moved forward. "Hannah and I have never gotten along. She's always had it in for me and my family."

Joannie's head bobbed vigorously in agreement. "So true. And she only got worse after Lawton died."

Ethan shrugged. "I dunno, maybe you should give her a break. After all, it's tough to lose a sibling, right?" He turned to Enola and extended his hand. "I'm Ethan Howell, by the way."

Enola took the proffered hand. "Enola Waincroft."

As Enola said her name, Joannie gave a little squeal and stepped forward, hand extended. "It's a pleasure to finally meet you, Enola. I'm Joannie Adams."

Enola looked puzzled for a second and then her expression cleared and she reached out to grasp Joannie's hand. "Oh, yes. The realtor."

Joannie's sharp gaze took in Enola's outfit and she let out a low whistle. "Love your outfit, especially that scarf! Hermès?"

"Yes. It's a replica of a one-of-a-kind design. Jackie O wore the original. Dies et Hore—the signs of the zodiac. One hundred percent silk. It cost a fortune, but . . . I just had to have it." Her fingers reached up to twine in the soft material. "I came to Cruz with the intention of helping get the mansion in shape for the gala, but I understand there's been a bit of trouble there."

"Hannah told Enola about the discovery Nick and I made . . . *all* the details," I said, giving Joannie a pointed look.

Joannie flushed. "I did tell a few people just what happened when I got back to the office," she admitted. "After all, Anderson didn't say we should keep any of it a deep, dark secret and quite frankly it was very upsetting to me."

I looked at her. "Why were you upset? You didn't even see the body."

"No, but you described it very vividly. It was almost as if I were in the room with you." She turned toward Enola and placed her hand over hers. "I'm so sorry you had to find out that way, and especially from Hannah Berger. Tact isn't exactly her middle name."

"Hannah has always had it in for me and my family," Enola said. "Her brother was obsessed with the legend, so she found it convenient to blame the Waincroft curse for everything that went wrong in her family, even her brother's illness. She was bitter as a teenager, and she hasn't changed one iota."

"Sure she has. She's gotten worse," Joannie said with a dry chuckle. "I was on my way here for a quick sandwich before my next appointment, but now I'm afraid I'm going to have to take it to go. An Emma Roberts, please, Nora."

"One Emma Roberts coming right up." I looked at Ethan. "And for you?"

"Oh, nothing today. I just came in when I saw Joannie and Hannah squaring off in case Joannie needed any help."

Joannie's cheeks reddened slightly and she ducked her head. "Oh, Ethan," she murmured. "Thank you."

He waved his hand. "No sweat. Anyway, I'm late for an appointment myself. I'll be by soon, though. I'm dying to sample that famous Thin Man tuna melt everyone raves about." He flashed us a quick smile and hurried out the door.

"At least the rain's letting up," Joannie observed. "A lot of the roads will be flooded, though. Bad for business."

"I would like to find out more about this body," Enola said suddenly. "I think I will check in at the Cruz Inn and then head over to the police station and talk to Detective Anderson, is it?"

"Yes. If you want to come back here around three when I close, Enola, I'd be glad to go with you," I said.

"Would you? I'd appreciate that," Enola said. "What's the quickest way to the Cruz Inn?"

"Normally it's down Centre Street, but that's probably been flooded out," said Chantal. "There's a back way, though, that takes a little longer. If you don't mind dropping me off at Poppies, I can give you directions. It's on the way."

"No problem." Enola scraped her chair back and stood up. "Let's go."

Chantal grabbed her jacket, and after blowing me a kiss the two women left. I handed Joannie the bag containing her sandwich and she handed me a ten-dollar bill. As I handed her back her change I said, "Before you leave, would you mind taking a look at something?" I removed the sketch of John Doe from my tote and handed it to Joannie. "Have you ever seen him before?"

Joannie looked at the sketch, frowning. "No. Should I?"

"It's a sketch of John Doe. The body in the casket."

"Oh." Joannie leaned in for a closer look, then shook her head. "No, sorry. Did Lacey do that? It's very good."

"She did one of the boy who took off from the mansion, too. I thought maybe I'd show them around, see if anyone recognizes him. So far the police have had no luck finding him." I paused and then added, "I think Hannah recognized the sketch of John Doe."

Joannie looked up sharply. "She did?"

"She denied it, but her reaction seemed to indicate otherwise."

"Are you certain of that?" She tapped her index figure on the sketch. "If she recognized him, I doubt she'd hide that fact. Hannah's basically a glory hound—there's nothing she'd like better than to be involved. What about the sketch of the boy? Did you show her that one?"

"Yes. She didn't recognize him either, but she said if I made her a copy she'd show it around the school."

"Hm, well, if I were you I'd take her up on that offer. She's got connections with most of the local schools. If anyone can track that kid down, it's her."

After Joannie left I leaned both elbows on my counter. Something was bothering me, but I couldn't pinpoint just exactly what that something was. I felt something furry brush my ankles, and I glanced down to meet Nick's golden gaze. "You sense it too, don't you, Nick?" I asked the cat.

"Merow," he said.

My apron pocket started to vibrate. I fished out my cell and glanced at the caller ID. Al Bennett. "I'm going to want an extra week's worth of lunch for this," he said the minute I answered. "I just got off the phone with my brother-in-law. Nothing's official yet, but they did find a lump on the back of his head. And there's more." There was a long pause and then he added, "The body was definitely exsanguinated."

I felt a lump rise in my throat. "Drained of blood?"

"Yep. They're just not certain if it was the cause of death or whether it was done after death. They need to do more testing." He let out a long sigh. "I almost feel like I'm in an episode of the *Twilight Zone*. It's definitely beyond weird."

I was forced to agree. As I disconnected from Al I heard a shuffling sound. I glanced down to see three Scrabble tiles at my feet. I picked them up. A *t*, an *a* and a *b*. Nick poked his head out from underneath my table and I shook my head as I laid the tiles on the counter.

"You felt these worthy of a repeat performance, eh? Sorry, bud, but this is one time I really think you're off. There's got to be some sort of explanation for the condition of John Doe's body other than he was a vampire's evening snack."

Nick narrowed his eyes and let out a soft grunt, no doubt chastising me in his kitty way for not agreeing with his conclusion. He ducked back under the table, no doubt to sulk, and I returned to my cleaning. I'd just finished putting the last pot away when the doorbell tinkled and Louis Blondell walked in. He shook his umbrella before putting it in the stand, whipped off his drenched slicker and hung it on the coatrack by the door before walking over to the counter.

"Lovely day outside," he said. He glanced at my blackboard. "Am I too late to get a sandwich? Nothing fancy, anything handy will do. Tell you what, I'll settle for roast beef on a roll with horseradish." As I pulled the rare roast beef out of my display case and set it on the slicer, Louis asked, "So, what's new? I hear Enola Waincroft's back in town."

"She sure is." I filled him in on the morning's events, ending with, "As for the body, she knows about it now. Hannah Berger was here and couldn't wait to tell her."

Louis shook his head. "Good old Hannah. Some things never change. The Berger and Waincroft feud dates back to the early seventeen hundreds, you know."

"I didn't know." I finished slicing the roast beef and now picked up a baguette, sliced it, and reached for the jar of horseradish. "What prompted it, do you know?"

"No one knows exactly—a lot more horseradish, if you don't mind— but apparently some ancestor of Hannah's insulted some ancestor of Enola's, and there was a lot of name-calling and insulting, and then this ancestor, a witch or a warlock, I can't recall exactly, put a curse on the Berger family."

"Really?" I spread a generous amount of horseradish on the roll and on the roast beef and set down my knife. "What sort of curse?"

"Dunno, but the Berger family has had their share of bad luck over the years, that I can tell you. Eustace Berger was killed in a mining accident, Beatrice Berger was decapitated in a freak accident during a rainstorm, Hannah's grandmother had a history of heart trouble that killed her, and Hannah's brother Lawton died a painful death of intestinal cancer . . . to name a few. Hannah even blames her lousy school grade average on the curse. Her brother Lawton was obsessed with the legend. No doubt Hannah got interested in it from listening to him." He motioned toward my pickle jar. "A dill pickle too, please."

I fished a large pickle out of the jar and wrapped it in wax paper. "Have you ever seen a website called Obscure Urban Legends?"

"Oh, yes. Lots of people have who are interested in things that go bump in the night. It's not a secret or anything." He chuckled. "And the manner in which the latest body was found isn't a secret anymore, either. I saw details on several websites devoted to supernatural happenings."

I rolled my eyes. "Swell. So much for Anderson's wanting to keep details under wraps, although she's got no one to blame but herself. She didn't tell us not to say anything, and Joannie blabbed to her whole office. No doubt it escalated from there."

Louis shrugged. "So, what's Enola's take on the legend?"

I wrapped up the sandwich and slid it and the pickle into a paper bag. "In a nutshell, the real story is that Robyn wasn't a witch and Bartescue wasn't a vampire, and Bartescue was framed for a similar death. That's why they left Cruz. The Waincroft legend is just that—a legend."

"Ouch. That is dull." He reached into his pocket, pulled out his wallet and passed me a ten-dollar bill. "So that means Enola isn't a witch. Too bad, that was always the most interesting thing about her. She did goth before it was in style. Still, all this controversy, finding that body in the same manner as the vagrant two centuries ago—there must be a story for *Noir* somewhere in there, d'ya think?"

"Maybe, if the ghostbusters don't get it first. According to Samms they're on their way here to prove Bartescue's existence."

Louis let out a low whistle. "Talk about complicating things. I bet Anderson's thrilled."

"Between that and pressure from Kay Trilby to release the crime scene, Anderson's probably wishing she were somewhere else right now," I agreed. As Louis turned to leave, I called out, "Hey, Louis, wait just a minute." I reached under the counter for Lacey's sketch of the boy and laid it in front of him. "Have you ever seen him around?"

Louis picked up the sketch and studied it. "Can't say that I have. What is he, about thirteen?"

I nodded. "He was in the mansion and nearly knocked me over trying to get away. I'm thinking he must have seen something, maybe the guy who did it. The police went looking for him but so far he's eluded them."

Louis tapped the sketch. "Have you asked Hannah Berger? If he's a student at Cruz High, she'll know."

"I did, and she didn't recognize him, but . . ." I pulled out the other sketch. "I'm pretty certain she recognized John Doe. She denied it, but I saw her face. She knows him from somewhere."

"Curious." He held out his hand. "Can I see that again?" I passed it to him and he stared at it for a full minute before handing it back. "You know, I can't be certain, but I think I have seen him around here. Recently, too."

"You have?" I cried excitedly. "Where?"

"Can't recall just offhand, but I'll think on it. It may come to me." He whipped out his iPhone and took a quick photo of the sketch, and one of the boy's as well. "Lacey did these, I imagine?" At my nod he added, "Someone should put a bug in Anderson's ear to hire her. Maybe I will next time I run into her." He held up his phone. "I'll mull this over and be in touch. Oh, and your next article's due right after the gala, by the way. But no pressure to wrap this mystery up."

I stuck out my tongue at Louis's departing back and then I went over to the back counter, grabbed my laptop, sat down at the table and fired it up. Nick lofted onto the chair next to mine and regarded me, his head cocked.

I looked at him. "Yes, we're going to do some research," I told him. I called up my favorite search engine and typed in "reasons why a body would be drained of blood," hit enter and sat back.

Five seconds later several pages popped up. Of course the first few entries mentioned vampires. I grimaced and ran my finger down the list, stopping at an entry that read, "The human body can be drained of blood in eight-point-six seconds."

I looked at Nick. "How about that? Who knew it took so little time?"

Nick looked back at me. "Merow."

I clicked on it and looked at the article that popped up. It was just a disclaimer from someone who'd made that statement, and the comments below just mentioned how "creepy" it was.

I sighed. A dead end? Maybe. But was that statement true?

I continued down the line. Another question and answer site, this time asking, "How long does it take to drain the human body?" The answer was interesting.

"Eight-point-six seconds with proper vacuum pressure *and* you need two holes."

Two holes—as in simulated bite marks?

I tried again, this time typing in, "How do you drain blood from a body?"

Several different choices came up this time—cupping, bloodletting, and blood transfusion—but none of them seemed to apply. I scratched behind my ear and stared at the screen.

"Okay, who would know how to drain a body of blood? Got to be someone in the medical profession, right? A coroner would know, but I certainly can't call Harvey Fishbein. And no, I can't ask Al. I can't afford to give him any more free lunches. So who else?"

"Ow-orr!"

I glanced down. Nick had somehow gotten the *Cruz Sun* and was pawing at one of the pages. I bent over and disengaged his paw, looked at the page he'd been tearing at.

The obituaries.

I slapped my forehead with my palm. "Of course. A mortician! Thanks, buddy!"

Nick's lips tipped up. "Merow."

I called up the Yellow Pages and got the number for the Cruz Funeral Parlor. Freddie Harmon, the head mortician, was one of my best weekend customers. Fortunately he answered the phone.

"Hi, Freddie, Nora Charles."

"Hey, Nora. Horrible day out today. Business here is really dead. Ha-ha."

I ignored his feeble attempt at humor and said, "I'm researching an article for *Noir*, and I'm wondering just how you drain a body of blood?"

"That's easy. You get a vampire to bite 'em in the neck." When I didn't laugh he added, "Yeah, I know. Poor joke, considering everything that's gone on the last forty-eight hours."

"I'm just trying to wrap my head around the fact someone would take the time to drain a body of its blood."

"Well . . ." I could visualize Freddie rubbing at his chin as he talked. "It actually doesn't take that long, if you have the right equipment and you know what you're doing."

"I heard it can be done in eight-point-six seconds?"

"That's right." Freddie's tone grew more animated as he warmed to his subject. "What we usually do is stick two pipes into the subclavian blood vessels. One allows the blood to drain and the other pumps a preservative into the body."

"And you use a vacuum?"

"Oh, yes. One pipe is attached to a high-pressure vacuum drain. It is most expedient."

"I don't suppose they're easy to obtain?"

"Well, that all depends on if you know where to go. Someone with a medical background would know, definitely. Have I helped you?"

"More than you know," I said, and rang off. I sat back, drumming my fingers on the tabletop, and slanted Nick a glance. One thing I was fairly certain of: it certainly seemed as if someone had gone to a lot of trouble to simulate the death that had taken place at Waincroft Manor two centuries before.

But why?

<u>**Chapter Nine**</u>

Three o'clock came and I had just flipped the sign on the door to *Closed* when the door opened and three men and a woman hurried in, dripping water everywhere. I hurried over to the front counter and plastered a wide smile on my face. "Good afternoon. May I help you?"

The tallest of the three men turned toward me. Eyes the color of chocolate dominated his face. Neatly cropped dark brown hair framed his forehead. He held out his hand. "I'm Grant Goodeve. I'm head of *Paranormal Phenomenon*."

Oy. The ghostbusters had landed.

He motioned toward his companions. "This is the rest of my team. Davey Dugan, Felix Santore, and Tammi Brandon. We were on our way to the Cruz Inn but apparently the road is washed out."

"The main road does flood, but there's a back one you can take. It's a few miles longer and tacks more time onto the trip, but it should get you there safely."

"Thanks. The rain's let up, but it's still bad out there." The man introduced as Davey gave a slight shudder. He was average height with light blonde hair and light green eyes, and a tiny mustache above a full upper lip. "Not fit for man nor beast, as the saying goes."

"It's perfect for our line of work, though. The ghosts are sure to be out in this," said Tammi Brandon. I took a minute to study her. She didn't look like someone who investigated ghosts; rather, she gave the impression she'd be more at home on a Miss America stage. Straight blonde hair with a few auburn streaks running through it swung across her shoulders down to the middle of her back. Her skin was pale—ghostly pale, I thought with a chuckle—peppered with a smattering of freckles across the bridge of her aquiline nose. She'd slipped off her rain slicker and I saw she wore a stylish dress with an asymmetrical hem in a brilliant shade of purple. "We saw your *Closed* sign but your door was still open, so we were wondering if we might get something to eat?"

"Yes," Grant Goodeve chimed in. "The boys and I have been on the road from LA all day, and Tammi drove here straight through from San Francisco, so we're all famished."

"Sure." I moved around the counter and over to the door, which I quickly locked. "No problem. The specials are still on the board."

They grouped around the counter, studying what was written there. Felix glanced at me rather shyly from behind his massive tortoiseshell glasses. He wasn't what you'd call classically handsome, but the dimple in his chin reminded me of a young Kirk Douglas. He pushed a hand through his damp, dirty blonde hair and asked, "Could I just have a grilled cheese and tomato? Wait, make that a grilled cheese, ham and tomato. On sourdough bread, if you have it."

Tammi looked at him, her lip curling. "That sounds pretty dull, Felix. Don't you want to try one of these specials? They sound delicious."

He shrugged. "I feel like a grilled cheese. So sue me."

"Wouldn't be worth the trouble, and I wouldn't get much for it." She glanced at the board again, then said, "I'll have the Joss Whedon. I was always a Buffy fan. Or to be more accurate, an Angel fan."

"Sounds good to me," remarked Grant, and Davey nodded assent. "Make that three."

"Three JW's and a grilled cheese ham tomato coming right up." I glanced over at the counter and saw that, thankfully, the coffeepot was still pretty full. "How about coffees all around. On the house?"

"On the house, sure. How can we turn that offer down? Bring it on," Grant said and laughed.

The four of them selected a table in the middle of the shop. As I poured the coffee I noticed that Felix sat apart from the other three and didn't seem to take an active part in the conversation, which from the little I could hear seemed to center around some type of meter. Tammi and Grant seemed to dominate the conversation, which went back and forth at an energetic pace. I returned to the kitchen and started putting together the sandwiches, and just as I put the last piece of mozzarella on the last Joss Whedon, I heard a sniff behind me. I turned and saw Felix leaning over the counter, coffee cup in hand.

"Could I bother you for a refill?"

"No bother at all," I assured him. I got the pot and filled the mug back up to the brim. "Do any others need refills?" I asked.

Felix glanced back over his shoulder, then shook his head. "Nah. Tammi and Grant have hardly touched theirs. Too busy arguing over what sort of meter is best for this type of job. Me, I like a K-11 DMF but that's not sophisticated enough for Miss Priss over there. She wants the Trifield 100XE. Like that'll work any better." He let out a snort. "We'll be lucky if we even get a blip on *any* sort of meter."

"You've been doing this awhile, I take it?"

"Grant, Davey and I have been doing this for the past six years. Tammi came on board just about a year ago. She and Grant hooked up somewhere."

I glanced over at the table. "They're a couple?"

"Oddly, no. Tammi used just enough charm to get Grant to hire her, and now she thinks she's in charge most of the time. The sad thing is, she's got Grant wound just enough around her little finger that he lets her. She probably thinks this will be just like last year."

I took the grilled cheese off the grill and started plating the sandwiches. "What happened last year?"

He looked at me over the rims of his glasses. "You don't watch our show, do you? Well, last year we made headlines when we got actual video evidence of the existence of a ghost over in a deserted lighthouse off the coast of Maine. Long story short, she figures if we can prove Bartescue actually returned and killed again, the same way as before, our ratings numbers will go through the roof."

"That would be quite a feat," I said. "You really got a ghost on video?"

He nodded, reaching into his jacket pocket. "I can show you." He whipped out an iPad, tapped at a few of the keys and then flipped the screen around so I could see. The video was dark and grainy, a blending of dark and gray shadow. I saw a figure off to the right and as it moved closer, I saw it was Tammi. A few seconds later the shadows on Tammi's left rippled and shifted, there was a sudden flash of light and then—a figure materialized out of nowhere, a man, it looked like. He was dressed in what appeared to be an eighteenth-century suit. His body was angled away from the camera so it was impossible to get a clear shot of his face, but he held out his arm, shook his finger in Tammi's direction and then—vanished.

I looked at Felix. "You're kidding, right?"

His lips twitched. "I can see you're not a believer. No, this is no joke. Actually, it's the best video evidence of the spirit of Peter Niven ever recorded."

"I take it Peter Niven is this ghost?"

"Yep. He died in that lighthouse and people claimed to have heard strange noises, believed that his spirit wasn't settled. Do you know since we shot this, the strange noises have dissipated."

"Meaning capturing the ghost on video freed his spirit?"

"Exactly." Felix smiled. "The same might be true of Bartescue. His spirit might be crying out for release."

I raised an eyebrow. "So after two hundred years he decides to kill a vagrant to get it?"

He shrugged. "Perhaps an opportunity never presented itself before."

I shook my head. It was much easier to believe the video of Peter Niven had been orchestrated, somehow, but if it had been, Felix apparently wasn't part of it.

"So how exactly do you track down ghosts? I'm sure they don't cooperate with a video every time."

He laughed. "If only it were that easy. What we do is attempt to collect evidence that we see as supportive of paranormal activity. To do that, we utilize a variety of electronic equipment: the EMF meter, digital thermometers, digital video cameras and audio recorders. We also, in some instances, conduct interviews and research the history of certain sites."

"What does all that equipment do?"

"Well, the meters help detect possibly unexplained fluctuations in electromagnetic fields. We use digital recorders to pick up any unexplained noises and EVP's that might be interpreted as disembodied voices. Then there are the ion meters, the ultrasonic motion sensors, infrasound monitoring equipment . . ."

I held up my hand. "Sounds like ghostbusting involves a lot of heavy lifting."

"Sometimes. We get criticized a lot because our methods aren't considered scientific enough." He drew air quotes around *scientific*. "Unfortunately, there is no science that can either prove or disprove the existence of ghosts or spirits. One has to take a lot on faith."

"And vampires? How are they different?"

"Tammi wants to treat it like a regular ghostbust, but how can you? A vampire is one of the undead. He's immortal. It's a whole different kettle of fish than a ghost. I guess we could try to get a digital image of him, but how can we? Vampires can't photograph."

"Oh, right. They show no reflection in a mirror."

Felix shook his head. "They don't get it, though. Grant is completely willing to trust whatever Tammi says. And him—" He jerked his thumb in Davey's direction. "He just goes along with whichever one of them seems to be winning."

"Which is usually Tammi, I'm guessing."

He raised his cup. "You got it."

I stole another glance at the table. Tammi sat back in her chair, arms crossed over her ample bosom, a self-satisfied smirk on her pretty face. Talk about looking like the cat who ate the canary!

Felix set his cup down. "I was admiring some of the home decorations on the drive in. Looks like people here really get into the spirit. There were plenty of spooky tableaux set up in the yards here—not like my neighborhood. About all they can muster up is stringing their porches with orange and purple lights. I saw one house with an insane asylum set up in the front yard—that was different."

"Yes, Halloween is popular here in Cruz," I said. I leaned one elbow on the counter and asked, "How did you guys hear about this? Newspaper, TV—one of those paranormal websites?"

"No, actually . . . oh my!" He gasped and took a step back from the counter. I turned around to see what had startled him and saw Nick on the back sideboard, tail held high. He stared in Felix's direction for a minute, his golden eyes gleaming, then started sniffing around the counter. He snagged a stray bit of chicken that had dropped out of one of the sandwiches and started chomping.

Felix cleared his throat. "Is that your cat?"

"Yes. His name is Nick."

"He's pretty big." Felix looked at Nick almost warily. "They say black cats are especially tuned in to paranormal phenomena."

"So I've heard," I said dryly. "Nick's not a black cat, though. He's a tuxedo."

"He's a member of the black cat family, though. I bet he's got heightened sensory capability," Felix said thoughtfully. "He almost looks as if he could talk to you."

"Nick has his own way of communicating."

Felix let out a soft chuckle. "I bet he does."

He turned and walked back to his group. I set the sandwiches on a tray and turned to look at Nick. He'd left his place on the counter and I saw his black tail disappearing beneath the table in the rear of the kitchen. A few seconds later I heard the distinct sound of tiles being batted around. Curious, I set down the tray and hurried over to the table. Five tiles were lying scattered on the floor. I picked them up. A *p*, *o*, *n*, *h* and a *y*. I didn't have to be a genius to see what Nick's tiles spelled out. A few seconds later a furry black and white face peeped out from underneath the tablecloth. "Merow."

"You're a showoff, but I couldn't agree more, Nick," I whispered.

Nick's lips tipped up slightly, and then he vanished back under the table. I picked up the tray and went into the main dining area. Grant and Tammi were huddled together, looking at something on a tablet, Felix and Davey hunched over them. They all appeared very interested in whatever it was that was on the screen. As I approached, Davey nudged Grant. He glanced up and when he saw me immediately set the tablet off to one side, facedown. The others returned to their seats as I set the tray on the adjacent table.

Grant sniffed at the air. "That smells delicious."

"Thanks."

I set Felix's grilled cheese in front of him and then put a plate in front of each of the others. I had to agree, the combination of grilled chicken cutlet, mozzarella cheese, and fresh basil did smell yummy. My stomach let out an involuntary growl.

Tammi took a bite out of her sandwich and then glanced out the picture window. "The rain looks as if it might be letting up," she said. "We might make it out to Waincroft Manor tonight after all."

I paused, tray in hand. "I doubt that. The road's probably still flooded out, but even so, Waincroft Manor is a crime scene. The police will have it cordoned off."

"That shouldn't be a problem for us," Davey said smugly.

I looked at him. "Why do you say that?"

He averted his gaze. "No reason."

Felix smiled at me. "We understand there's to be some sort of benefit held at that mansion soon?" At my nod he went on, "Well, Grant's plan is to contact the woman in charge and convince her that not only will our presence be good publicity for her benefit, but if Bartescue's spirit is indeed around—well, I'm sure she doesn't want him interfering with her project."

Tammi turned to Grant, a petulant look on her pretty face. "You should ask that Mrs. Trilby to let us occupy the mansion exclusively while we're here. All those volunteers milling around, cleaning and straightening things, will be distracting to our research. It will disturb the electrical forces we need to connect with."

Grant scowled at Tammi. "One step at a time, Tam. I'm certainly not going to start making unreasonable demands on the woman before she even agrees to let us in the place."

Tammi jumped back as if she'd been stung. "Unreasonable! How is asking for privacy to conduct our investigation unreasonable? You know as well as I do this can be a twenty-four-seven job. It would be better for us to have the mansion all to ourselves."

Grant frowned. "I'm not about to push the matter with her, Tam. From what I understand the woman's a real piece of work."

Tammi started to say something, then slumped lower in her chair, her lower lip thrust out in a childish pout.

I ventured another question. "Just how long will validating the spirit of Bartescue take?"

"Depends." Tammi gave a careless shrug. "It could take a day, or a week, even an entire month. Ghosts have no sense of time as we have. It would go faster if . . ." Her voice trailed off as Grant shot her another look.

"What we really need are more details about the body," Grant said, tapping his pen against his notebook. "I've put in a call to the coroner but he hasn't returned it." He started to flip pages. "I thought I wrote down the names of the people who found the body. They were connected with that gala. I can't seem to find my notes, though."

I stepped forward. "I can save you the trouble. I'm the one who found the body."

There was a rustling sound and then Nick jumped on the front counter. He puffed his chest out and meowed loudly. I chuckled. "He's reminding me that I've been remiss. Actually, he and I found the body."

Grant turned his attention back to me. "Then you saw the vampire marks, right?"

"I don't know if I'd call them vampire marks, but I saw two red marks on his neck."

"Did they look anything like this?" He whipped out his iPad, fiddled with the keys, and then passed the screen over to me. I stared at a picture of a column of neck, with two holes near the jugular, drops of red blood dripping down.

I handed him back the iPad. "Similar. Maybe not quite so gory-looking."

"Good, good," he muttered. "Now we're getting somewhere." He tapped his finger impatiently on the table and stared off into space. "It would really help," he muttered, "if I could actually see the body."

I looked at him curiously. "Why?"

"I might be able to make contact with his spirit, find out firsthand what really happened."

"You mean you could actually speak to him?"

"Not exactly. Ghosts don't have ears or vocal chords."

"Then how?"

"Emotion is the universal language, Ms. Charles. We receive messages fueled by emotion all the time, but we rarely recognize it. If a ghost has a developed level of consciousness, it is able to project specific 'messages' or emotions to us. If the ghost projects a negative emotion, we may become scared. Alternatively, if the ghost projects a positive emotion, we may feel comforted or happy. That's just a general overview of how a ghost can communicate. Emotions can be very complex. It takes a great deal of practice to interpret and fully understand the message a ghost might send."

From the passion in Goodeve's voice, it was apparent that he believed he had the power to communicate with spirits. Either that or he'd missed his calling and should be an actor. "No one's claimed the body as far as I know," I said. "They still haven't identified the victim."

"No?" He stared off into space again. "Then I'd guess it's still at the morgue."

Davey leaned forward and said, "I can call—"

Grant's head shot up and he glowered at Davey. "It doesn't matter," he said brusquely. "We can work around that."

Tammi suddenly let out a squeal and pointed at the window. "Look! It's getting lighter. I do believe the storm is letting up."

Grant took another bite of his sandwich, then scraped back his chair. "We'd better take advantage, then, and get over to the Cruz Inn. We've got plenty to do, anyway, before we go to the mansion tomorrow. Equipment to be checked out, notes to be written . . ."

"You really should check with Detective Anderson before you do anything else," I cautioned them. "You'll save a lot of time and trouble."

"Oh, that won't be nec—" began Davey, and once again Tammi cut him off.

"Advice noted, Ms. Charles. We'll surely do that," she said with a bright smile. "Thank you for all your help." She took Davey's arm and fairly pushed him in front of her.

I watched them march out the door with a vague feeling of unease. Nick hopped up on the counter, cocked his head at me, then lifted his paw and placed it on my arm.

"Yes, I am troubled, Nick. Those ghostbusters seem to know an awful lot about what's going on. It's as if someone's feeding them information.

But who would do that? And why?" I tapped my nail against the table. "I think the key could be that vagrant. Why would someone want to murder him? What's more, why would they stage the murder to look as if it were committed by a vampire? It doesn't make much sense, does it?"

Nick cocked his head and widened his golden eyes. "Merow," he said.

"I'm glad you agree. It makes sense to the killer, though. The question is why?"

And as I was pondering all this, the door flew open and Enola stalked in, her cape trailing behind her dripping water, her eyes blazing. She raised her hand and pointed at me in a dramatic fashion.

"Nora," she said, "You have to help me. This Detective Anderson—she thinks I killed that man."

Chapter Ten

For a second I was so flabbergasted by her announcement I just stared at her, and then I finally found my voice. "What are you talking about, Enola? Where did you see Detective Anderson? I thought you wanted me to go with you to the police station?"

She flopped into a nearby chair and put her head in her hands. "That was my plan, but when I got to the Cruz Inn, Detective Anderson was there in the lobby, waiting for me." She raised her head, and I saw tears starting to form at the corners of her eyes. "The detective said she received an anonymous tip, but I know better. It was that witch Hannah Berger. That woman has always enjoyed making my life difficult, and now she's poisoned the police against me. Ooh, I could just *kill* her."

I walked over and settled myself in the chair next to Enola. "One thing I can tell you about Dale Anderson. She's very thorough, and she doesn't make snap judgments. I'm sure she hasn't reached any sort of conclusion about you, or about the murder, at least not yet."

Enola just sniffed and slouched lower in the chair. I waited a few moments, and when Enola remained silent I asked, "Want to tell me just what Anderson said to you?"

"Well, first of all she started asking me about my family and where I'd been the last few years, and why I chose now to return to Cruz." Enola rubbed the sides of her arms, as if to ward off a chill. "I told her just what I told you, that I went to stay with my aunt, and the only reason I returned to Cruz was to see if I could help with the restoration of the mansion for the gala."

"Did she ask you anything else?"

Enola hesitated, then said, "Yes. She asked me when I arrived in Cruz. I told her this morning. She wanted to know the exact time, can you believe that?" She held up a bare wrist. "I told her I haven't worn a watch in years. I stopped being a slave to a clock years ago. Then she asked me again was I certain this was the first time I'd been back to Cruz, and after I told her yes yet again she showed me a photo of a man and asked me if I'd ever seen him before. I told her I had not." Enola expelled a long breath. "Then she asked me what my plans were, and I said I was going to stay and help out with the gala. Then she said that it would be in my best interests not to leave town for a while, and that she might need to speak with me again."

Enola shifted in her chair. "She did not come out and accuse me of murder, but I could tell from the way she looked at me she's considering it. I am, no doubt, high on the suspect list, if not numero uno, and I am sure I have Hannah Berger to thank for that."

We heard a soft creak and our heads swiveled in the direction of the door that led to my upstairs apartment. My sister Lacey, bundled in a terry-cloth bathrobe, a Kleenex pressed to her nose, breezed across the threshold. "Nors, have we got any peppermint tea down here? We're all out upstairs—" She stopped speaking as her gaze settled on Enola. She blinked, and then cried out, "Oh my gosh! Enola Waincroft! You look fabulous."

"Lacey! It has been a long time." Enola smiled. "You look great too."

"Oh, no. I look a fright. I've got this horrible cold I can't shake." My sister twirled a blonde ringlet around her middle finger. "What brings you back to Cruz after all this time? Are you going to help out at the gala?"

"That was my intention," Enola said stiffly. "Of course, that will all depend on whether or not I am thrown in jail."

Lacey gasped. "Jail! Why would you be in jail?"

"Enola said she thinks Anderson believes she might have had something to do with the murder at Waincroft Manor," I said.

"Oh, that." Lacey rolled her eyes. "It's kinda Detective Anderson's mission to make life miserable for everyone. I wouldn't worry. Even if she throws you in the slammer, why, Nora can get you out. She did it for me."

I cut my sister a black look, which, of course, she paid no attention to. She sat down next to Enola and started chattering away, telling her every little detail about her arrest and how Nick and I had finally brought the real murderer to justice. Figuring it was best just to let her talk, I busied myself cleaning up the kitchen. I was just putting the last pot away when I spied Nick over in the far corner, by the back door. He had something white between his paws.

I walked over to him and bent down. "What have you got now?" I asked sternly. I rolled him over on his side and saw the object—a small white envelope. I gently plucked it out of his claws and turned it over. *Nora Charles* was printed in block letters across the face.

I looked sharply at Nick and shook the envelope. "Where did you get this?" I murmured.

Nick's paw shot out and pointed toward the back door.

"Did someone slip this under the door?"

Once again, the paw motioned toward the door. I walked over, jerked it open and stepped outside. The rain had stopped, but the streets were wet and it was extremely foggy outside. A movement in the bushes over to the left of the garage caught my eye and I whirled in time to see a flash of black vanish among the foliage. After giving the street a quick once-over, I stepped back inside and closed and locked the door. I carried the envelope over to the table and sat down. I slit the edge of the envelope cleanly with my nail and shook it.

One single sheet of paper fell out. I picked it up, unfolded it, and read the words printed there:

Ask yourself who would benefit from keeping John Doe's identity a secret.

I drummed my fingers on top of the note. An interesting point. Who would benefit? I dallied briefly with the notion of John Doe being in witness protection, but quickly rejected that train of thought. I knew from lots of past experience that people in the witness protection program were guarded and monitored closely, particularly in instances where they might be sought after by criminals. Of course it was possible John Doe might have eluded his watchdogs and been killed by whoever was after him, but would they go to all the trouble to drain his body of blood?

I stared at the note I held in my hand. Who had left it for me, and why? What did they know about all this? I'd seen a flash of black. The only person I'd seen recently draped all in black was Enola. Could she have slipped this under the door before she entered Hot Bread? But no, that didn't make any sense either. Enola was right there in the shop with me, and anyway, Enola didn't know anything about John Doe. Or did she?

"Nora? Are you all right?"

I glanced up to see the woman in question looking at me anxiously from the doorway. My sister had gone over to the stove and was busy putting a kettle of water on. Apparently she had finished regaling Enola with the details of her one and only encounter with the law.

I scraped back my chair and stood up. "I'm fine. I just thought I'd tidy up a bit while you and Lacey were talking."

"Lacey told me what you did for her," Enola said. "I know you said you only treat PI work as a hobby, but you apparently are quite good at investigative work. I would pay you to help prove my innocence."

"I'm sure it won't come to that, Enola. I don't see how Anderson could possibly think you had anything to do with that man's murder. For one, you were nowhere near the mansion, and for another, you don't know the victim, right?"

"It is hard to say," she responded. "I have no idea what the victim looks like."

"I can help you with that." I pulled out the sketch of John Doe and handed it to her. "Have you ever seen him before?"

Enola stared at the sketch, then handed it back to me with a slight shake of her head. "No. I have never seen him before."

"Then you have nothing to worry about. If you don't know him what possible motive would you have for killing him?"

"I am a Waincroft, with the accompanying curse," spat out Enola. "That seems to be enough for most people."

My cell rang, and I glanced at the caller ID. I saw it was Joannie Adams, so I mouthed "One second" and depressed the answer button. "Nora Charles."

"Nora! Great news!" Joannie Adams's voice held a note of jubilation. "Do you believe it, I just got a call from Anderson. As of tomorrow, Waincroft Manor is no longer a crime scene."

I almost dropped the phone. "You're kidding! That was fast."

"Wasn't it? Anderson said her team has gotten all the forensic evidence they can, so there's no point in holding up any of the preparations for the gala." Joannie lowered her voice. "Personally, between you and me I think Kay Trilby had a lot to do with it."

I could believe that. "Did you hear anything about those paranormal investigators? They were in here earlier, and the guy in charge was planning to contact Kay. He wanted to try and get her support for them to occupy the mansion and track down Bartescue."

Joannie sniffed. "I didn't hear anything like that, and I certainly can't picture Kay agreeing to anything so ridiculous."

"They were going to try and persuade her their presence would be good publicity."

"That sort of publicity could go either way. Anyway, can you meet me out there tomorrow afternoon, say around three thirty, four? I've already called Cathy, and she's getting in touch with Hannah."

"Sure. I'll call Chantal and let her know."

I hung up and turned to the others. "Anderson's releasing Waincroft Manor effective tomorrow."

Enola looked at me anxiously. "So my house is no longer an official crime scene? That is a good thing, right?"

"I hope so." I recalled the ghostbuster's assertion that they might get into the place tonight to inspect it. I looked at Enola. "You do know that there are paranormal investigators in town, right?"

Enola's eyes snapped wide. "You are kidding! And don't tell me they want to investigate Waincroft Manor to see if they can find the spirit of Anton Bartescue?"

"Yes. They were going to talk to Kay Trilby about getting permission."

"Kay Trilby! Why her? It is *my* house," Enola screeched.

Before I could answer, Lacey slid her arm around Enola's shoulders. "You own the property, right?"

Enola nodded. "Yes."

"Well, then all you have to do is tell them they can't conduct their investigation. If they do, they're trespassing, and you can have 'em thrown in jail."

I gave my sister a sharp glance. "And just how do you know that? Don't tell me you've learned something from Peter and Hal?"

She stuck her tongue out at me, then leaned her elbow on my counter. "No, smarty. I heard it on a rerun of *CSI*."

I rolled my eyes, but Enola leaned forward eagerly. "That is exactly what I will do. I will press charges if they even dare to set foot on my property."

"I don't think you can do that, Enola," I said, giving my sister a sidelong glance. "While I hate to contradict the writers on *CSI*, I do remember a friend of mine worked on a story once that involved abandoned property. The subject couldn't press charges against the vandal because it was claimed the property in question was abandoned, even though he owned it."

Enola's brow creased. "I do not understand."

"It's called Elements of Abandonment. Two things must occur for property to be considered abandoned: an act by the owner that clearly shows he or she has given up rights to the property and intent to abandon. In that case, the owner had moved away and was not living anywhere near the property. He's said many times he wasn't returning to it. The house was left unguarded in an area of town easily accessible to the public. And while I'll grant Waincroft Manor isn't all that accessible, you can see the similarities, right?"

"Nors might have something there," Lacey said grudgingly. "The property on *CSI* wasn't abandoned. It was an old apartment building they wanted to tear down but some families still lived there, or maybe squatted is the better word."

"It doesn't matter," Enola interrupted, a note of impatience creeping into her tone. "Can't I get an injunction or something?"

"You'd need a lawyer for that," Lacey interjected. "I know a good one. Two, in fact."

"I have a lawyer. I shall call him the minute I get back to the inn."

"Think about it," I cautioned. "By the time you fill your lawyer in on the details and he gets the injunction, why, those people might have gotten all they need. Plus, if you make a scene and draw attention to yourself, the news media will eat that up and those people will play it for all it's worth, believe me. Kay will most likely discourage them, but in the event she doesn't, I think it's best to just leave the whole thing alone. After all, its not like they'll find any evidence of Bartescue's existence, right?"

"Of course not," said Enola, but her tone didn't exactly sound convincing. "Fine. I will leave them alone. But I do not have to like it." She rose and slipped on her cape. "I will meet you at the house tomorrow at three thirty. But when I get back to the inn I am calling my lawyer. It can't hurt to make him aware of what's going on here, just in case."

Gathering her cape around her, Enola swept out the front door. Lacey turned to me and shook her head. "Wow. She's even more volatile than I remembered."

I tapped at my chin. "She certainly seems to be nervous about something."

"She was always a bit on the excitable side," my sister mused. "It's probably leftover agita from dealing with Anderson. Anyway"—she leaned in a bit closer to me—"I spoke to LB a little bit ago. He told me Anderson was releasing the mansion. That's what I wanted to tell you, but Joannie beat me to it. Apparently Anderson and Kay Trilby had quite a conversation."

That remark brought a smile to my lips. "I'll bet they did. I would have loved to be a fly on the wall for that one."

"Me too." Lacey grinned. "Don't worry, I'll get something else interesting out of him. His cousin's in town, the one he thought he might have to work for, and they're getting together Saturday at the Poker Face. He asked me to go with him, so I said yes. I figured it would be a good opportunity to pump him for information."

"The Poker Face this Saturday, huh?" I cast her a sideways glance. "If I'm not mistaken, this Saturday is Lance's turn to work the night shift."

"Is it? I didn't realize." She lifted her hand to study the tips of her fingernails. "Well, that doesn't really matter, does it? We've both moved on."

"Uh-huh." I figured getting information wasn't the only reason my sister had accepted LB's invitation. She was dying to walk in there, looking like a million bucks, on another man's arm, determined to show Lance just what he was missing—whether he wanted to know or not.

"Oh, and by the way," she said, "you'll be paying for my outfit. I saw a beautiful red dress in Sew Nice. Isaac Mizrahi. Deep V neck, lace sleeves. Only a hundred and fifty dollars."

"That's all? You don't want me to spring for a five-hundred-dollar Dior original like Enola had on?"

"Yeah, I have to admit, her taste in clothes has vastly improved since she left Cruz. She could stand to lose that black cape, though. It's creepy." Her fingers grazed my shoulder as she sailed past me. "If I get enough good info out of LB, maybe I'll up my ante. Give him a few beers and he spills like a waterfall."

If Lacey came up with something worthwhile, I'd be happy to spring for an entire wardrobe, but I'd never tell my sister that. She disappeared up the stairs to our apartment, and I was about to follow when my cell rang. I picked it up, saw that it was Al Bennett, and quickly answered. "Hey, Al. What's up?"

"I just got off the phone with my brother-in-law. He can't come for dinner tonight because he has to wait at the morgue." He paused dramatically, and then blurted out, "John Doe's body is being claimed."

I gripped the phone. That could only mean he'd been identified. "I don't suppose you happen to know who it is that laid claim?"

His tone sounded smug as he replied, "As a matter of fact, I do. It's the FBI."

<u>Chapter Eleven</u>

I couldn't speak for about a tenth of a second, and then I blurted out, "The FBI? Are you sure?"

"Of course I am," Al said with just a hint of reproach in his tone. "If I weren't absolutely certain I wouldn't have said it. I can tell you Jenny's pissed. She was making his favorite, breaded pork chops stuffed with apples. We thought about holding off until nine o'clock when he gets done, but if I eat that late I get bad indigestion. Acid reflux. It's a bitch." He burped into the phone. "Well, guess I'll see you tomorrow. I'll have one of those Michael Bublé burgers, medium well. Lots of ketchup."

I hung up and sank into a nearby chair, struggling to make sense of what I knew so far. There was a paper and pen on the table. I pulled it over and started to write:

1. Al confirmed that the body was indeed drained of blood. Why would someone do that?
2. The staging of the vagrant's murder is similar to the murder of another vagrant in Waincroft Manor two hundred years ago—supposedly by a vampire. Who would do that, and why?
3. The FBI is picking up JD's body. How does that tie in?
4. Nick is playing with a mysterious note that reads *Ask yourself who would benefit from keeping John Doe's identity a secret.* Who could have left this for me?

I set the pen down and studied what I'd written. The answer to number four was pretty obvious now: the FBI. And it was obvious to me that Samms knew more about all this than he let on as well. One and two were the puzzlers. They seemed to indicate that the killer wanted to make it seem as if the vagrant had been killed by a vampire, in the same fashion as that other vagrant had two centuries ago. Why? What purpose would that serve?

I drummed my fingers on the tablecloth. I really couldn't think of any logical purpose miming that old murder would serve, so I returned to number four. Why would it be to the FBI's advantage to keep John Doe's real identity a secret? Two possibilities came to mind. Either John Doe was an agent himself or . . .

"An informant," I cried. "John Doe was an FBI informant."

"Merow." Nick sat up on his haunches and pawed at the air as I got up and started to pace.

"Okay," I said. "That makes sense but it still doesn't explain how he ended up at Waincroft Manor inside a coffin. What was he doing there in the first place?" I paused in my pacing and eased one hip against the counter. "The way I see it, there are two possible scenarios. Either John Doe was killed at the mansion, drained of blood and put in the coffin, or he was killed somewhere else, drained of blood and then brought to Waincroft Manor and put in the coffin. Either way, it just doesn't make sense, unless the bloodletting and coffin staging were done deliberately, to make it appear that a vampire were the killer." I tugged at a stray curl and frowned. "That makes no sense, though. Why would someone want to do that?"

Nick's head snapped up. *"Er-owl,"* he said.

"Yes, it is very puzzling. Almost as puzzling as who could have left me this clue." The logical answer, of course, was that it had to be someone with ties to the FBI. But who? Daniel could be eliminated. Not only wasn't he around, but leaving cryptic notes definitely wasn't his style. The same could be said for Samms, who'd already advised me to steer clear of the case. Rick Barnes? The DOJ official worked in the FBI offices, but he wouldn't be privy to that info, and it was doubtful he'd reveal it if he could. I looked at Nick. "I wonder if this anonymous someone knows the answer to the rest of my questions."

"Er-rup," Nick said softly, his golden eyes not meeting mine.

I looked sharply at my cat. "What's up, Nick? Does your magical kitty sixth sense have some sort of idea who our mysterious note leaver might be?"

"Merow?" He blinked at me as though he didn't understand my question, and I wasn't buying that for a second.

"Okay, be mysterious, Nick. I'll worry about who it might be later. Right now, I think, the focus should be on finding that boy who ran out of the house. He saw something, I'm certain of it, and not just the body in the coffin either. Who knows? Maybe it was a vampire, and the kid saw him turn into a bat and fly away."

I swear that cat rolled his eyes at me before he ducked back underneath the table.

I walked over to my middle drawer, opened it and removed the sketch, then picked up my cell and punched in the number of the Cruz PD. When the switchboard answered, I asked to speak to Detective Anderson.

"What's it about?" the operator asked. The voice was one I didn't recognize. Another new hire, no doubt.

"It's regarding the John Doe found at Waincroft Manor."

"Hold, please."

I only had to listen to the intolerable Muzak for about twenty seconds before I heard Anderson's voice, sharp with something between apprehension and annoyance, come over the line. "Yes, Nora. What is it?"

And hello to you too, Detective Anderson. "I was just wondering if the ghostbusters had contacted you."

"Ghostbusters?"

"Those paranormal investigators. They were in my shop earlier."

"Oh, them. Yes, they were here. I told them under absolutely no circumstances did I want them tripping around that mansion until the perp is apprehended. They didn't like that much."

"I'll bet."

"They're of the mind that Bartescue is the perp, and their interference will aid in apprehending him. The leader, Goodeve, was going to try and speak to Mrs. Trilby, but I doubt he'll have much luck with her either."

"I doubt that too. Have you made any progress on finding that boy?"

"No, nothing yet. We put a BOLO out on him and sent it to neighboring counties, but so far nothing."

"I see. Well, would a sketch of the boy be helpful?"

Now just a hint of suspicion entered Dale's tone. "A sketch?"

"Yes. My sister Lacey used to work at the St. Leo Police Department as a part-time sketch artist before they had budget cuts. I had her make a sketch of him and it's quite good, actually. I wondered if that might help you."

Dead silence and then: "It might. Can you send it over?"

"I'll email you a photo. Just a second." I hesitated then said, "She made one of John Doe as well. Do you want that one too?"

Anderson hesitated just a fraction of a second and then said, "Sure, why not. Send 'em both."

I put her on hold, switched my phone to camera mode, took a quick shot of the sketches and sent them. I switched back to phone mode. "Let me know that you got them okay."

"Something's coming in now on the general email. Just a second." There were a few moments of silence, and then, "Got it. Your sister did these?"

"Yes. Do you like them?"

"As a matter of fact, I do. The one of the kid especially. He looks like he could spring off the page and talk to me. She worked at St. Leo, you said?"

"Yes." In a casual tone I added, "If you'd like a reference, talk to Samms. He's the one who recommended her for the job."

Another moment of silence, and then: "What's your sister doing now?"

"Right as this moment, she's nursing a bad cold."

"Very funny. I meant, does she have a job?"

"Oh, yes, she does. She works for me."

"So not a real job then," Dale remarked.

"I beg your pardon," I said.

"Don't get all huffy, Nora. I meant not a real job in her profession." There was a brief pause and then she continued, "Think she'd like to go back to sketching, or is she firmly entrenched in the glamorous world of sandwich making?"

My heart gave a little leap in spite of the sarcasm. "I think she might consider it."

"Have her drop her résumé off at the desk. Oh, and thanks for this. We'll put out another BOLO with it attached."

Anderson rang off and I set down my phone with a soft chuckle. Nick lofted onto the counter and I bent over to stroke his soft black fur. "Well, one good thing. All this just might have gotten Lacey another job." Nick cocked his head and blinked, and then raised his paw and pointed at my phone. A second later it rang.

I shook my head at him. "I do so hate when you do that, Nick." I glanced at the number on the screen, saw it was Louis, and answered.

"I remembered where I saw John Doe," Louis said without preamble. "It was a few weeks ago, at a yard sale."

I raised a brow. "You go to yard sales?"

"Hey, sometimes you get really good bargains. Anyway, this was more like a block sale. You know, where a few families all join together and have one gigundo event. I saw him picking through some of the things at one of the tables." Louis paused. "I think I know why he might have looked familiar to Hannah Berger. She was one of the people participating in the sale, and I'm pretty certain the table he was hanging around was hers."

<u>Chapter Twelve</u>

I thanked Louis and hung up, then glanced at the clock on the wall. There was plenty of time before my field trip to the coroner's office to swing by Staples, get a copy made of the boy's sketch, and then hightail it over to the high school for some more face time with Hannah. I felt a sharp tug on my apron, and I glanced downward. Nick was squatted at my feet, watching me expectantly, golden eyes wide.

"Sorry, buddy. You can't come with me to the high school. They have a strict no animals allowed policy. You stay here and rest up for our trip to Salinas."

Nick sat back on his haunches and let out a soft *grr*. I filled his bowl with some of his favorite lobster salad as a sort of consolation prize for not being allowed to accompany me, and left him hunched over his bowl, slurping happily as I shrugged into my jacket and walked the four short blocks to my destination.

• • •

Cruz High hadn't changed one iota since I'd graduated twenty years ago, except for the office, which had been relocated to just inside the main entrance, right next to the main study hall slash auditorium and library. I noted their Halloween decorating was well underway. I saw two boys struggling with a dummy. This one had on a long black cape and I was betting it was Count Dracula. I sincerely hoped they weren't going to stick him in a coffin.

As I pushed through the glass door to the office, I noticed that two out of the five desks were empty. Apparently most were gone for the day. A young girl who looked to be about sixteen was seated at the first desk, typing furiously on a keyboard, her eyes glued to her computer screen. She glanced up as I approached, and the force with which she pushed her chair back caused the pumpkin perched on the edge of her desk to teeter precariously. She pushed the pumpkin back into place and hurried forward with a wide smile. "Can I help you?"

I returned her smile. "I hope so. I was looking for Hannah Berger? Has she left yet?"

The girl, whose badge read *Carla Michaels*, looked a bit surprised. "I think she's still here," she said with a quick look around. "There's a parent teacher conference tonight, and she's supposed to be here till eight. She probably just went to the ladies' room or something." She nodded toward a bank of chairs on the left side of the office. "You're welcome to have a seat and wait. I'm sure she won't be long."

"Thanks, but first can I ask you something?" I reached into my tote and pulled out the sketch of the boy, laid it on the counter. "Does this boy look familiar to you? Is he a student here?"

Carla picked up the sketch and studied it for a long moment before regretfully shaking her head. "I've never seen him before. Too bad, because he's really good-looking." The edge of her lip drooped downward. "We could use a few more good-looking guys like that around here."

With that, she returned to her desk and her computer. I moved over toward the chairs, pausing before a low table that had a stack of yearbooks piled on it. I saw one dated the previous year and tucked it under my arm. I eased myself into a hard-backed chair near the door and thumbed through the volume. First I looked through all the portraits of the graduating class, and then I flipped through each page, paying careful attention to the group shots of the various sports teams and clubs at Cruz High.

In none of the photos did I see anyone who remotely resembled the boy at Waincroft Manor.

The office door opened and Hannah strode in. Her gaze sharpened when she saw me. "Nora. What are you doing here?"

I set the yearbook down on the chair and rose. "I had a copy of that sketch made. I thought I'd bring it over to you."

I held it out to her. She took it, eyes narrowed, and stuffed it in her jacket pocket. "Thanks," she mumbled. "I'll show it around." She hesitated and then added, "I'm sorry about the way I behaved earlier, in your store. Enola Waincroft was just about the last person I ever expected to see, today or any other day, here in Cruz." Her voice lowered to a whisper and she glanced quickly around before she added, "She's evil, like all the Waincrofts."

"Oh, Hannah, really. How can you say that?"

The woman's lips clamped together. "I can say it because it's the truth. My brother died before his time, and that rotten curse was to blame."

"You don't believe that. There are no such thing as curses, or witches, or . . ."

"Or vampires? And yet you saw the proof of that yourself," Hannah said.

I wasn't going to get in an argument with her over that, so I decided to try another tack. "I heard you participated in a block sale a few weeks ago." At her nod I went on, "I understand that the vagrant who was killed was there too. Someone remembered seeing him hanging around your table."

Her expression looked guarded and she said carefully, "Was he? I don't recall."

I took a step closer to her and pulled John Doe's sketch out of my bag. "Are you sure? Take another look."

She hesitated, then barely glanced at the sketch. "Sorry," she said, her lips thinning to a straight line. "I don't know him."

She was lying, I was certain of it but there was no way I could call her on it. I made one last plea as I shoved John Doe back into my tote. "Hannah, a man was killed, murdered brutally. This is nothing to fool around with. If you know something . . ."

"What I know is, I've got reports to fill out and I've got things to do to get ready for the parent teacher conference tonight," she said crisply. "I told you I'd show that sketch of the boy around to some of my colleagues, and I will. I'll let you know if I find out anything."

And with that she turned her back on me and walked to the back of the room, sat down at a desk, and started hammering away on her keyboard. I watched her for a few more minutes, debating continuing the conversation, but then a crowd of laughing teens bustled in, swarming around the counter, and Carla stepped forward to help them. They were gone a few minutes later and so was Hannah.

Back outside on the high school steps, I let out a giant sigh. I couldn't prove it, of course, but I was convinced Hannah Berger knew a lot more than she let on. But getting her to reveal it was going to take some persuasion.

Chapter Thirteen

 As I walked down Main Street I replayed the previous hour's events over in my head. I was more certain than ever Hannah had recognized John Doe, so why was she denying it? Did she truly not remember, or just not want to get involved? Or was there more to it? I was so wrapped up in my thoughts I didn't see the man loom up before me until it was too late. I collided with his chest, and we both cried out "Oof" at the same time.

"Ms. Charles. I didn't think I'd run into you again today, and not in the literal sense, either." Ethan Howell flashed me a wide smile.

"My fault entirely," I said. "I'm afraid I wasn't watching where I was going."

"I can't say I was either." He gestured toward a nearby brick building. "I just gave my last guitar class of the day, and I was a bit thirsty. I know it's early, but can I buy you a drink? To make up for my clumsiness?"

I was about to refuse, but then thought perhaps I could put the run-in to good advantage. "I can always make time for Lance's iced tea," I said. "Lead the way."

The Poker Face is Cruz's only bar and grill, and it's located a stone's throw from my shop. It had originally been an old fire station that the original owner had converted into a bar. Lance and his brother Phil had eventually bought it and turned it into one of Cruz's premier hot spots. Ethan and I walked in and I immediately ducked as a large plastic bat suspended from a wire swooped down at us. I started for the large cherrywood bar, but Ethan touched my arm and motioned to a small table for two near the picture window overlooking the main street. We'd barely seated ourselves when Lance appeared. He slung a towel over one shoulder and raised one eyebrow questioningly at me.

"Well, Nora, long time no see. I've heard you've been pretty busy, though, what with the shop and volunteering for committees and, oh yeah, finding dead bodies and all."

I stuck my tongue out at my former high school flame. "Very funny." I craned my neck around. "Where's Alexa? She usually helps out at the bar around this time, right?"

"She's working at the museum today, but we're going over to the theater at Pebble Beach tonight. She got tickets to the symphony."

I raised an eyebrow. "She's definitely broadened your horizons." I saw him look curiously at Ethan and added, "Lance, have you met Ethan Howell? He just opened a music store a few doors down."

Lance inclined his head in greeting. "So, what can I get you? If you're the adventurous sort, Jose's whipped up a pot of caramel coconut coffee."

I wrinkled my nose. Jose was a good short order cook, but his coffee-making skills had long been a secret source of amusement around town. "I'll just have a raspberry iced tea, please."

Lance's eyes twinkled. "What if I said Alexa's been giving Jose lessons on how to prepare coffee?"

I made a face at him. "I'll still have the raspberry iced tea. Not a big fan of coconut."

"Chicken," Lance muttered under his breath. To Ethan he said, "And you?"

"I'll have a Coors on tap."

As Lance moved off toward the kitchen, the door opened and two women came in. They started toward the bar, and then one of them turned and saw Ethan. She nudged her companion, who also turned to gawk at him. The two of them took stools at the far end, giggling. Ethan sighed and leaned back in his seat. "I recognize them. They've been in a couple times this week, inquiring about lessons." He leaned across the table and lowered his voice. "I'm willing to bet, though, that neither one of them has ever plucked a guitar string in her life."

"How could you tell?"

He pointed to my short, square nails. "For one thing, both of 'em have perfectly manicured nails—no, wait, talons might be a better word. Got to be five inches at least. Kinda hard to play guitar with nails like that." He reached out, plucked a napkin from the container on the table and started to fiddle with the ends. "I suppose I should be flattered with all this female attention, but quite frankly I'm not in the market for romance right now. I've got to get my business up and running."

I thought how distressed Joannie would be to hear that. "How is your business coming along?"

"Quite well, thanks. In addition to the music lessons, I sell and rent instruments, and I just signed a contract with a few of the high schools in the area to supply them."

"Would Cruz High be one of them?"

"They were the first one I called, seeing as I live here now, but they already have a supplier and they don't want to switch right now. I tried to make an appointment to see the principal, but—" He held up both hands in a gesture of surrender. "No go."

"Oh, that's too bad."

He shrugged. "It was worth a try. Can't win 'em all, right."

I nodded. If Ethan had gone to the high school office, no doubt Hannah had been somewhere around. That might account for her reaction to seeing him.

Lance returned and set a tall glass of iced tea in front of me and a frosted mug of beer in front of Ethan. He also set down a bowl of salted peanuts before tossing me a grin and heading back to the bar. I reached for the bowl, grabbed a fistful of nuts, popped one into my mouth. "Lance knows how I feel about his cooking," I explained. "I once told him the only palatable thing here were the nuts, so every time I come in he gives me a bowl. Fortunately Jose's cooking has improved greatly since Alexa has been giving him lessons."

"Alexa, that's his girlfriend, huh?" At my nod, he took a long pull on his beer. "That was some scene at your shop today. That Hannah person is a real character, eh? She sure doesn't like Joannie, and she definitely didn't like that other gal, Enola, right?"

"Their disagreements stem from a family feud," I said carefully. "I'm really not too familiar with the details."

He fell silent, sipping his beer. I took another sip of my iced tea and set down my glass. "You mentioned you had contracts with some of the high schools in the area?"

He nodded. "Yep. I'll be supplying instruments for the bands and the music classes. Hopefully, it'll turn into something lucrative."

I was just about to pull the sketch of the boy out to show him when he held up a finger and reached into his pocket. He whipped out his cell, glanced at the number and sighed. "Joannie Adams. She probably wants to know if I'm interested in looking at another rental." He sent the call to voicemail and slid the phone back into his pocket. "She is one persistent lady, but I guess I can understand it. After all, she's single and supports herself. She probably needs all the commissions she can get."

Apparently Ethan didn't realize a commission wasn't the only thing Joannie was interested in. "Are you planning to put down roots here in Cruz?"

He shrugged. "Maybe. I'm not sure yet. I thought I'd see how my business goes first."

The door to the bar opened again, and Tammi Barton hurried in. She stood in the foyer for a minute, looking around. Her gaze fell on our table and I saw her eyebrows rise. Then she turned on her heel and walked out of the bar. "Well, that was strange," I murmured.

Ethan looked up sharply. "Pardon?"

I gestured toward the closed door. "One of those paranormal investigators just came in. She seemed to be looking around for someone, and when she saw us sitting here she turned and left." I ran my finger around the rim of my glass. "I didn't realize I was that scary."

Ethan took another sip of his beer, set the mug back on the table. "I wouldn't take it personally. Folks like that are always a bit strange anyway, right? I didn't know we had paranormal investigators in Cruz."

"Apparently they heard about the dead body and connected it with the legend of the house. They want to see if they can contact the vampire's spirit, or something."

"Really?" Ethan frowned. "Isn't that dangerous? What happens if they do contact him?"

"I can't even begin to imagine."

Ethan took a final pull on his beer and rose. "I've got to get going, but . . . just how well do you know that girl—Enola?"

"Not all that well. We went to high school together twenty years ago, but we didn't hang in the same circles. Why?"

"Well . . . the last thing I like to do is gossip, but . . ." His fingers closed over the handle of his beer mug. "I'm positive I've seen her before."

"Have you been to San Francisco? She owns a curio shop there."

"No, no, it wasn't in San Fran. It was in Branson, I'm sure of it. She's not exactly the type of woman one forgets, and she's rather distinctive, with that long black hair, and that cape." He paused. "It was real recent, too. Day before yesterday."

Day before yesterday? But Enola had said she'd only driven up from San Francisco this morning? My mind was whirling. "Do you remember exactly where she was when you saw her?"

He nodded. "Yeah, that's the odd thing. She'd just come out of the building across the street from Branson High. A funeral parlor, I think. Kinda creepy, if you ask me."

A funeral parlor? What the heck was Enola doing there? I caught a flash of movement out of the corner of my eye and turned my head in time to see a young boy on a ten-speed whiz by. My heart gave a little leap.

Unless I was mistaken, it was the same boy who'd barreled into me at Waincroft Manor!

<u>Chapter Fourteen</u>

I gulped down my iced tea, thanked Ethan for the drink and raced outside. I looked up and down the street but there was no sign of the boy. I pulled out my cell and made a quick call to Anderson. She wasn't around, but I left a message and then hurried the few blocks back to Hot Bread and let myself in the rear door. Nick, squatting by the refrigerator, rose when I entered and followed me as I pounded up the stairs to my apartment. I checked in on my sister, who was dozing in front of the TV. I shut her door and went into my den and booted up my laptop. Nick lofted onto the desk next to it, watching me with a wide, curious golden gaze.

"First things first, Nick," I said. "Let's get our directions for tonight." As he yowled his approval, I googled the Monterey County Coroner's Office in Salinas and found it to be approximately eighteen miles away, a good half-hour drive. I printed out directions and then glanced at the clock. Al had said they could have held dinner up until nine, which probably meant that the FBI would arrive at the coroner's office sometime between seven thirty and eight thirty. It was four thirty now so I figured Nick and I should leave right after dinner, at six thirty, to get there around seven, just to play it safe. That left a couple of hours in between to do some more detective work.

First I looked up funeral parlors in Branson. The one across the street from the high school was the Collins Funeral Home. I dialed the number and an almost sepulchral-sounding voice answered. I played my PI card and explained what information I needed. The Lurch sound-alike informed me that Allan Collins would have been working that day, and he was off until Thursday. I left my name and number and resolved to call again if I didn't hear from Mr. Collins. I also dialed Enola's cell number and got voicemail. I hung up without leaving a message.

Next, I looked up the Cruz High School website and spent the next twenty minutes poking around it. Although Hannah had said she'd never seen the boy, it was possible he was a new student and their paths just might have never crossed. I clicked on the tab marked "Students" and each of the subsequent tabs that appeared. Lots of names were given, but no accompanying photographs. I clicked on some of the other tabs: Bulletins, Academics, Counseling, Resources—none had any photographs until I clicked on the tab marked "Athletics." Several group photographs came up:

Varsity Football, Basketball, Baseball, Cheerleading. I studied each photo and the names carefully, but none resembled the boy I'd seen. If he went to Cruz High, he wasn't sports-minded. I'd never have thought that from the way he sprinted across that field. I'd have pegged him for the track team for sure. I clicked on the track photo twice, but no dice.

On impulse I clicked on the tab marked "Staff." On this tab there was a portrait photo next to each staff member. They were in alphabetical order, so I didn't have far to go down the list until I came to Hannah Berger. The picture wasn't an especially flattering one. Hannah's hair was pulled back in its usual severe bun, she wore very little makeup save for two slashes of red on her lips, and her blouse was a dull tan, yet her eyes seemed haunted by sadness. No doubt she still felt the loss of her brother keenly.

I pulled up some other nearby high school websites but they were all pretty much the same. No individual student photos, and the only group ones were the sports teams. No sign of the mysterious boy on any of these either. At quarter to six I called it a day and went to the kitchen to prepare supper. Lacey wasn't very hungry after an earlier grilled cheese pig-out, so she was satisfied with a bowl of broth and then adjourned to her bedroom, wide awake after her catnap and wanting to watch the end of the Johnny Depp marathon. I polished off a bowl of broth and then a hot turkey sandwich. Nick hovered close by, hoping for a few slivers of white meat, and I dropped some in his bowl. I listened to his contented slurping while I formulated my plan for the evening. I'd park close enough to the county coroner's office so I could see, but not be seen. I was ninety-nine percent sure the FBI agent picking up John Doe would be Leroy Samms.

I finished eating and changed out of my khaki slacks and tan striped T-shirt into black jeans and a matching black mock neck sweater. I bundled my hair into a ponytail and pulled a black ski hat out of my drawer, just in case. I pulled on a black fleece jacket and was ready to go. Nick was waiting for me by the stairs, already dressed for the occasion. We went downstairs, piled into my SUV, and took off.

• • •

I was glad we'd left a little early. Traffic was unusually snarly, and I attributed it to at least three accidents along the way. It went a little faster once we were on CA1-S, and in no time I was taking the Pacific Grove exit. About ten minutes later I pulled up across the street from the low white building and checked my watch. It was just a few minutes past seven. In spite of the traffic, we'd made good time. I shut off the car and glanced over at Nick in the passenger seat. He was stretched out comfortably on his side, head on one paw, the other shielding his face. I heard the sound of light snoring. I pushed my seat back and reached in the side pocket for the latest issue of *Cosmopolitan*, and settled back. I flipped through the pages idly, pausing at one quiz.

How can you tell if your boyfriend's the right one for you? Five signs on how to tell!

A very good question, I thought. How can you tell?

I looked at sign number one: *Being around him is always fun, even when the situation isn't.*

That could easily apply to both of them, I thought. How many times over the last few years had I found myself in danger, only to be rescued by either Samms or Daniel, or both—the situation sure hadn't been fun, but I'd appreciated their presence.

For that matter, the same could be said of Nick.

I looked at sign number two and burst out laughing: *He knows about your weirdo hobbies and he's into it.* Oh, boy. Definitely a tie. Both Samms and Daniel understood my penchant for finding bodies, although Samms was more inclined to tease me about it than Daniel. And, considering they both worked for the FBI, they were most definitely into it as well. I moved onto question number three. *Supports your ambitions and goals one hundred percent.* I was considering this when I heard a loud pounding on my window. I turned my head and saw Leroy Samms glaring at me. I glanced over at Nick, who'd raised his head and opened his mouth in a wide yawn. I slid the magazine back into the side pocket, rolled down the window and gave Samms a big, wide smile. "Well, well, fancy meeting you—"

Samms held up his hand. "Save it, Red. What are you doing here?"

"Oh, it's such a lovely night, Nick and I decided to take a ride."

"And you decided to what, just park for a while across the street from the county coroner's office?"

I let my jaw drop and I hoped to heaven my expression looked surprised enough. "Is that what that big white building is?"

He inclined his head and I followed his gaze to the large sign on the lawn: *Monterey County Coroner Office.*

I clamped my lips into a thin line. "Fine. Okay, you got me. I knew it."

He expelled a breath, and I had the feeling he was having a hard time keeping from rolling his eyes. "Excellent. Progress. So, now that we've established that, what are you doing here?"

I twisted in my seat so that I could see him full-face. "I wanted to see just what FBI agent was going to show up to claim the vagrant's body," I said.

Both of Samms's eyebrows lifted. "How did you know that?"

I deliberately widened my eyes. "Know what?"

"You know darn well what. How did you know the FBI was picking up the body tonight?"

I slumped back in my seat. "I have my sources. You know as well as I do it's not good to rat out an informant."

"Nora . . ." he began, and I knew I was in for a lecture. Since the best way I know of to avoid getting a lecture is to start giving one, I ignored his interruption and continued talking.

"That's why Dale called you to come down to Waincroft Manor, isn't it? She recognized the corpse as either an FBI informant, or maybe one of yours. So, were the two of you working on something? Is that what got that man killed?"

When his eyes darkened and the muscle started to work in his lower jaw, I knew I'd struck a nerve. "Oh my God, that's it, isn't it. What were the two of you working on?"

A long, dark sedan rounded the corner and pulled into the county coroner's driveway. Samms leaned into my window. "Got a piece of paper and a pen?"

I fished in my tote, handed them to him. He scribbled something down, then handed the items back to me.

I looked at the paper. "Moe's Bar and Grill? Really? What has that got to do with—"

"It's about ten minutes from here off the main drag of Salinas," Samms interrupted me. "Go there, get a table and wait for me."

"While you do what? Take care of the body?"

"If you want me to tell you anything you'll keep quiet and head out. Now."

I could tell from the stubborn set to his jaw that I wasn't going to find out anything more unless I did as he asked. I nodded, and Samms stepped away from the window. I rolled it up, started up the SUV and pulled away from the curb.

Nick sat up straight in the passenger seat and cocked his head at me. "Er-erup?"

"We're going somewhere to wait for Samms to come across with some answers," I told him. I looked down at the magazine jammed into the side pocket and shook my head.

"Definitely not supportive," I mumbled.

• • •

I followed the directions Samms had scribbled down and found North Street without much trouble. The bar stood on the corner's edge and was totally black, save for the battered stone front flanking heavy oaken doors with lights on either side. A wooden plaque right above the doors read in large block letters, *Moe's Bar and Grill*, and the title was repeated in thick black letters on the large picture window that took up almost all of the building's right side. Fortunately there was a parking spot right in front of the building, and I maneuvered the SUV into it without too much trouble. I hopped out, but when Nick started to follow I shook my head.

"Sorry, fella. This bar probably isn't like the Poker Face. They most likely have a no animals allowed policy. You wait here, okay?"

Nick made a grumbly sound deep in his throat and eyed me balefully for a few seconds before settling back on the seat, his head on his front paws. I pushed aside any pangs of guilt I felt at leaving him there, made sure the windows were cracked open, then locked the SUV and hurried inside.

I stepped inside and stood for a moment on the threshold, letting my eyes adjust to the dim lighting. A life-sized skeleton beckoned to me from the corner, a large rat at its feet. Ghostly music played softly in the background. A young girl wearing an almost nonexistent black skirt and white blouse appeared almost instantly. "Table for one?" she asked in a bored voice.

Samms had said to get a table, so I nodded. "For two please. I'm expecting someone."

She showed me to a small table off to the left of the bar. The tables were all covered with orange and black checked tablecloths, a large orange candle in the center. She placed two plastic menus on the table. "Your server is Addie," she said. "She'll be with you shortly."

A dark-haired Filipino boy came over and placed two glasses of water down on the table. As I sipped mine, I glanced at the menu. The fare seemed almost as enticing as what Lance served at the Poker Face: burgers, club sandwiches, appetizers. I set the menu down and a shadow fell across the table, and Samms eased himself into the chair next to mine. I pushed my menu off to one side and smiled at him. "Charming place. Come here often?"

"More than I'd like."

I looked at him. "Is this where you used to meet your CI, John Doe?"

"Once or twice." He gave a swift glance around. "By rights I shouldn't tell you a thing, but I know you. You'll chip away at this and poke your nose in where it doesn't belong until you get answers, so I figure this'll save us both a lot of trouble. Besides, I'm hungry."

A pretty brunette wearing a black shirt and matching slacks came over to our table, pad and pen in hand. I figured this must be Addie. She gave Samms a wide smile, showing off her perfect white teeth. "Hey, Lee. Nice to see you again." Her gaze shifted to me then back to Samms. "Your usual?" At his nod, she glanced at me. "And your friend?"

"I'll have what he's having," I said, hoping that I wouldn't regret that choice, but right now I was more interested in what Samms had to say than anything else. Addie picked up the menus and departed, and I leaned my chin in my palm. "Okay. I'm listening."

"What I say to you is extremely confidential, okay? Not one word to anyone, and that includes Chantal, your sister, Ollie. No one."

"How about Nick? Can I share details with him?"

He rolled his eyes and then said, "John Doe's real name is Emanuel Delgado. We called him Manny. He used to be a programmer, and a damn good one until there was a fire at the company where he worked, and he got injured rescuing a coworker."

"So that's how his fingers got burned."

Samms nodded. "Yep. He got a pretty big settlement from the company and between that and disability he was pretty well set."

"Then he wasn't a vagrant?"

"Not in the strictest sense of the word. He wasn't hurting financially, but mentally . . . well, he started dressing the part of a hobo, hanging around the shelters, the docks, places like that. He said once he'd always been curious how the downtrodden lived."

"So he became one of them?"

Samms nodded. "Sort of. He got a kick out of playing the vagrant role, and he was good at getting people to confide in him, and I'm not just talking about harmless hobos here. He came through with info on a couple of cases when I worked St. Leo. A few of 'em were murder cases that might still be open if not for Manny." He let out a slow breath. "I hadn't heard from him since I left St. Leo, and then all of a sudden he called me a few weeks ago, out of the blue. Said he'd heard I was FBI now, and he might have a lead on a cold case, one with a reward. He wanted to know if I was interested in his information."

Samms fell silent as Addie reappeared and set two bottles of Heineken in front of us. Samms grabbed the bottle, took a long pull on his beer and sat back, eyes closed.

"You were saying," I prompted. "Manny called you with information on an old case."

"Yeah." He opened his eyes and looked at me. "I said sure I was interested and he said good, he'd be in touch. Then a few days later he called again. He wanted to meet at our old place, the park in St. Leo. He said he was really onto something and he might even have the case solved. I went to the park at midnight but he never showed." His fingers tightened around the beer bottle. "The next day Dale called me. The minute she saw the corpse, she knew who it was. She'd had a few dealings with Manny herself and thought I might be interested." He let out a breath. "The whole thing's a puzzle."

Addie reappeared with a large basket of cheese fries that she set in the middle of the table and two burgers that I had to admit smelled heavenly. In spite of the fact I'd already eaten, I suddenly felt ravenous. I squirted ketchup liberally on the burger and took a large bite.

"Umm, this is really good!"

"Coming from you, that's a high compliment," said Samms. He popped a cheese fry into his mouth and chewed it deliberately before adding, "To be honest, the rest of their food isn't that good, but their burgers are beyond belief."

I had to agree. "It's cooked to perfection. Whoever seasoned this burger did a terrific job. This date might not be that big of a bust after all."

He slid me a glance. "You consider this a date?"

"It's you and me in a pub, having dinner. That qualifies as a date." I took another bite and savored it before I asked, "What was the case he had a lead on? Maybe there's some sort of a clue in that as to what he was doing at Waincroft Manor."

Samms picked up his napkin and dabbed at his lips. "That's the thing. I don't know what case it was. He just said that he was in the process of gathering evidence that would close the case, and he wanted to make sure he got the reward money."

"I thought you said he was well-off."

"The money wasn't for him. He wanted to donate it to Saint Paul's Shelter in St. Leo, because they'd always been good to him when he was down and out." He passed a hand across his eyes. "Manny was a good guy. He certainly didn't deserve to die like that."

"Exsanguination was the cause of death?"

"We're still not definite on that. The body was drained of blood, and without blood, it's hard to run tests to tell if he might have had any poisons or medications in his system, but we're not giving up. He had a good-sized bump on his head, but we're not certain that was the cause of death." He ran his hand along his jawline. "Maybe once I figure out what case Manny had info on, pieces of this puzzle will start to fall into place."

"I agree. So where do we start?"

Samms shot me a sharp look. "*We* don't start anything. I'm working this case."

I turned on my sunniest smile. "Of course you are. But maybe I can help."

He leaned in a bit closer to me, and I caught a whiff of his aftershave, a combo of musk and sandalwood. "I told you what I did to satisfy that insatiable curiosity of yours. Now you have to promise me, Red, for your own safety, you won't do any more probing. If you want a story for *Noir*, I'll give you an exclusive once the case is solved. Stay away from Waincroft Manor."

"You're forgetting that I'm on the decorating committee at the mansion, plus I'm doing the catering. It's kind of hard for me to stay away."

He wiped some ketchup from the side of his lip with his napkin. "Fine. Then just stick to the decorating and the catering, and refrain from investigating. I need you in one piece for Saturday night."

My eyes narrowed. "What's Saturday night?"

He sighed. "I was going to surprise you, but I thought we'd have dinner at the Seaside Grill, and then I got tickets for *Phantom* at the Bay Theatre."

"*Phantom!*" I squealed. "*Of the Opera?*"

"Is there any other?" He grinned. "I asked Chantal when I heard they were coming and she said it was your favorite play. It's one of mine too." He leaned forward. "So promise me, will ya, Red, that you won't take any unnecessary chances and you'll leave the investigating to me? Can I have your word on that? Are you even listening to me?"

My attention had been momentarily distracted as the door to the bar opened and a familiar figure walked in. Grant Goodeve, one of the paranormal investigators. He sidled up to the bar, and I leaned forward a bit in my seat. Moe's was definitely a long way from Cruz. If Grant had wanted a drink the Poker Face was much more accessible, and there were other bars in towns much closer than Salinas. What was he doing here?

Samms leaned forward and hissed in my ear, "Red!" so loudly I jumped.

"Goodness, what?" I snapped. "I'm sitting right across from you. You don't have to shout right in my ear."

"You're a million miles away," he chided. "Did you even hear what I said?"

"Yes, yes. Saturday night, dinner at the Seaside Grill, tickets to *Phantom.*"

"That's not all I said. I want you to promise me . . ."

I rose abruptly and held up my bottle. "I need a refill, and I can't wait for our waitress. How about you?"

"I could go for another. But first I want you . . . hey! I'm not done."

I pushed back my seat while Samms was still talking and edged up to the bar. There was an empty stool a few down from where Grant sat, and I slid onto it. The bartender, a good-looking guy with light hair and a pencil mustache, set a napkin in front of me almost immediately.

"Hey, good-lookin'," he said. "What can I get you?"

Normally I would have flirted a bit but I had other fish to fry. "A Heineken, please," I said with a smile. A pudgy, dark-skinned man sat on the stool beside me, and a stout, dark-haired woman on the stool in between him and Grant. From the whispering and snickering going on it was pretty obvious this was a hookup that seemed to be going well. With any luck, they'd leave shortly and then I could—what, exactly? Confront Grant? Ask him why he was here instead of the Poker Face? And then have him tell me that it was none of my business?

Just as I was thinking this was a bad idea and I should return to my table, the man and woman abruptly stood up and the man tossed a twenty on the counter; then, arms wrapped around each other, they headed for the door. I glanced around and then moved over one stool. Grant was talking on his cell phone, a bottle of Bud in front of him, and he was paying no attention whatsoever to me. I hesitated, then moved over so that now I was on the stool right next to him. His back was angled toward me, so I leaned over as far as I dared, pretending to feign interest in the bowl of nuts that was perched on the counter. Grant was obviously irked about something, because he raised his voice slightly—not a lot, but enough so that I could catch what he was saying.

"Of course I'm pissed," he hissed into the phone. "I only missed the body by that much. I could have gotten a good video of it, bite marks and all . . . you didn't tell anyone else about the body being claimed tonight, did you?" A few minutes of silence, and then, "That's what I thought. I didn't think you'd pull that on us. I tried to find out where they'd taken it, but that guy Fishbein was less than cooperative. He said if I wanted to find that out I'd have to hold my own séance and contact the guy's spirit. Can you imagine?" He let out a deep sigh. "Guess I can kiss getting an exclusive video of *that* goodbye."

I couldn't imagine Harvey Fishbein coming up with a line that good but apparently he had. I was super-curious, though, as to just who was feeding these people all this information. I knew darn well it wasn't Al, and it certainly wasn't Harvey. Davey's mysterious contact was the obvious choice, but unless Al Bennett was double-crossing me and feeding them the info, how had they known about the body being claimed tonight?

A young girl came in, motioned to the bartender and whispered something. The bartender nodded, then said, "Anyone here own a Prius? License Plate GHST85? You're parked in a tow zone."

"Oh, crap!" Grant flung down his phone on the bar and slid off the stool. "I'll be right back," he yelled over his shoulder as he made a beeline for the door. I glanced quickly around. No one was looking. I reached out, grabbed his phone, and hit redial. It rang once, twice, and then a deep voice answered.

"Cruz Police Department. How can I direct your call?"

Chapter Fifteen

Well, at least I had a good idea of where the ghostbusters were getting their information. Now I had to determine who at the Cruz PD was giving it to them. Out of the corner of my eye I saw Samms start to rise from his seat. I set the phone down, quickly grabbed my bottle of Heineken and headed back to the table. Samms glared at me as I lowered myself into my chair.

"Just what was that all about?" he asked.

I raised the almost empty bottle. "What? I told you I was thirsty." I took a quick sip and set the bottle down. "Sorry I forgot to order you another one."

He leaned back in his chair and folded his arms across his chest. "Don't play dumb with me, Red. I was watching you very closely. I saw you move over next to that guy and grab his phone the minute he sprinted out the door. So, you'd better spill it."

"Fine. That was Grant Goodeve, the head ghostbuster on *Paranormal Phenomenon*. I overheard a little of his phone conversation, enough to know that he just missed getting a video of Manny's body."

Samms's face darkened. *"What!"*

"Ssh." I leaned in a bit closer. "He was talking to someone and telling them that he'd just missed you claiming the body. He asked whoever it was if they'd told anyone else, and then he said that Fishbein was less than cooperative, and said if he wanted a video he'd have to contact the guy's spirit."

Samms's eyes widened. "Harvey said that? He's got more of a sense of humor than I gave him credit for."

"Yeah, well, that's not the best part. When he jumped up to move his car I decided to see what the last number he'd dialed was, and I got the desk at the Cruz PD. I can't think of any reason why he'd be calling the police, or vice versa—unless, of course, he wanted to talk to Anderson about getting into Waincroft Manor."

Samms drummed his fingers on the tabletop, his eyes slitted as he thought. "I worked with those guys, although quite a few have left since then. None of the men under me would ever do something like that."

"I agree. But Dale's been hiring a lot of new people lately."

He nodded. "Some of 'em retired, and some of 'em left because, quite honestly, they didn't like working for a woman."

I was tempted to ask, *"A woman? Or Dale in particular?"* but figured I should leave well enough alone. "Maybe one of her new recruits isn't as trustworthy as she thinks."

He rubbed his hand down his empty Heineken bottle. "It wouldn't be the first time something like this has happened. Cops starting out don't make a great salary, and if they've got a family to support and someone comes along and offers 'em a lot of money—heck, it happens. Tomorrow I'll go over there, get the lowdown on all the new hires, see if I can pinpoint who the ghostbuster's mole might be." He leaned closer to me. "Me, not you. You stick to making sandwiches and decorating the Waincroft mansion, and I'll stick to solving the case. I'm still not convinced your friend Enola doesn't know more than she's letting on, either."

I shifted in my seat. "Speaking of that . . ."

I told Samms what I'd found out from Ethan Howell. Samms listened, and when I'd finished, gave a brisk nod. To his credit, he refrained from saying "told you so," saying instead, "I'll check it out." I decided not to mention I'd already left my number at the funeral parlor with a request for a call-back.

The door opened and Grant hurried back in. He walked over to the bar and asked loudly, "Say, did anyone happen to find a phone—oh, there it is." He reached over and grabbed it, fiddled with it a few minutes, then shoved it in his pocket. He dipped his hand in his other pocket, pulled out a bill and dropped it on the counter. With a quick wave at the bartender, he vanished out the door.

"He's in a big hurry," I observed. "I wonder where he's going."

"Maybe he remembered a hot date."

"He looked at his phone, and then he couldn't get out of here fast enough. Maybe there was a text message on it. Maybe it was a lead on where they took Manny's body."

Samms shook his head. "Couldn't be. No one at Cruz PD or anywhere else, for that matter, is privy to that information. Not even Harvey Fishbein. So, unless my men were followed, which is doubtful, cross that off your list."

"Okay, then my other choice is maybe one of the other ghostbusters called him. Maybe they got into Waincroft Manor and they were texting him to come on down."

"If they got into Waincroft Manor tonight they'd have had to hire a boat. That road's still flooded from the storm. It won't even be accessible till tomorrow."

I tapped at my chin with my forefinger. "Not from the main road, no. There's a back way there, though."

"Yes, but that way has a lot of twists and turns. They wouldn't know how to navigate those roads in the dark. If he got a text it has nothing to do with Waincroft Manor. And even if it did, they aren't going to find any evidence that Bartescue has risen from his grave."

"That doesn't mean they aren't going to try and manufacture something."

His eyes widened and he let his jaw drop. "Nora! You think they're fakes? You mean they haven't found real ghosts?"

I rolled my eyes. "Very funny. One of them, Felix, showed me a video of this ghost they were supposed to have found. I didn't say anything, but it sure looked faked to me."

Samms let out a loud guffaw. "Ninety-nine percent of those TV shows about ghosts and the likes are faked, Nora. They're classified as reality shows, but do you ever see the credits at the end? They've got writers and directors just like any other television show."

"Still, it's rather convenient, their turning up here at just this time, don't you think? Maybe you should be checking into whether or not any of these people might have some sort of past with Manny Delgado?"

"A long shot, if you ask me, but . . . yeah, I'll check it out. You never know." His hand shot out to cover mine. "I'll do that. You take your cat on home and give him a big saucer of milk. He looked pretty lonely, out there in your car."

I started. I'd completely forgotten about Nick. What kind of human was I? "You're right," I said, rising. "I should go."

He fixed me with a stare. "Straight home."

I batted my eyelashes. "Of course. Don't I always follow instructions?"

That got me a half smile. "Do you really want me to answer that?"

I leaned over, gave him a quick kiss on the lips. "No," I said. "I don't. I'll see you tomorrow." I gave him a saucy wave and headed for the door. Once outside, I let out a long breath. It had been quite a night, and I'd learned a lot. Now, if only these clues would make sense! I walked the few steps over to where I'd parked my SUV, and had to chuckle as I saw Nick's head pop up and peer out the window on the passenger side. I walked over and tapped on the glass.

"Miss me, buddy? Sorry to keep you waiting so long."

Nick yawned, then swiveled his head so he was looking straight ahead. I followed his gaze and saw a white object stuck between my windshield wiper blades. I groaned. It had to be either an advertisement or a ticket. I leaned over and picked it up and saw it was neither. It was a white envelope, similar to the last one, with *Nora Charles* printed exactly the same way, in block letters across the face.

I gave a quick glance around, but the street was deserted. I walked around the car, unlocked it, and slid behind the wheel. Nick leaned over, butted my elbow with his head. I waved the envelope in front of him.

"Did you see who left this?"

Nick stretched, then curled himself back up into a ball on the seat and closed his eyes. If he knew, he wasn't telling.

I slit the envelope with the edge of my nail, and another single sheet of paper fell out. I picked it up and read the words printed there:

The cold case is the key—but instead of looking outside the box, put it in a whole new one. Watch out for smoke and mirrors and unnecessary distractions. Things are not as they appear.

"Oh, come on!"

I banged my fist against the steering wheel. Whoever left this had to have overheard Samms and me talking. I racked my brain, trying to remember who'd been seated around us. There had been a young couple, an old man and . . . I had a vague impression of someone seated at a table near the kitchen. It was a dark corner, and the figure had been merely a shadow. I tugged on a strand of hair, hard. I'd aced observation in my PI class, but where were my powers of observation when I needed them most? I'd definitely been asleep at the wheel for that one. I'd been so preoccupied with the body, and the ghostbusters, I'd paid zippo attention to my surroundings. I shoved the paper and envelope into my tote and turned the key in the ignition.

I slid a glance at Nick. "You must have seen who left that note," I said.

Nick's eyes were closed. Apparently he'd decided this was as good a time as any to grab forty winks. He let out a loud snore. I sighed.

"This is one of those times when I wish you could talk. But if you could, just what would you say?"

I had to admit, I was afraid to find out.

• • •

It was almost ten when I let myself in the back door of Hot Bread. I slipped off my jacket, booted up my laptop, and then went over to the stove and put the kettle on for a cup of hot tea. Nick hovered around my feet, rubbing against my ankles—hungry as usual. I pulled out a can of whitefin tuna and spooned it into his bowl. He walked over, sniffed at the contents, and then looked up at me with his big golden eyes.

"Merow?"

"No, you are not getting any leftovers," I said sternly. "You like the tuna, Nick."

He looked again at the bowl, then at me. "Merow?"

"If you're that hungry, you'll eat it."

The kettle started to whistle and I hurried back to the stove, poured water into a large mug. I selected a chamomile teabag and plopped it in. I carried the mug back to the table. Nick had hunkered down in front of his food bowl, apparently resigned to his fate of eating canned cat food instead of leftover lobster salad, and I could hear his slurping sounds. I reached into my jacket pocket and pulled out my cell phone. I hit the message button, and saw I had two. The first was from Samms: "Hey, Red. You'd better be at home. I'll be driving by to make sure your car is in your driveway." I chuckled and then hit play for the second message. "Nora, it's Hannah Berger. There's something I need to tell you, concerning what we talked about today. I think I may have recognized the man in that sketch after all. He may have taken something from my table at the sale. But I've got to make certain of something, I guess I'll text you later. Maybe we can meet up, if not tonight, then tomorrow." I saved the message and hit redial. It went into Hannah's voicemail. "Hannah, it's Nora. I'm home now. Call or text me when you can."

I set the phone down. There didn't seem to be anything more I could do on the Hannah front, so I snatched up my purse. I pulled out the mysterious note, which I propped up right next to my laptop. I took a sip of tea, then called up my favorite search engine and typed in, "Open FBI Cases that offer rewards." I gasped as more than a half million hits came up. My query was definitely in need of some refining. I thought a moment, then typed in, "Open FBI Cases offering rewards for information on crimes that occurred in California" and hit enter.

Even more hits! Damn. Narrowing it down to California made it worse.

How was that even possible? Was this state such a hotbed of unsolved crime? Apparently so.

I tried again. "Open FBI cases offering rewards in Monterey County, CA."

This still got too many hits. I groaned. Maybe I'd have better luck on the FBI's own website. I typed it into the browser. When the homepage came up, I typed in "open cases offering rewards."

Twenty-five hits. Hm, big difference. I went down the list. Believe it or not, the Lindbergh Kidnapping was still listed. There was a kidnapping that had occurred in Los Angeles five years ago—I ruled that one out. LA seemed a bit far. A ten-thousand-dollar reward for any information leading to the apprehension of two credit union robbers seemed pretty viable— until I saw it was in Minnesota. Two strikes.

I looked again at the note. *Instead of looking outside the box, put it in a whole new one.* Just thinking about what that bit of advice meant made my head hurt. I wasn't even touching the "smoke and mirrors" reference. That had migraine written all over it.

I went down the list and by the time midnight rolled around I'd narrowed it down to three. One offered a fifteen-thousand-dollar reward for any information on an organized criminal ring believed to have burglarized more than seventy-five jewelry stores of almost nine million dollars in jewelry. The burglaries centered on national, mall-based stores and had victimized sixteen different companies across the United States. I recognized one of the names as a prominent jewelry chain that had stores in California, one in nearby Carmel. The second was a twenty-five-thousand-dollar reward for any information on an armored car heist of a shipment of antique gold coins and artifacts en route to the Monterey Museum of Art. But it was the third that really grabbed my attention. A fifty-thousand-dollar reward for any information on an armored car heist that had occurred outside of Salinas a few years ago.

I pulled up the account and read it with interest. The armored car left the First National Bank branch in Salinas and pulled into a gas station. The guard had just started fueling up when two men with rifles approached. They knocked the guard over the head, beat him up and left him at the side of the road along with the driver, who they also beat up. They took off with the truck. Another car pulled in shortly thereafter and reported the incident. Police found the armored car down a deserted side road, over four million in cash gone. To date the perps had not been caught, and none of the stolen money recovered.

I leaned back and closed my eyes. That definitely sounded interesting. In most robberies, the money turns up at some point, usually leading a trail back to the robbers. In this case, however, nothing had been heard of either the money or the robbers in two years.

I plugged in "Salinas Armored Car Heist" and the date into the search engine and several news accounts came up. I read each one, and they all said pretty much the same thing. The assailants had both worn stocking masks and hats pulled down low. The taller man's cap had slipped a bit, and the guard had seen the man was bald, but that was as much of a description as either man could give. The FBI had originally thought it might have been an inside job, but the guard and driver checked out. Spotless records, no evidence of anything untoward. There was no mention of names, however. I looked up the numbers of the First National Bank in Salinas, and ArmLink, the armored car company. It was too late tonight, of course, but tomorrow I'd do a little checking into those employees' backgrounds.

Nick lofted up onto the chair beside mine and opened his mouth wide in a yawn. I reached over to scratch him on the white streak behind his ear. I found this particular cold case puzzling. Why wouldn't a trace of either the money or the robbers have shown up in all this time? There could be several reasons for that. The crooks might have been arrested on another charge before they could spend the cash, and might even now be doing time for another crime. As for the money, well, they could have hidden it somewhere . . .

"Oh my God!"

I sat bolt upright, startling Nick, who jumped off my lap. I rose and started to pace.

Put it in a whole new box. That's exactly what I was doing. Of course, by doing that the result was pretty fantastic, but . . .

It made sense. A crazy kind of sense, but sense.

"Merow!" came impatiently from the chair next to mine. I bent down and scooped Nick into my arms. He cocked his head and blinked at me, obviously waiting for me to explain my earlier outburst.

I gave his white streak a quick scratch. "It's pretty far out there, but it's the only thing I can think of that might account for Manny's being at Waincroft Manor. He didn't get a lead on the robbers themselves. He got a lead on what they stole. That money from the armored car heist is hidden somewhere in Waincroft Manor."

Nick lifted his head. "Merow."

I got up and started to pace. "If the robber stashed the money in Waincroft Manor, it had to be someone familiar with the place, right?"

Nick blinked.

"Enola? That's a real long shot. Why would she need to steal money? She makes a good living from her aunt's curio shop, right?"

Although what had Joannie said? Waincroft Manor ate up a lot of her income in taxes. But still, the thought of Enola engineering such a daring robbery was stretching pretty far. I stroked Nick's head. "Tomorrow I'm making a few phone calls, see what else I can find out about this bank robbery, and who was involved. Maybe then some of these puzzle pieces will fall into place."

Nick looked up at me and opened his mouth in a wide yawn.

"Right. It's late. We need our beauty sleep."

I shut out the lights and then Nick and I climbed the stairs to our apartment. I undressed and got into bed, and then I checked my phone one last time before shutting out the light. There was no text or message from Hannah, but by now, I hadn't really expected to get one.

Chapter Sixteen

At nine o'clock the big breakfast rush was under control, so I felt justified in excusing myself and heading upstairs to make a few phone calls. Lacey's door was shut tight—still sleeping, no doubt—so I went into my den and shut the door. I dialed the number of the First National Bank and after a few minutes a perky-sounding girl's voice said, "First National Bank! How may I direct your call?"

"Good morning," I said, trying to inject the same amount of perkiness into my tone but not succeeding. "My name is Nora Charles. I was wondering if I might speak with your manager? Parker Peterman, correct?"

"Yes, Mr. Peterman is our manager but he's out of town at the moment. Can I direct your call to Anita Elk, his assistant?"

Damn. "I'd rather speak directly with Mr. Peterman. When will he be back in the office?"

"He should be in tomorrow. But Ms. Elk is very knowledgeable and perfectly capable of handling any concerns you might have."

"Fine."

A few minutes later another female voice, even perkier sounding than the first, came over the line. "Anita Elk speaking. How may I assist you?" Without waiting for an answer she went on, "We have a wonderful promotion this month. Put five hundred dollars in one of our CDs and you'll get three point five percent! That's practically unheard of! And if you're in business, we also have a promotion for business checking accounts."

I interrupted her mid-spiel to inform her I was a freelance reporter (not a total lie) and explained that I was in the midst of doing a story on unsolved crimes. "I'm researching the armored car robbery that took place a few years ago. Would you know anything about that?"

"Armored car robbery? Hm, I'm sorry, I don't, but then again I've only been the assistant manager here a few months. Our manager, Parker Peterman, would probably remember it. I believe he was the assistant manager at the time."

"Great. Could you ask him to return my call."

"Certainly. Ms. Charles, right? C-h-a-r-l-e-s?" There was a pause during which she presumably scribbled down my name and number and then she said brightly, "Are you certain you're happy with your current bank, Ms. Charles? The interest rate on our loans this month is very good."

I thanked her for her time and hung up before she tried to interest me in a retirement account.

Next I dialed the number of ArmLink Armored Car and asked to speak to their HR department. A few minutes later a bored female voice said, "ArmLink HR, Emmie speaking. How can I help you?"

"Good morning," I said in my best professional tone. "My name is Nora Charles. I'm a freelance reporter doing an article on cold cases, and I was wondering if I could speak to someone who could verify some information on two of your employees."

The tone turned from bored to guarded. "What sort of information?"

"I've got some questions regarding an armored car heist that happened about two years ago. I'd like to speak to someone who can give me some information on the ArmLink employees who were involved."

A long pause, and then: "Just a minute."

The dreaded Muzak came on, but fortunately I didn't have to listen to it long. After a few minutes a gruff male voice came over the line. "Barney Hicks here. I'm the Director of Personnel. Would you mind telling me exactly who you are and what it is you're looking for?"

I repeated my spiel once again. When I finished, Barney said, "As far as I know, the crooks were never caught and the money never recovered. Our company was found to be not at fault in any way. I really can't say any more than that."

"Yes, I'm aware of that. I was wondering if you might be able to provide me with contact information for those men."

"Contact information?" He sounded puzzled.

"Yes. I'd really like to interview them. Get the story firsthand."

"They were already interviewed and cleared by the FBI," Hicks said brusquely. "If you need more information for your article you should contact them directly. I have nothing else to add, except that my employees are above reproach and I stand behind every one of them."

"I understand that but—"

Click.

"Hm." I looked at Nick, who was playing with one of his catnip mice at my feet. "Well, I blew that all right, although Mr. Hicks seemed a little disturbed by my questions. Maybe he's not as convinced of his employees' innocence as he'd like people to believe."

Nick didn't answer, just kept chewing on the catnip mouse's tail. Well, maybe I'd have better luck quizzing the bank manager tomorrow, one way or another. I sighed. I went back downstairs, and just in the nick of time too. There was a line that stretched almost to the door. For the next half hour, Mollie and I worked preparing breakfast specials, and finally when the last customer had been served, Mollie let out a giant sigh and grinned at me.

"We haven't had a line like that in a long time. It must be that William Hurt Hotcake Sandwich. They were flying out of here like, well, like hotcakes."

I grinned back. "You know, Mollie, when you need to ask for a favor, you don't have to butter me up by complimenting my sandwiches."

Her jaw dropped. "I don't do that, do I?"

"Yeah, you kinda do. And it's not necessary, so spill. What do you need?"

"I hate to ask, because you've already given me so much time off, but . . . that witch MacGruder is giving us a science quiz tomorrow and I really need extra time to study for it. Science isn't my strong suit."

I remembered Florence MacGruder from my own high school days and was frankly amazed the woman was still there. We'd all thought she was a hag even then. "Sure, you can have the extra time. When do you need to leave?"

She wrinkled her nose. "Could I go now? I can work all day Friday to make up the time."

"No need for that, but if you want to, you can." As she took off her apron I walked over to my tote and pulled out the sketch. "Before you go, could you take a look at this?"

Mollie peered over my shoulder at the sketch. "Say, he's kinda cute. Who did that, Lacey?"

"Yes. You don't recognize him? You've never seen him at Cruz High?"

She leaned in for a closer look. "You know, I think I have seen him somewhere," she said at last. "But not at school, though." She whipped out her iPhone and snapped a photo of the sketch. "Kara Wait's in my study group. I'll show it to her. She's on the school newspaper. If anyone might recognize him, it's her."

"I'd really appreciate that, thanks." I gave her arm a quick squeeze. "And just make sure you ace that quiz."

Mollie shrugged into her jacket, gave me a quick wave and took off, and I settled down at the table in the back with a steaming mug of coffee. Nick lay stretched out full-length in front of the refrigerator, eyes closed, obviously catching up on his beauty sleep. I decided he had the right idea, so I stretched my legs out too, propping them up on the chair across from me. I leaned back, took a sip of my coffee, and closed my eyes. No sooner had I done so than my cell started to vibrate. I reached into my apron pocket and looked at the number. When I saw Collins Funeral Home on the screen, I set down the mug and depressed the answer button on my phone.

"Ms. Charles?" asked a reedy voice. "This is Allan Collins. My assistant left me a message that you are inquiring about a Ms. Enola Waincroft?"

"Yes." I crossed my fingers and sucked in a deep breath. "I'm working with the Cruz police on a case. Ms. Waincroft is a witness, and we need to verify her whereabouts in conjunction with her testimony. I understand she was at your establishment on Saturday, the third of this month?"

"The third, the third . . . yes, she was here. She came to get the key to Waincroft Manor she'd messengered to us."

I swallowed. "She messengered you a key to the mansion? Could I ask for what purpose?"

"Why, for the delivery, of course."

Delivery? "Just for my records, Mr. Collins, exactly what delivery was that?"

"The coffin."

I almost dropped my phone. "I'm sorry, I'm not certain I heard correctly. Did you say coffin?"

"Yes. She placed the order about two weeks ago. She wanted a coffin delivered to the Waincroft estate. Was rather specific about what she wanted, too."

"What do you mean?"

"I mean, she didn't want one of our stock coffins. It had to be made of knotted pine, and the interior had to be lined with bronze satin. She even faxed me a drawing of just what she wanted." He paused. "Does any of this help you?"

"Yes, and thank you for calling back so promptly." I disconnected and stood, tapping my phone against my chin. Why on earth would Enola order a coffin? So she could put a dead man's body in it?

At least now I knew just where the coffin had come from; but it seemed every time one question was answered, two more even more puzzling ones cropped up. I winced as I thought about Samms's reaction to this since he hadn't trusted Enola right from the start.

Nick butted his head against my elbow. "Murp," he said. "Merow."

"True. Enola might have a perfectly logical explanation for why she ordered a coffin—although I'm at a loss to think what it might be." I dialed the number of the Cruz Inn and asked to be put through to her room. After a few minutes I was informed there was no answer. I thanked the switchboard operator and hung up, then dialed Cruz High. A young girl answered, and I asked to speak to Hannah Berger.

"Sorry. Hannah didn't come in today."

"She called in sick?"

"Dunno. All I know is she didn't come in. I'm not sure if she called in or not."

I thanked the girl and hung up. The whole thing just didn't hit me right. I doubted greatly Hannah had missed more than one or two days in her entire career at Cruz High. I debated calling Anderson, but since a person isn't officially considered missing until after forty-eight hours, there probably wasn't much she could do. In the end I did call, but was informed that Anderson was out and they weren't sure just when she'd be back. I hung up, thinking it was probably just as well. I hated feeling helpless, but there really wasn't anything more I could do. And then another disturbing thought occurred to me.

I hadn't been able to reach Enola either. Were their disappearances connected?

Chapter Seventeen

My regular lunch crowd started to shuffle in, so I didn't have too much time to dwell on either Hannah or Enola. Chantal hurried in the back door a few minutes past twelve, apologizing profusely for her tardiness. We worked filling orders for the next hour, and when the last customer had been served, finally collapsed at the table in the back.

"Whew," I exclaimed. "What a morning, in more ways than one."

Chantal looked at me. "You sound as if you've made some progress."

"I have, I think. For one thing, I found out that Enola hasn't been entirely truthful." I quickly filled my friend in on Enola's ordering the coffin, and Chantal's eyes almost bugged out of her head.

"Ooh," she said, "that is so . . . macabre. Why on earth would she do something like that?"

"An excellent question, and one for which I have no good answer. I'm ashamed to say the first reason that popped into my mind was that she wanted it to put the body in."

"Don't feel too guilty. That was the first thing I thought of too," Chantal confessed. "But, chérie, that makes no sense. Enola is not a murderer. She has no motive for killing that man. She does not even know him, right? To be honest, the only person I could picture her killing would be Hannah."

"Funny you should say that," I said, and then filled her in on recent events regarding the other woman.

Chantal held out her arms when I'd finished. "Look, chérie. I have goose bumps. I hate to say it, but I do not have a good feeling about Hannah, or Enola either."

I studied my friend for a minute. "Something else is bothering you, Chantal. What is it?"

My friend avoided my gaze. "I am not sure if I should tell you, chérie."

I slid into the seat across from her. "Well, you know I'll just nag you until you do, so . . . out with it."

"Fine." She placed her hands in front of her on the table. "After our talk the other day, I did a reading on Daniel last night. The Chariot and all four aces came up. Sure signs of danger."

I felt the hairs on the back of my neck start to rise. Chantal's readings were usually amazingly accurate. As a matter of fact, it's scary how accurate they can be. "Are you certain?" I asked.

She nodded. "The final card, though, was the World. It usually indicates success in work-related matters. So while Daniel's mission is dangerous, the signs are indicative of a favorable ending."

I let out the breath I'd been holding. "Let's hope so," I said. I glanced at the clock on the wall and added, "Do you think you could do me a favor and close up here and meet me out at Waincroft? I've got a few errands I've got to run."

"No problem. And in between customers I'll keep trying to get hold of Enola and Hannah. Worst-case scenario, we'll see them at Waincroft Manor this afternoon, right?"

"Right." I nodded grimly. *If either one shows up.*

• • •

I put the whole Daniel reading out of my mind with an effort and got to the high school office a few minutes before two thirty. There was a different girl behind the reception desk, a freckle-faced redhead with her hair done in two pigtails. She gave me a wide smile as I approached, displaying her braces proudly. "Good morning, can I help you?"

I returned the smile and saw *Melinda* printed on her name tag. "Good morning, Melinda. I'm looking for Hannah Berger."

Melinda's smooth brow furrowed. "Hannah? I don't think she came in today, but let me check." She turned toward the desk in the back, where a dark-haired woman of around thirty sat, pounding away on a keyboard. "Sofie! Did Hannah Berger come in today?"

Sofie glanced up and pushed her tortoiseshell glasses up on her nose. "No, come to think of it, she didn't." She got up and walked over to the front counter, where she picked up a black and white notebook. She looked at it and frowned. "She didn't call in, either. That is odd, but . . ." She set the notebook down and tugged at a stray curl. "I know the conference ran late last night and Hannah was one of the last to leave. Maybe she overslept this morning and just decided to take the day off."

I personally didn't think Hannah would do that without calling in, but I refrained from saying it. "Is there someone who worked here last night I could talk to?" I asked.

Sofie glanced at the clock. "If you want to hang out for a bit, Ali Larter's due in at two forty-five. I know she was here last night. She might be able to tell you more."

"Thanks, I'll do that."

I eased myself into one of the chairs, and to pass the time started thumbing through one of the yearbooks on the coffee table. The one I'd chosen was two years ago, and the photo right inside the front cover depicted the principal and the superintendent of schools, handing an award to a distinguished-looking woman with dark brown hair, dressed impeccably in a suit that looked as if it came right off the pages of *Vogue*. The caption below the photo read *Principal Magill and Superintendent of Schools Crosby with Cruz High's biggest benefactor, Kay Trilby*. I took another look. I hadn't recognized Kay. On the few occasions I'd seen her, her hair had been a soft silver shade. As I stared at the photo, something niggled at me, a feeling of familiarity I couldn't explain. I set the book aside and was about to pick up another when the door burst open and a tall blonde in form-fitting jeans and a sweatshirt burst through with a bright, "Hello, everyone. How's things?"

Sofie glanced over at me and nodded briefly before turning to the blonde. "Ali, there's a lady here who wants to ask you about Hannah Berger."

I stepped forward and introduced myself. Ali gave me a quick once-over, then held out her hand. "I've gotten takeout from your shop a few times. It's nice to finally meet you. Sofie says you want to ask me about Hannah Berger?"

"Hannah had some information for me—for a story I'm working on for *Noir*. She said she'd call or text me after the conference, but I never heard from her."

"Well, we were here pretty late. The conferences usually only last until eight, eight thirty tops, but this one went on till nearly ten." Ali's pert nose wrinkled. "Come to think of it, Hannah was getting pretty antsy. This guy Jerry teased her about it, and she snapped at him that she had someone very important to meet and she was going to be late. I thought it might have had something to do with that phone call, but it must have been because she was supposed to hook up with you."

I leaned forward. "Hannah got a phone call?"

"Yeah, she got one around eight thirty. Wasn't on very long, but she was pretty mad at whoever it was." She ducked her head and added, "I don't usually eavesdrop, but we were the only two here, and it was kind of hard not to overhear."

"Could you hear what she said?" I asked as Ali paused.

Her brow furrowed as she thought, and finally she shook her head. "Not really. She was talking pretty low. She said something about the law, I think, and then at the end her voice got a little louder and she said, "I knew there was a reason you were here." Other than that, though . . ." Ali spread her hands. "Once the last parent was out of here, so was Hannah. Honestly, I didn't even think she could move that fast. I always thought the only speed she knew was slow."

I smiled a little at that remark. "You have no idea who she might have been talking to, or where she might have gone?"

"No, sorry. Oh, wait a minute!" Ali turned on her heel and made a beeline for the desk farthest in the back. The woman went straight to the phone and grabbed a pad that was next to it. "I remember she wrote down something when she was on the phone. She took the paper with her, but she has a heavy hand. You can see the impression of the words on the paper. See!" She held it out to me.

I reached into my tote bag, whipped out a pencil, and ran it over the area. A few seconds later the message was visible. *SS, ten p.m.* I glanced at Ali. "Can I have this?"

"Sure. If you want, you can leave me your number. I'll call you if we hear from Hannah."

I reached into my bag, found a Hot Bread card and handed it to her. "I'll do the same, thanks."

I left the office and went outside, pausing to take a minute to review what Ali had just told me. Something about the law. What? Breaking it? Obeying it? I took out my phone and punched in the number of Cruz Realty. Luck was with me, and Joannie Adams answered the phone.

"Hey, Nora. Is something wrong? Has something else happened at the mansion?" Joannie cried.

"No, I'm not canceling. I just wanted to ask you a question. Do you remember if Hannah ever referred to her brother as Law?"

"Oh, sure. All the time. She rarely called him Lawton."

"And he died suddenly?"

"Yes. He was diagnosed in April and had to quit his job. He was really upset about that. He died, oh, about six weeks later."

My heart was starting to pound in my chest. "Do you remember what he did for a living?"

"Sure. He was a driver for that armored car company ArmLink—oh, my next appointment just came in. I'll talk to you later."

I hung up and tapped the phone thoughtfully against my chin. Hannah's brother had worked at the same armored car company that had been robbed. He'd gotten sick in April, two years ago, right after the robbery. Both Joannie and Enola had mentioned that Lawton Biggs had been obsessed with the legend of Waincroft Manor. And Manny Delgado had been at the house, presumably trying to track down the money from the armored car robbery. I gave my head a quick shake. What I was thinking was impossible, wasn't it? And yet, it was the only thing that made sense.

Hannah's brother had to be one of the two masked robbers. He also must have been the one in charge of hiding the loot until it was safe to get it, and he'd chosen Waincroft Manor. But he'd died before he could tell his partner where he'd hidden the money. Manny Delgado had somehow managed to figure out the money was hidden there, but unfortunately for him, so had someone else.

The other robber.

I hurried over to my SUV parked in the driveway. I slid behind the driver's seat, put the key in the ignition and was just about to turn it when I heard a scratching sound in the back. I turned my head slightly and caught a flash of black and white as Nick leapt into the passenger seat. He sat erect, tail wrapped around forepaws.

"Merow."

I shook my head. "I should have known you'd be here." I turned the key and the engine purred to life. "Feel like taking a drive to Waincroft Manor?"

Nick blinked twice and then lay down on the front seat.

I chuckled. "I knew you would."

• • •

In the late afternoon light, the mansion looked more foreboding than ever. The *Road Flooded* signs were still up on the main drag, indicating there might still be remnants from yesterday's storm. Fortunately, I knew the back way. As I approached the rear of the mansion, I saw what appeared to be a car hidden behind a clump of bushes. I pulled over, put the SUV into park and alighted. Nick did as well, trotting along beside me as I made my way over to the car. It was a late-model Buick that had seen lots of wear and tear. The driver's door was partially ajar. I reached into my tote bag and pulled out a Kleenex before I grasped the handle and pulled. The door opened with a loud creak, and I poked my head inside. The interior was in better shape than the exterior, but not by much. I reached over, Kleenex still in hand, and opened the glove compartment. I pulled out the owner's manual, a couple of mail-order catalogs, and then found what I was looking for—the registration and insurance card.

Sure enough, this was Hannah Berger's car.

I looked over at the mansion. I so did not have a good feeling about this. I pulled out my cell and called the Cruz police station. I asked for Detective Anderson and was told that she was over in Parkerton, her old stomping grounds, consulting on a case. Swell. I hung up and called Samms's number, but it went straight to voicemail. I hesitated, then decided to leave a message.

"Hey, Samms, it's Nora. I'm over here at Waincroft Manor. I haven't been able to get in touch with Hannah Berger, and I just found her car parked here in the bushes behind the mansion. I'm going to check out the house, see if I can find any clues. Call me back, please."

I slid my phone back into my bag and looked at Nick. "What do you say, Nick? Ready to investigate?"

In answer, Nick started up the path ahead of me at a steady trot. I had to half run, half walk to keep up with him. As I climbed the steps I couldn't shake the feeling I was being watched. I paused and glanced around. I thought I saw a bush at the far end of the property rustle a bit, but when the movement wasn't repeated I chalked it up to a bird or a squirrel. Nick rubbed against my ankles, impatient. We hurried up the rest of the steps, and when I reached the porch the first thing I noticed was the front door stood slightly ajar.

I hesitated. My common sense was telling me to stop right here, call 911, and wait on the porch for the police and/or Samms to arrive.

But my gut was telling me otherwise.

Nick was up on his hind legs, pawing at the door. "Nick, stop," I called out, but too late. The door creaked inward and my cat was inside like a flash of black lightning. I had a flash of déjà vu as I stepped over the threshold. The last time Nick had snuck inside this house, I'd found the vagrant's body in a coffin.

I stood for a minute, letting my eyes adjust to the inky blackness. I moved forward cautiously. "Nick," I called. "Where are you?"

"Merow."

I moved slowly forward, my heart beating so loud I was certain it could be heard at least ten miles away. I heard another meow, and I inched forward, following the corridor to the right. A few more steps and it led into the same large dark room as last time, only now there was no coffin square in its center.

There was just Hannah Berger, slumped against the newel of the staircase, her eyes wide and sightless, the scarf knotted around her neck flecked with spots of red that looked like blood.

Chapter Eighteen

Once again I waited on the porch of Waincroft Manor as blue and red strobe lights from police cruisers illuminated it. The police had responded in record time to my 911 call, and as I walked down the steps I saw Dale alight from one of the squad cars, jaw set, eyes narrowed. Her sour expression didn't change one iota as she caught sight of me, but her left eyebrow twitched slightly and she quickened her steps to meet me halfway.

"We've really got to stop meeting like this," I said. My light attempt at humor was not well received. Dale scowled, then whipped her notebook and pen out of her jacket pocket and held them poised in front of her.

"Where's this one?" she asked without preamble.

"Same place as the last one, sans coffin."

Dale's stance relaxed slightly. "I guess that's an improvement. Male, female? Anyone we know?"

"Female, and yes. It's Hannah Berger. She looks like she's been dead a while, a few hours I'd guess."

Dale's head snapped up. "Hannah Berger! What on earth was she doing out here? Oh, wait, she's on that damned committee too, isn't she?"

"Yes, but I don't think one had anything to do with the other. For one thing, we weren't supposed to meet here until late afternoon, and for another . . ." I reached in my pocket and fished out the note. "I went by Cruz High earlier. Ali Larter said Hannah got a call late yesterday that seemed to upset her. We found this on her desk."

Dale took the note, read it, and her frown deepened. "What the hell does this mean? SS, ten p.m. Is SS a person, a place, or what?"

I shrugged. "Your guess is as good as mine."

Dale arrowed me a look, then folded the note in two, slid it between the pages of her notebook and slid it into her jacket pocket. Two other officers climbed out of the second patrol car and hurried over to us. Before they could say anything Dale barked out, "Ben, Mike, inside with me. Did one of you call Fishbein?"

The one addressed as Mike nodded his head so hard I thought I could hear his teeth rattle. "Yes, ma'am. He'll be here as soon as he can."

Dale grimaced, then made a shooing motion with her hand. "Wait for me at the top of the stairs." As the officers shuffled off she turned back to me. "You know, for a moment there I was afraid this corpse might have been that missing boy. I got your message and sent a patrol car right out, but nothing." She lifted her shoulders. "Teenagers can really fly under the radar, but this one is a real pip. No one seems to know a damn thing about him. It's like he's a ghost himself."

"Oh, he's no ghost. He's very real, trust me." I rubbed at my side. "I'm still a little sore from where I fell when he bowled me over. It's certainly odd, though, that no one knows anything about him. Is it possible he's not a student locally, that he might have just been in the area, visiting someone?"

Dale's eyes narrowed to slits. "Hm, that's a thought. Did you see any other kids around that day? Maybe he was part of a group?"

I shook my head. "He appeared to be alone. You know, kids that age like to wander off, and I imagine a big, deserted house would hold a certain amount of appeal for an adventurous boy, even if he wasn't familiar with the history."

"Good point," Dale admitted, and I caught a note of grudging admiration in her tone. "We'll check that angle out too. That sketch your sister made has been a big help." She raised her finger and jabbed the air in front of my nose. "I'm serious. Tell her to drop off her résumé."

"I will. It's just been so . . . hectic. I forgot to mention it to her. But I'm sure she'll jump at the chance."

"Merow."

We both looked down and saw Nick twining himself around Anderson's ankles. "Nick, don't bother the detective," I said, but Anderson surprised me by actually smiling.

"He's not bothering me. He's actually rather cute, when he isn't helping you ferret out corpses, that is." She looked down at Nick and said, "Can you and your assistant, here, stay put while my men and I go inside? And stick around for a while, I might have some more questions for you."

Nick looked at Anderson and his head moved forward, almost in a nod. Then he purred loudly. Anderson hurried up the steps and motioned to the two officers, then they all trooped inside. I sighed and sat down on the porch steps. Nick settled next to me, arranging himself so that he nestled in the crook of my arm. "Remind me to speak with Mollie again and see if her friend found out anything about that boy," I said to him.

"Merow."

I ran my hand down his smooth, silky back. "I doubt there were two murderers. The same person killed both Manny Delgado and Hannah, and the most logical choice I can think of is Lawton's partner, the other bank robber."

Nick looked at me, his golden eyes wide, then suddenly he sat up straight, his ears flicked forward. I heard the sound of tires crunching on gravel and looked up to see Samms parking his dark blue sedan next to Anderson's cruiser. He got out of the car, turned toward the house, and paused as he caught sight of Nick and me on the steps. Then he raced forward, taking the steps two at a time, until he was standing right in front of me. The next thing I knew I was in his arms, crushed against his broad chest.

"Geez, Red," he whispered into my hair. "When are you going to find another hobby?" He pushed me away from him a bit so he could look into my eyes. His hand came up, brushed against the side of my face. "I got your message and I was on my way to Hot Bread when I caught your 911 call on my scanner. Who is it this time?"

"Hannah Berger."

"Hannah Berger?" He raised one hand to scratch at his forehead. "Who would want to kill her?"

I looked straight into his eyes. "I think I know."

His eyes widened a tad. "You do? Who?"

"I don't have a name, but I've got a theory, and it's a good one, if I say so myself. If I'm right it not only explains her murder, but Manny's too."

He leaned against the porch railing and crossed both arms over his broad chest. "Okay, Red, you've got my attention. What's your theory?"

I let out a long breath. "I think Lawton Biggs's partner killed them." Samms listened in silence for the next few minutes as I painstakingly explained what I thought must have happened. When I finished he was silent, stroking his chin with his long fingers and staring out into space. After about five minutes of that I stamped my foot impatiently. "For God's sakes, say something."

He raised his gaze to mine. "It's a pretty theory, but that's all it is. A theory. You've no proof."

"What, two dead bodies aren't proof enough for you?"

"Heck, Nora, you know what I mean. Manny told me he had information on a cold case, but he never said anything about it being the bank robbery. There's nothing that ties it to either of these murders."

"I know. I researched cases with large rewards, though, and this one had the largest one. It also interested me because in most bank robberies, the money turns up at some point. This one, nothing."

"I looked into it too," Samms said. "I read the interview accounts. Lawton Biggs wasn't working that day and both the driver and the guard checked out clean."

I felt a sharp pang of disappointment arrow through me. "Are you certain?"

He laid his hand on my shoulder. "Yes, Red. I'm positive. Manny had a lead on something, but I greatly doubt it was the money from that robbery. I'm still digging into what it could possibly be."

"Well, then, let's not overlook the fact that whoever killed Manny went to great lengths to make it appear as if a vampire were responsible, what with draining the body of blood. It stands to reason that it would be someone familiar with the legend of Waincroft Manor, and more than one person has commented on the fact Lawton was obsessed with the legend."

His brow arched. "Yeah, Lawton was, but not necessarily his partner."

"If he was that obsessed, I'll bet a month's worth of Hot Bread receipts that he talked to his partner about it. Who knows, maybe they both decided that Waincroft Manor was the ideal place to stash their loot."

"If that's the case, then Lawton's partner would know where he hid it."

"Not necessarily. They might have split up after the robbery to cover their tracks. Lawton might have told his partner he'd hide it in the mansion and then when it was safe they'd get together and get it, but Lawton got sick and died shortly afterward. There are a lot of nooks and crannies that make ideal hiding places in that house. Without Lawton's help, his partner wouldn't know where to look."

"Even so, it's a long shot. Whoever drained that body of blood had to have medical knowledge. Most bank robbers don't have that."

"Maybe so," I grumbled. What Samms said made sense, but my theory did too, and I was unwilling to give up on it, at least not yet.

He touched my arm. "What makes you think Hannah's murder is connected to the robbery?"

"I went by Cruz High earlier. Ali Larter said that Hannah got a phone call last night at eight thirty, and she seemed very upset. She overheard Hannah tell whoever called her that she knew the real reason they came to Cruz, and then she said they couldn't disrespect law like that. I'm sure she was talking about her brother. Maybe she couldn't wrap her head around the fact that he'd been involved in something so shady. Maybe she went to confront this person, and she might even have threatened him with exposure."

Samms shook his head. "Once again, you're stretching and making a lot of assumptions. You're trying to make the facts fit around your theory, Nora."

"Well, hello, Lee. What are you doing here?"

We both turned. Anderson stood on the porch behind us, holding a plastic bag in one hand. Samms inclined his head toward Dale. "I heard the 911 on the scanner and thought maybe you'd need my help," he said smoothly.

Dale glanced from Samms to me and back to Samms, then wiggled the bag in the air. "We need to wait for the coroner's report, of course, but it appears Ms. Burger was strangled." She waved the bag around again. "With this."

I leaned in for a closer look. Inside the bag was an ivory-colored scarf. It looked expensive, and the design on it was definitely unusual. The signs of the zodiac. I sucked in my breath. I wasn't mistaken, I'd seen this very scarf just yesterday, draped around Enola Waincroft's neck. We'd all commented on how beautiful and unusual the scarf was. I averted my gaze, but it was too late. Anderson's eagle eye had caught my reaction, and she pounced on it like Nick on one of his catnip mice.

"Does this scarf look familiar to you, Nora?" she asked, waving the bag in front of me.

"I may have seen a similar one," I said. "It's hard to tell, what with that scarf all bunched up in the bag and the big bloodstain on it and all." I pointed to said bloodstain. "You said you thought Hannah was strangled, right? Then how did blood get on this scarf?"

"A good question. I'm hoping it might be the killer's blood. We'll know more after the lab has a go at it. Now, getting back to the scarf. Where did you see one like it?"

Fortunately I was spared answering as we all heard the sound of crunching gravel. Joannie parked her car a short distance away from Anderson's cruiser and she, Chantal and Enola all got out and started toward us. Anderson thrust the bag containing the scarf at one of the other officers and hurried down the steps to head them off.

"Ladies, I'm afraid you can't go in here," she called out to them. "Waincroft Manor is off-limits right now."

"Again?" Joannie let out a loud moan. "Good Lord, who's dead now?"

Anderson eyed her. "Did I say anyone was dead?"

"You don't have to." Joannie spread her arms wide. "All the police cruisers and flashing lights say it for you."

Enola stepped forward, her hands thrust deep into the pockets of the expensive black wool blazer she wore. "Waincroft Manor is my property," she rasped. "Therefore, I have a right to know what's going on."

Dale matched her defiant stare with a frosty one of her own. "What's going on is your home is a crime scene again. Rest assured, though, my people and I will do all we can to hurry things along so as not to interfere with any of the plans for the gala." She switched her stare to Joannie. "As I'm sure Mrs. Trilby will want."

"You needn't get so huffy, Detective," Joannie blustered. "Mrs. Trilby is just trying to . . ."

"Oh, yes," Dale said. "That she is. I'm sure Nora will be glad to fill you all in later, but right now I need you all to *get the hell out of my crime scene!*"

"Geez, you don't need to get all ballistic on us, we're going," Joannie sniffed. "I'll have to inform Mrs. Trilby there's been yet another delay."

"Oh, yes," Dale sneered. "By all means inform Mrs. Trilby. I look forward to hearing from her. Again."

As Dale and Joannie traded barbs, I grabbed Enola's arm and pulled her over to one side. I was aware of Samms's gaze on us as I whispered hoarsely, "The scarf you were wearing yesterday, the one with the zodiac signs? Where is it?"

She cleared her throat and looked down at the ground. "I'm not sure."

"You're not sure?"

"I-I can't find it. I must have lost it somewhere," she said. "Or I misplaced it in my room. I looked for it this morning and it was gone."

I inclined my head toward Dale. "Well, I think it's been found. It turned up around the corpse's neck. Anderson thinks it might even be the murder weapon."

"Oh, *no!*" Enola lifted her hands out of her pockets and put them up to her face. I started as I noticed the large bandage wrapped around her thumb and the side of her hand. I reached out and grabbed her wrist, pulling it closer for a better look. "What happened? Did you cut yourself?"

Enola snatched her hand back. "Yes. I ordered a large hunk of cheddar cheese from room service and the knife slipped as I was cutting it. Fortunately the cut was not too deep, but some blood did get on my scarf."

"Did the inn doctor have a look at it?"

She appeared puzzled. "No. I had a bandage in my suitcase, and I know enough about first aid to take care of myself."

I eyed her. "Are you telling me the truth, Enola?"

"Of course I am," she huffed. "Why would I lie?"

Why indeed? "Well, there's blood on that scarf, and Anderson's going to have tests run on it, so if it should turn out the blood is yours . . ."

Enola licked at her lips. "I think I was still wearing the scarf when I cut myself—yes, I remember now! I was. I took the scarf and put it in one of those bags the inn leaves to send it out to be cleaned. I even wrote out specific instructions to make sure they would handle it properly. It is *silk*, after all." She paused. "Did you tell Anderson the scarf is mine?"

"No, I managed to avoid that question. There's something else, though." I looked straight into her eyes. "Would you like to tell me about the coffin?"

Her eyes darted about nervously. She gave a choked laugh. "Coffin?"

"Can it, Enola. I know all about the coffin you ordered. And if I know, you can bet it won't be long before Anderson knows too."

She looked down at the ground. "It was supposed to be a joke. I thought the decorating committee would find it amusing, finding Bartescue's coffin in the house. I came here a few days early, intending to set it up with a vampire dummy inside. Imagine my surprise when I discovered it had already been found, and there was a real dead body inside it!"

I looked straight into her eyes. "Tell me the truth. Did you know the John Doe they found inside that coffin?"

She made a crossing motion over her chest. "No. I did not. I swear to you, I did not kill that man. And I did not kill Hannah, either."

I stared at her. "Enola, no one mentioned the name of the second victim. How did you know it was Hannah?"

Enola stared at me in silence for a moment, and then cleared her throat. "Are you certain? I thought I heard Detective Anderson mention Hannah's name."

I shook my head. "No, she didn't. Come clean with me, Enola. How did you know it was Hannah?"

She sighed. "Okay, fine. I called Hannah at the school last night. I wanted to find out more about the body, but she was her usual disagreeable self. She finally agreed to meet me here at ten thirty. I was late getting here, it was actually more like ten forty-five, or maybe closer to eleven. Anyway, when I got here, I saw her car parked out front but there was no sign of her. I went inside, and I found her, propped up against the stairwell. I went over and touched her, just to make certain she was dead—I got out of there as fast as I could."

I frowned. Enola had been Hannah's caller? "What time did you call Hannah, do you remember?"

She bobbed her head. "Oh, yes, because that cable talk show I like so much on channel twenty was just starting. It was right at nine o'clock."

After Hannah's other mysterious caller. "And you're positive you weren't wearing your scarf?"

She waved her hand impatiently. "I told you, I got blood on it when I cut myself, and I put it in the bag for the inn cleaning service. There was nothing around Hannah's neck when I found the body. She was just lying on the stairs, her sightless eyes staring heavenward—oh my gosh!" Her fingers dug into my arm. "Of course! I've been set up. Someone is trying to frame me for these murders."

"Who would want to do that?"

"I don't know? Maybe they figure the Waincroft Curse makes a neat, tidy little package. It's always been a convenient scapegoat for people's problems, especially Hannah."

I shook my head. "If Anderson should find out about the coffin, and about the fact that you spoke to Hannah last night, you will look guilty to her. You should have come clean with everything right from the beginning." I turned my head and saw Anderson talking on her phone. She glanced over and stared hard at Enola, then snapped her phone shut and started toward us. "Too late," I murmured under my breath.

"Ms. Waincroft," Anderson barked out. "Might I have a word?"

Enola slid me a look. "You mentioned you knew some good lawyers. Would you mind calling one of them for me?"

Chapter Nineteen

I returned to Hot Bread after closing time, only to find customers still in the shop. Grant, Tammi, Davey and Felix occupied the large rear table. Lacey looked up as I put my tote down on the counter.

"Sorry," she said, spreading her hands. "They got here just as I was about to lock the door, and I didn't think it was good business to turn customers away, even them." She leaned in closer to me and whispered, "The tall good-looking guy and the girl have been arguing since they came in. The other two look bored or scared, or maybe a combination of both. And, they haven't ordered anything yet."

Sure enough, I could hear Tammi's nasal whine raised above Grant's calmer tones. I sighed. "It figures, after the day I've had, that they would be the icing on the cake."

Lacey peered at me. "Yeah, you look drained, Nors. What happened? Don't tell me you found another body?"

"Well, since the account will most likely be on the evening news, yes. Hannah Berger."

"Hannah!" Lacey's eyes popped. "Who would want to kill her?"

I leaned against the counter. "It appears suspect numero uno is Enola. Remember that distinctive scarf of hers, the one with the zodiac signs? It was wrapped around Hannah's throat."

"Oh my gosh! What did Enola have to say? Or does she even know?"

"She knows. She and Chantal and Joannie showed up for the look-see, which is canceled again, by the way. First she tried to tell me she'd misplaced the scarf, then later she changed her story. She said she cut her hand and got blood on the scarf and put it in one of those bags to be sent out to be cleaned."

"Well, her story's easy enough to check, right?"

"Right, which is why I'm inclined to think she's telling the truth. She thinks someone's trying to frame her for Hannah's murder, and possibly the other one as well."

"Why that one? She didn't know the guy, right?"

Out of the corner of my eye I saw Davey and Felix approaching the counter. "I'll tell you later," I whispered, and then turned to face the newcomers with a wide smile. "Hello, fellows. Ready to order?"

"I don't know," Davey sighed. He stared at the chalkboard that had all the specials listed. "Everything sounds so good. It's hard to decide."

I tapped at the item written at the bottom of the board. "How about this? It's really a breakfast special but you can eat it any time of the day."

Davey's face split into a grin. "The Bill Murray/Dan Aykroyd Ghostbuster Special," he said. "Wow, how can we resist! What is it?"

"Egg, cheese and ham between two waffles with a side of bacon or sausage."

"Ooh, sign me up." Davey rubbed both his hands together. "Grant and Tammi just want a bagel with butter and coffee, though."

I scribbled the orders down and then turned to Felix. "How about you? Are you game for the ghostbuster special?"

He shot me a shy smile. "If it's all the same to you, could I get a grilled cheese and tomato on whole wheat?"

Davey pulled a face. "Man, don't you get sick of it?"

Felix lifted his shoulders in a shrug. "Hard to get sick of something you love," he said softly. He looked at me. "We realize it's past your closing time, so we'll take those orders to go, but could we have some coffee while we wait?"

I poured hot coffee into four mugs and set out a pitcher of cream and a bowl of sugar. Davey put some cream and sugar into his mug, then put it on a tray with two other mugs and started for the table where Grant and Tammi were sitting. Felix remained at the counter, staring into his mug.

I put generous slices of cheddar on whole wheat, added some fresh tomato, then slid it onto the panini maker. I sliced two bagels, slathered them with butter, plated them and put them on a brown tray. Then I went to the fridge, got out the waffle mix, and returned to the cooking area, where I poured the mix into the waffle maker and pressed down the lid. I glanced back at the counter. Felix was still standing there, brooding over his mug of coffee. I walked over with a smile. "You don't feel like sitting with your friends?"

He shrugged. "That's okay, I can live without hearing Tammi and Grant argue again about what a waste of time this all is, and why did he ever listen to her, and we should have gone to explore that abandoned mine in Arizona instead of here."

"I take it you haven't had any luck getting into the mansion?"

Felix shook his head. "No. Detective Anderson was pretty adamant. Tammi wanted Grant to disobey, she even offered to go out on her own, but he wouldn't hear of it. Said he didn't feel like bailing her out of jail." He leaned forward and said in a low tone, "I have to side with Grant. This second murder doesn't appear to have supernatural overtones at all. The energy from that poor woman's spirit might well neutralize any chance we might have of contacting Bartescue. If he's even still around, that is."

I put two eggs on the grill. "What, you think Bartescue's spirit got scared away?"

"It's possible. I mean, he definitely had nothing to do with the second murder. The woman died from strangulation, and no blood was drained from *her* body."

I leaned both elbows on the counter and looked Felix straight in the eye. "And just how do you know all this, Felix? I know for a fact the police didn't release those details, just that another body was found at Waincroft Manor. Someone's feeding you guys information, aren't they? Someone on the Cruz PD?"

Felix shifted his weight uncomfortably. He glanced quickly over his shoulder at his coworkers, then back at me. "I could get in trouble," he murmured.

"You guys are definitely going to get in trouble if you keep this up. And you're not the only ones."

He looked at me with a puzzled expression. "What do you mean?"

"If Anderson finds out one of her men is leaking confidential information, she'll fire him like that." I snapped my fingers in the air. "She'll blacklist him, too, so it's doubtful he'll get another job in law enforcement around here anytime soon."

Felix wrung his hands. "We didn't mean to get anyone in trouble. But when Davey said his cousin got this job on the Cruz PD, and we heard about that first murder, Grant said it was a golden opportunity. We could get inside information on the investigation that would help us stay one step ahead of everyone."

I cocked a brow at him. "And Grant didn't consider the possibility that should this get out, he might be responsible for ruining someone's career?"

Felix offered me a thin smile. "Probably not. Grant, Davey and Tammi rarely think of others." He picked up his mug and took another long sip of coffee. "You'd think Davey would be more considerate of his cousin, considering this is his first job and all. And he didn't even think he'd get it. He was so afraid that he'd have to come work for us."

His words made a lightbulb go off in my head, bringing to mind the recent conversation I'd had with Lacey. "Oh gosh," I said. "Davey's cousin is LB—Larry Bolton? Officer Bolton? He's the one who's been feeding you information?"

"Ssh," Felix cautioned, putting a finger to his lips. We both glanced over at the ghostbusters' table, but we needn't have worried. Tammi and Grant were engaged in a lively conversation, oblivious to everything around them. Davey sat listening to them, a bored look on his face.

"Look." I leaned in closer to Felix. "I won't say anything, but if I were you, I'd encourage Davey to stop taking information from LB. Anderson's no fool, and trust me, it won't be long before she figures it out. Believe me when I tell you Larry will suffer consequences. Anderson doesn't take stool pigeons lightly."

Felix nodded. "I'll try," he said. "That's all I can do."

I removed the waffles, placed the egg on top, and added ham and cheddar. I removed Felix's grilled cheese from the panini maker and wrapped everything up, slid it into two large paper bags. Felix sniffed the air as I placed the bags in front of him.

"Wow, this all smells great." He handed me a fifty-dollar bill. As I made change, he said, "I'll mention what you said about using Larry to get advance info to Grant, but I can't make any promises that he'll stop."

"If I were you, I'd try real hard to convince him. Believe me, it'll be better for all of you in the long run. In the meantime—"

"I know." He made a motion of locking up his lips and throwing away the key. "Mum's the word."

Felix held up the bags, and the others scraped back their chairs and followed him out the front door. I walked over, closed and locked it, and had just flipped the sign to *Closed* when I felt my cell vibrate in my pocket. I slid it out and checked the caller ID. Seeing the number for First National Bank on the screen, I pressed the button eagerly. "Nora Charles."

"Ms. Charles? This is Parker Peterman, manager of the First National. I'm returning your call."

"Thank you for calling back, Mr. Peterman." I repeated the spiel I'd given his assistant, ending with, "I was hoping you could give me some details about the robbery."

"Of course I remember the incident, Ms. Charles. I was the assistant manager here at the time. I do believe that our manager at the time, Paula Fredericks, gave a complete statement to the police, which should be on file."

"Oh, yes, I've reviewed that," I lied glibly. "I was just wondering if you perhaps had anything to add, if you remembered anything unusual about that day, for instance. Anything out of the ordinary that happened?"

"Not really. It was business as usual."

Damn! "Nothing at all happened? Nothing that would be considered a departure from the usual routine?"

"No, nothing . . . oh, wait! There was one thing. I'm not sure if Paula mentioned it in her report because it really wasn't the bank's responsibility, but . . ."

"Yes," I prompted as Peterman hesitated. "I promise you, all my sources on this will be kept confidential, Mr. Peterman. No one will ever know where I got my information."

"Okay, then. The armored car driver wasn't the regular man."

My heart gave a little leap. "No?"

"No. For as long as I could remember, we always had the same driver on that run. The guard changed frequently, but the driver was always the same. And that day it was a different man. They said the regular one was ill, and we all thought it was odd, because that guy never missed a day, even when he was sick as a dog. But he did that day."

My heart was pounding so loud I was certain Peterman would be able to hear it. "I don't suppose you remember the regular driver's name?"

"As a matter of fact I do. It was Biggs. Lawton Biggs."

Chapter Twenty

I disconnected and then just sat for a minute, trying to make sense of the million and one thoughts running through my head. Nick must have sensed something was up because he rose from his post in front of my refrigerator, lofted onto the table and sat, sphinxlike, staring at me with wide golden eyes.

"It's all starting to come together, Nick," I said. "There are a lot of clues here. I just have to make some sense out of them." I scraped back the chair and started to pace back and forth. "Okay, here's what I've got so far. Hannah's brother Lawton worked for ArmLink, the armored car company. Lawton was supposed to drive the armored car the day it was robbed, but he called in sick, which Peterman said was very unusual. Now, assuming that Lawton did have something to do with the robbery, what might make a dedicated employee like him consider committing a federal crime?"

Nick sat back on his haunches. "Er-owl."

"Exactly," I said. "People like Lawton would only consider doing something like that if they were in a desperate situation. What would make someone desperate?" I dragged my hand through my hair. "Well, considering the nature of the theft, it was something he needed money for, and a great deal of it. So why do people usually need a great deal of money? Number one reason I can think of—they're in debt. Now, why would Lawton have been in debt? Joannie said Hannah and Lawton both lived in the family house, which was free and clear. He probably made a decent salary. What would he have spent a great deal of money on?"

Nick let out a resounding purr. I reached down to pet him. "You're right. We need some expert advice on this, and I know just the person." I jumped up from the chair and started for the door. "Come on, Nick. We're going to visit the one person in Cruz who just might have the answer."

• • •

Luck was with me as I entered the Cruz Sweet Shoppe and saw Betty Callahan sitting behind the register. Betty was a lifelong resident who knew more about the goings-on in our town than even our other permanent fixture, librarian Jemina Slater. I always remembered my mother saying, "If you want to know any gossip, Betty's your gal." I sincerely hoped this might be the case as I approached the counter. Betty glanced up, and her wrinkled face creased in a broad smile.

"Well, well, Nora Charles. I'd begun to give up hope that you'd stop in to visit me." She laughed, her voice hoarse as a result of years of chain-smoking.

"Hey, Betty. Sorry I haven't been by."

"Oh, I understand. After all, you've been busy, what with your mama's business to take care of, not to mention solving all those mysteries."

"Merow."

Betty leaned over the counter and smile at Nick, who squatted beside my feet. "My, what a handsome fellow. I take it this is the other half of the Nora and Nick investigative duo?"

"Merow," Nick said. He lofted onto the counter in one quick motion and butted his head against Betty's arm.

"Nick," I admonished him. "Betty might not like you jumping on her counter."

"Oh, he's fine." She waved her hand carelessly. "There's no one here but us anyway." She leaned closer and peered at the cat. "He's pretty agile for one so large." She let her fingers roam over Nick's smooth fur, then gave his head a pat and turned back to me. "So, Miss Nora, what can I do for you? Some candy, gum . . . information, perhaps?"

I grinned sheepishly. "Am I that obvious?"

"Not really. I'm just playing percentages. Most people come in for some sort of information or gossip, then they stay for the goodies . . . or maybe a winning lottery ticket."

I laughed. "That last item would be nice, but you're right. I need some information."

Betty rubbed both her hands together and leaned both elbows on her counter. "Okay, then. Fire away. What do you want to know?"

"You've heard about the latest murder at Waincroft Manor, right?"

"Sure, sure. Poor Hannah. She wasn't too well liked—no, wait, scratch that. She wasn't liked at all, but I can't think of anyone who might have hated her enough to kill her, if that's what you're interested in."

"Actually, I wanted to ask about Hannah's brother."

Betty's eyes narrowed. "Lawton? What about him? He's been dead a few years now."

"I heard a rumor that he'd gotten in a spot of trouble before his death."

"Oh, that." Betty pulled a stool out from under the counter and plopped down. "Hannah never liked to talk about it. I think she figured if she didn't mention it, the problem would go away." She made a tsking sound with her tongue. "But that's the problem with gamblers. Their problems never go away. They never lose that fever."

"Lawton had a gambling problem?"

Betty's head bobbed up and down. "Oh, yes. It started out small, but then it mushroomed into a big debt. There was even talk of him being indebted to some Vegas mob." She leaned in closer to me and lowered her voice. "Hannah came in here one day all upset and spilled her guts to me before she realized what she was saying. Of course, she blamed his obsession on the Waincroft curse. She said that ever since he was a little boy, he'd been fascinated by the legend of Bartescue and he used to sneak inside, hunting for the vampire. One Halloween she had to actually drag him out of there, which was no easy feat. Lawton probably knew his way around that house better than the people who built it. Anyway, she was deathly afraid that he'd gambled away their house."

I felt a tingle run down my spine. "It was that bad?"

"Oh, yes. She was pretty much beside herself. Then, a few weeks later she came in here and pulled me over to the side. "Betty," she says, "that business with Lawton's been all cleared up. I'd much appreciate it if you'd forget I ever spoke to you about it." So I said, sure, no harm done. Not long after that—gee, maybe a month or two—Lawton started feeling worse. He'd been tired and run down, but it got to the point he could barely get out of bed. Hannah hauled him to the doctor and he was diagnosed with liver cancer. He died a few weeks later. Hannah blamed that on the Waincroft curse, too." Betty expelled a long breath. "I guess it's easy to see how circumstances made her the way she was, but I told her she shouldn't blame that supposed curse. If anything, she should blame Silverman."

"Silverman?"

"Yeah, Fred Silverman. He worked at the First National. He was a guard, I think. He and Lawton got friendly when Lawton did those weekly runs to the bank for ArmLink. He's the one who got Lawton hooked on gambling. Whenever their schedules were in sync, they used to take weekend trips to Vegas, Tahoe, some of the Indian casinos in Arizona. Heck, once Hannah told me they were even talking about flying to Atlantic City for the weekend." She shook her head. "The two of 'em should have known better. You know, if ArmLink had ever found out about Lawton's problem, he would have been fired like that." She snapped her fingers in the air. "Silverman knew how to cover his tracks, though. He taught poor Law all sorts of bad habits. When I mentioned it to Hannah, she said the curse probably brought 'em together. She just wouldn't give up on that idea."

I tried to keep my tone casual. "Whatever happened to this Fred Silverman? Does he still work at First National?"

"Hell, no. He left the bank, oh, let's see. I think it was either right before or right after that big robbery." She paused and crossed her arms over her chest. "And that, Nora Charles, just about sums up all I know about Lawton Biggs. Did it help you any?"

I smiled and reached in my purse for my wallet. "You've helped more than you know, Betty. I'll take two Twix bars and a pack of spearmint gum."

As Betty rang up my purchases, she said, "How's things with you, Nora? How is Lacey doing, working at Hot Bread?"

"She's doing better than expected, although I'm hopeful that she might get another job in the art field one day. She's really pretty talented."

"Seems to run in the Charles family. You're talented with words, your sister has a gift for drawing, and your mother was right up there with Gordon Ramsey, if you ask me. She made a mighty fine sandwich. You've inherited that talent, too." She cocked her brow. "How'd your sister take the news of Lance seeing Violet's niece?"

"She says she's fine with it, but deep down I think it bothers her that Lance could ever look at another woman after her."

Betty shot me a knowing smile. "That sounds like your sister. She always had a way with the men. Speaking of men, how's your boyfriend, the good-looking FBI agent, Daniel, right? I haven't seen him around lately."

"Daniel's away on a case. I have no idea when he'll be back." I almost added *or if*, but restrained myself.

"Oh," Betty said. "That explains it then."

I looked at her curiously as I took the bag from her outstretched hand. "Explains what?"

"Those longing looks passing between you and that guy who used to be our head of Homicide. Samms, right? Are you dating him now?"

I blushed. "We've been out a few times," I said at last.

Betty threw her head back and let out a good, loud laugh. "Oh, you are so coy, Nora. You remind me so much of your mama!" She placed one hand over her heart. "Oh, to be so young and fancy free, and have two handsome gents a'courtin' me. Enjoy it," she said with a saucy wink. "Believe me, it doesn't last forever."

• • •

Back on the street, I opened the bag, pulled out a Twix bar, unwrapped it and took a large bite. Nick watched me, head cocked.

"Well, one good thing. After talking to Betty, I really do think my theory is a good one. It certainly sounds as if Lawton would know the perfect place to hide something in that mansion. I think our next move should be to find out everything we can about this Fred Silverman, what do you think?"

"Merow," Nick said.

The door to the Sweet Shoppe suddenly flew open and Betty appeared in the doorway. She motioned for me to come closer, so I retraced my steps. When I got to within a foot of her, she reached out and grabbed my arm.

"I just remembered. Shortly after that Silverman guy quit and left Cruz, the FBI came around asking questions about him. I'm pretty sure they interviewed Hannah, on account of he and Lawton were so tight." She sighed. "Too bad, isn't it? No one can ask her for details now."

Chapter Twenty-one

I returned to Hot Bread, Nick at my heels, and immediately put in a call to the First National Bank. The perky girl who answered the phone assured me that the manager was there, but meeting with customers. I left my name and number with a message that it was urgent, to please call back, and then I decided to do some research on my own. I fired up my trusty laptop and typed "Fred Silverman" into the search engine. After scrolling through all the hits on Fred Silverman, TV producer, I came to the Public Records Now site. I typed in "Fred Silverman" and hit the enter button. Twenty records came up. I went through each and every one of them. Five were deceased, three were teenagers, and six were in their eighties, way too old. Out of the remaining six, three were in the twenty- to thirty-five-year-old range, way too young. The remaining three were between the ages of forty-eight and fifty-two, which was a better fit. A quick check of the candidates' previous addresses, though, didn't yield Cruz. Only one listed California—Santa Monica, specifically—as a former address. Fred W. Silverman, currently residing in Greeley, Colorado.

I looked at Nick, who was lounging on the table, positioned so that he could see the computer screen. "What do you think, buddy? Shall we give it a whirl?"

Nick blinked, so I hit "view details." A list of choices came up, ranging from ninety-five cents for phone and address information, all the way to thirty-nine ninety-five for a detailed account that most likely included when the man cut his first tooth. I hesitated, and then backed out of that site and went to the White Pages site. I plugged in "Fred W. Silverman, Greeley Colorado." Only one name popped up, and of course, the telephone number was unlisted. I sighed.

"What do you think, Nick? Should we spring for ninety-five cents and this guy's phone number?"

Nick shrugged and stretched himself full-length across the table. Apparently he was leaving the financial decision in my court. I sighed, reached for my tote bag, and pulled out my Discover card. Ten minutes later I was dialing the number of Fred W. Silverman. It rang about eight times and I was just about to hang up when I heard a male voice answer, very cautiously, "Hello?"

"Hello! Fred W. Silverman?"

"Who wants to know?"

"My name is Nora Charles, Mr. Silverman. I'm a former reporter for the *Chicago Herald* and I'm currently working on—"

"I don't want any subscriptions to any newspapers," he cut me off. "And I don't live in Illinois, I live in Colorado. What would I want with a Chicago newspaper?"

"I'm afraid you misunderstood me, Mr. Silverman," I said patiently. "I said I'm a *former* reporter, and I'm working on—"

"See, this is the reason my number's unlisted. You damn telemarketers have no idea how troublesome you are . . . how did you get this number, anyway? I'm calling my lawyer."

"Wait, wait," I cried. "Don't hang up. I just have a few questions for you, Mr. Silverman, and if you cooperate, there's a fifty-dollar gift card in your future."

"A fifty-dollar card? Really?" I could hear the greed and the interest in his tone. It was startling how many people would cave whenever free money was involved.

"Yes. I just need to ask you a few questions, if you don't mind?"

"Well, sure. Go ahead." The tone had changed now, from guarded to definitely affable. "Ask away."

"Did you ever reside in or near Cruz, California?"

"I lived in Santa Monica. That's about a six-hour drive to Cruz, if I remember correctly. It's up by Monterey, right?"

"That's correct. So you didn't know anyone in the Cruz area? Or work around there?"

He laughed lightly. "Those damned freeways are one of the reasons I moved. Heck, no. I managed an In-and-Out Burger in SM for years before I bought my own little hardware store here in Greeley."

Disappointment shot through me. "So you're not the same Fred Silverman who used to work for the First National Bank in California?"

"Nope, sorry." A pause and then . . . "Does this mean I don't get the gift card?"

"Unfortunately, it does."

"Bummer," he muttered, and then I heard a loud click. I looked over at Nick. "Well, that was a waste of ninety-five cents," I said. "Back to square one." I drummed my fingers on the table. Asking Samms was out of the question, and even if Daniel were around, what were the chances he'd tell me? No, if I was going to find out anything about this mysterious Fred

Silverman, there was only one person who could help me. I picked up the phone again and dialed Hank Prince's number. My former CI answered on the second ring.

"Nora, you must be psychic. I was just about to call you." Hank's jovial voice, a refreshing change from Fred W. Silverman's nasal whine, boomed over the wire. "I'm going to be headed out your way soon."

"You are?" I squealed. "That's great, Hank. So you're finally taking a vacation?"

"Sorta kinda. I'll tell you all the details when I see you. So, you called me. What do you need?"

"What, I have to need something to call you?"

He laughed outright. "That's been my experience, yes. So spill. What is it?"

"How well you know me. Okay. Do you still have that contact in the FBI? The one who specialized in cold cases?"

"Bartie Winslow? Sure, he's still around. You need info on a cold case?"

"I need whatever you can get me on a robbery that involved an armored car in Salinas a few years ago, and on the whereabouts of a Fred Silverman in particular."

"I vaguely remember that," Hank said. "The robbers got away with something like four mil, right?"

"Right. The robbers were never caught and the money was never recovered, but . . ." I hit the highlights, starting with finding Manny Delgado's body all the way up to my conversation with Betty. "I just have this feeling that money's hidden in Waincroft Manor," I finished.

"Well, if this Fred Silverman was Biggs's partner, it's obvious that he's not going to let anyone stand in the way of his recovering the money," Hank said. "What does Daniel think of all this?"

"Daniel's still in London."

"Oh. Well then, what does Lee Samms think of all this?"

"Samms thinks I should butt out and stay safe."

"Good advice, but you're not going to take it, right?" He let out a long sigh. "I sense Louis Blondell's fine hand in all this. He wants a front-page story for that magazine of his."

"Louis did mention this would make a good story, but there's another reason for my interest. Anderson seems to like Enola Waincroft for both murders. I think she's innocent, and tracking down Fred Silverman seems to be the best way to start proving it."

"Okay, then. Give me a day or two."

"I might not have that luxury. Can you tell your friend to make this a top priority? Pretty please? I'll make an extra-special sandwich for you when you come out here, I'll even name it after you."

"Such bribery. I guess your mama taught you the way to your CI's heart is through his stomach, huh?" He laughed. "Fine. I'll see what I can do, but I'm not making any promises."

"Your best effort is all I ask."

"Yeah, yeah. See you soon."

I hung up and looked at Nick. "Okay, Hank will get back to me, but in the meantime, Louis said that he recognized Manny as hanging around Hannah's table at that block sale. Hannah herself admitted he was there. She said she thought he might have taken something from her table, but she wasn't sure, and right after that was when he called Samms, so he must have found something that gave him a clue as to the money, but what?"

My phone vibrated, and I snatched it up. The number on the screen wasn't Hank's, but Ollie's. I answered and right away Ollie said, "What's wrong, Nora? I know something is, I can hear it in your voice."

Once again I reviewed the previous happenings, ending with my theory as to Manny and Hannah's yard sale. "I'm positive he found something there, but what?"

"Hm. Does Hannah have a will?"

I started. "I have no idea. Why do you ask?"

"Because if she died intestate, without a will, or even if she had one leaving everything to Lawton, who predeceased her, everything will go to the state. Meaning—"

"Meaning we should get in there and have a look around before they seal up the place," I cried. "What are you doing this afternoon?"

"Oh, you know me. I'm always up for a little B&E. I can be there in about an hour."

I rang off and saw Nick watching me. "No, you can't come with us," I said. "But you can help me pick out a good housebreaking outfit."

My phone vibrated again. This time it was Hal Frey. "Hey, Hal. What happened with Enola?"

"That's why I'm calling. I'm trying to get a bail hearing for Enola. Anderson formally charged her with both murders."

"Both!" I cried. "But Enola didn't know John Doe."

"That's where you're wrong," Hal said. "John Doe was really Manny

Delgado. Apparently he was some kind of police or FBI informant."

"Yes, I know. Samms told me."

"Oh. Well, here's something you don't know. The main reason Anderson arrested Enola was because she lied about not knowing Manny."

I almost dropped the phone. "What?"

"Yes. Apparently Anderson was suspicious of Enola from the start, and ordered copies of her cell phone records. Not only did she find out Enola ordered a coffin sent to Waincroft Manor, but there's evidence of Enola having more than one phone conversation with Manny Delgado. One not long before his body was found."

Chapter Twenty-two

Hal promised to keep me posted on what went down with Enola. I rang off and frowned. Enola had lied about many things, but I still didn't feel that she was a murderer. There had to be a logical explanation for her having spoken to Manny Delgado, but at the moment, I hadn't the faintest clue what that might be.

I ran upstairs to my apartment, switched into jeans and a dark long-sleeved shirt, then brushed my hair back into a ponytail and tucked it under a baseball cap. Nick sprawled across my comforter, watching me, and when I was finished dressing he sat up and let out a loud meow of approval.

"I'm glad you like it," I told the cat. "But you're still not coming with us."

Nick let out a *grr*, turned his back on me, and sprawled back across the comforter.

I stopped in my den for a moment to retrieve a legal pad and a pen from my desk, then went back downstairs to the shop to wait for Ollie. The afternoon had turned chilly, so I put water in the kettle for a quick cup of tea, and while it was boiling, took my pad and pen over to my table and sat scribbling some notes. I finished just as the kettle started to whistle. I got up, returned a few minutes later with a steaming cup of lemon ginger tea, and perused the notes I'd written. I'd put down two columns: one was headed *Manny Delgado*, the second *Hannah Berger*. Underneath Manny's I'd written:

1. Was informant for the police and the FBI.
2. Louis saw him at block sale, hanging around Hannah's table.
3. Hannah recognized him from Lacey's sketch—thought he might have taken something but did not say what.
4. Manny called Samms and said he had a lead on a cold case, wanted to be certain he got reward money.
5. Manny's body turns up, drained of blood and stuffed in a coffin at Waincroft.

Under Hannah's name I'd written:

1. Very protective of her brother Lawton—told Betty Callahan that she was afraid his penchant for gambling would cost them

their house.

2. Told Betty shortly after that armored car robbery that the problem with Lawton and the house had been resolved—did she know about her brother's part in the robbery?

3. Blamed the Waincroft curse for all the misfortunes in her family—hated Enola and vice versa.

4. She recognized John Doe's sketch, but denied it at first.

5. Got a mysterious phone call the night she was killed—the note read, SS, 10 p.m.

6. Nick and I found Hannah's body at Waincroft Manor the next day. Enola's bloodstained scarf was around her neck.

I took a calming sip of tea and then added another note under Hannah's column:

7. Who is SS? Did he/she have anything to do with Hannah's death?

After some deliberation, I added another note, separate from the rest:

Ghostbusters—the wild card. Why did they show up now, at this particular time? What is their connection, if any, to these murders? Their appearance just seems too . . . convenient.

I'd just finished writing that last note when a loud knock sounded at my back door. I jumped up and let Ollie in. His gaze swept over my outfit, and he gestured at his own dark slacks and shirt. "Looks as if we both had the same idea. Try to be as inconspicuous as possible, especially in broad daylight."

I chuckled. "Would you like a cup of tea before we go?"

Ollie nodded assent, and as I went to fix it he settled at the table and pulled my pad over in front of him. "I see someone's been writing down case notes, just like they taught you in PI school." His hand reached up to touch a springy gray curl. "Mark my words, it won't be long before you'll be itching to go into PI work full-time. I can see it now—Sampson and Charles, Investigators."

"What, not Charles and Sampson?" I teased as I set his tea in front of him. I pointed to the last entry under Hannah's name. "I have a feeling that this SS is the key to the whole mystery."

"Could be," Ollie said. He took a sip of tea and set the mug down. "It is odd that's all Hannah wrote. It's almost as if she were afraid someone would find her scribbling, and she wanted to keep the meeting a secret."

"Good point. I never thought of that."

Nick had come downstairs and now he wound himself around Ollie's ankles, purring loudly. Ollie reached down to pet him on the white streak behind his ear. "What's up, Little Nick?"

"He's cozying up to you because I told him he had to stay here, aren't you, Nick?" I said with a stern look at the cat.

Nick's head swiveled around and he regarded me with a wide-eyed, "Who me?" stare.

I folded my arms across my chest. "Yes, you."

Nick lay down at Ollie's feet, put his head on his paws, and started to purr.

Ollie laughed. "Oh, let him come, Nora. What harm can it do? Nick's a good detective, maybe he can ferret out a clue."

"Or another body," I grumbled.

Nick got up, walked over to me, and sat up on his haunches, pawing at my pants, his eyes wide and pleading. "Er-rup."

I shook my head, but I felt my resolve starting to melt. "Is this how you got your way with your former human? Using your catly charm?"

"Speaking of his former human." Ollie reached into his breast pocket and pulled out a postcard. "Guess what I got in the mail today."

I walked over and took the card from Ollie. The front was a montage of pictures of the Carmel Mission. I flipped the card over and read the message, scrawled there in what I had come to recognize as Nick Atkins's nearly illegible handwriting:

Just a brief note to let you know I'm OK. Hope you are doing well *mapping* out strategy. "N"

I tapped the postcard against my chin. "How odd, to hear from him after all these weeks without a word."

"Odd on many levels, if you ask me," said Ollie. "Am I mapping out a strategy? A strategy for what? Do you think that message might be written in some sort of code again?"

"Maybe." I pointed to the postcard. "Mapping is underlined. Why?" A sudden thought occurred to me and I hurried over to the island, yanked open the middle drawer, and removed the mysterious notes I'd received previously. I brought them back to the table and laid them in front of Ollie. "They're all printed, so it's hard to tell, but . . . do you think Nick Atkins could have sent these?"

Ollie scanned them both, frowning as he did so. "It certainly seems like Nick's cryptic style. If he is working in espionage, he might have known Delgado was an informant, which would answer the first one. As for the second—" Ollie tapped at the paper with his forefinger. "It sounds like one of those riddles Nick used to love."

"His advice certainly helped." I took the postcard back from Ollie. "The second one was on the windshield of my car, and I was certain I saw a dark figure in that bar, watching me. Damn, it was probably him."

"Well, can you beat that." Ollie scratched at his ear. "Nick Atkins, watching over you like a guardian angel, offering help from afar. That doesn't sound like the man I worked with for years."

I grimaced. "If he really wanted to be helpful he could tell me the murderer's name."

"If he knew it, he'd probably find a way." Ollie let out a sigh. "It's all so very cloak-and-dagger. I'm starting to believe that Atkins really is a spy."

Ollie and I started for the door, and I noticed that Nick hung back, walking in a circle in front of the refrigerator. As I laid my hand on the doorknob, he squatted down, looking mournfully at the two of us.

"Oh, all right," I said. "But you be sure and behave yourself."

Nick rose and immediately scampered over to us, head and tail high, eyes gleaming.

I waved my finger in the air and gave one final order.

"And no more bodies!"

Chapter Twenty-three

Hannah Berger's house was located about a half hour away from Hot Bread. While not considered to be in Cruz proper, it was still well within the official town line. A line of pine trees ran along one side of the house, and beyond was a marshy wooded lot. There was a lot of property, which included a garage and a shed, both of which had seen far better days. I could well understand Hannah's panicking at the thought of her brother possibly losing the family home; not only for the obvious sentimental reasons, but because the property, not necessarily the house, could be worth a great deal of money if a developer got their hands on it. It would have, no doubt, netted a tidy profit at some point and provided Hannah with a generous nest egg for her golden years—years she'd never reach, now.

The house itself was modeled after an 1880s farmhouse. I'd never been inside myself but I'd heard others talk about it. The house had been described as elaborate and quite large in the Queen Anne style, and most of the rooms boasted gorgeous wood paneling. Personally I thought it would be a shame to let the property go to a developer, when someone could acquire this at an estate sale for a fraction of its value. A handy person could do wonders with the place. As Ollie pulled his jaunty convertible to a stop at the side of the road, I pointed to a sign on the lawn: *Open House.*

Ollie switched off the ignition, pocketed the keys. "At least we don't have to worry about committing a B&E," he said and chuckled.

I pulled the visor of my baseball cap down over my eyes. "Damn. And I was getting good at 'em, too."

I headed for the front porch, with Ollie and Nick bringing up the rear. I looked around and didn't see a doorbell. I opened the screen door and my hand was poised to knock when the door was suddenly flung open and a familiar voice cried out, "Nora Charles? Is that you under that baseball cap?"

I flushed at Joannie Adams's effusive greeting. "Joannie, hi. I didn't know you had this listing."

Joannie waved her hand. "Oh, Hannah mentioned a few weeks ago that she was interested in selling, and I've already talked to her lawyer. Since she died intestate, the state will take over the proceeds, but if I can scrape a quick sale together, well . . ." She rubbed her hands together. "I'll get a pretty good commission out of it." She looked past me at Ollie and Nick, standing on the porch. "What are y'all doing here anyway?" she asked.

Ollie moved forward and said smoothly, "I'm afraid it's my fault. I heard about Hannah's unfortunate demise, and I admit, I was rather curious to see her home. I'd heard that the property was quite outstanding, and I'm in the market for a good investment."

Joannie, sensing a prospective buyer, turned to Ollie with an effusive smile. "Are you now?"

Ollie smiled affably. "Yes. I made quite a killing in the stock market last month. Let's just say I've got cash at the ready, just waiting for the right investment."

Joannie glanced at her watch before turning another dazzling smile on Ollie. "I do have a prospective buyer coming, but he's already fifteen minutes late, so . . . the early bird gets the worm, right?" She spread her arms wide and motioned for us to enter. "This is the foyer. You'll want to note especially the deep baseboards and the brass fittings . . ."

Joannie linked her arm through Ollie's and proceeded to extol the virtues of the house. Nick and I took that opportunity to scurry quickly up the staircase that led to the second floor. I had no idea what I was looking for, but I hoped that I'd know it when I saw it. There was a long hallway with four closed doors, and I went over to the first door on the left and opened it. I saw a large, canopied four-poster bed and two generous-sized dressers, done in a dark oak. One dresser had a silver hairbrush and comb on it, and beside that was a framed photograph of a man and a woman. The woman wore what looked to be a short white dress and she carried a small bouquet of carnations in one hand. The man had on a dapper suit and a boutonniere in his lapel. Both wore wide smiles. I had no doubt that this must be a picture of Hannah's parents—their wedding picture if I had to hazard a guess. There was a large closet on the other wall. I walked over and opened the door. Inside were rows and rows of plain blouses, all whites and grays and taupes, and several hangers with skirts and slacks all in the same color palette. Several pairs of shoes were strewn across the bottom of the closet—all sensible, low-heeled shoes in one color, a basic black that went with everything. I felt a wave of pity for Hannah surge through me and I shut the closet door. As I turned, I saw Nick, sprawled on his back, all four paws in the air. He had a slip of paper clenched in his forepaws. I walked over and bent down.

"Say, buddy, what have you got there?"

Nick looked at me. "Merow," he said. I gently disengaged the paper from his claws and looked at it. It looked to have been torn from a ruled pad, and written across it was a string of numbers. I slid the paper into the zip compartment of my tote and motioned for Nick to follow me.

Moving back into the hallway, I paused at the stairwell to listen. Joannie's voice sounded a bit further away. She must have taken Ollie into the kitchen. Saying a silent prayer that Ollie would stall her with as many kitchen questions as he could, I opened the door of the room directly across from Hannah's bedroom. This room was furnished much more sparsely. A twin-sized bed with a threadbare mattress dominated the center of the room. Two high dressers stood on one side, all the drawers open, and a quick glance assured me they were all empty. Likewise the closet, save for a few wire hangers.

This, no doubt, had been Lawton's room.

I went back into the hall again and moved swiftly down to the next door. Opening it, I let out a tiny gasp. This room appeared to be more of a storage room. There were boxes upon boxes stacked on two of the walls, and a long folding table square in its center, with items bearing Post-it tags still on them.

"Mother lode," I whispered to Nick. "This is what Hannah probably was trying to sell at the block sale."

I left the door slightly ajar so that I would be able to hear when Joannie and Ollie started to make their way upstairs, then I walked back to the table and started to peruse what was on it. At first glance it appeared to be mostly junk: there were a few old and slightly cracked plates with a Post-it indicating they could be had for the thrifty price of twenty-five cents, an ashtray, a few platters. At the far end of the table there looked to be some more masculine items, and I figured these might have belonged to Lawton. There was a scratched and worn wood dresser valet, a tarnished silver money clip, an assortment of combs, two pairs of sunglasses. At the very end of the table there was a large book, what my mother would have called coffee-table style. I walked over and picked it up. There was a photograph of an old mansion on the cover and I looked at the title: *Marvelous Old Mansions: An Architect's Guide.* What the heck? The dust jacket was dirty and torn in a few places. I wondered if Lawton had picked this up at a garage sale himself. I started to put it back, when suddenly I felt something furry twine around my ankles. I jumped, and the heavy book slipped from my hands and crashed to the wood floor.

I glanced over at Nick, who had moved away from me and was occupied with something beneath the table. "Thanks a lot, Nick." I picked up the book, and as I did so two articles fell to the floor. I picked them up to look at them. One was a yellowed edge of parchment paper, with some odd markings on it. The other was a photograph of two men, standing in front of what appeared to be the entrance to a casino. One man was short and squat, with thick dark hair and a weak chin. He wore a dark T-shirt that had *ArmLink* emblazoned on the chest, and he had the same squinty eyes and thin lips as Hannah, so this, no doubt, was Lawton. The other man was taller and thinner. He wore a massive pair of dark glasses that obscured most of his face, but the most arresting feature was the man's hair, or rather, his lack of it. He was totally, completely bald. I tapped the photo against my chin, trying to remember the account of the robbery given by the injured guard. If memory served, he'd described one of the robbers as "totally bald." I stared at the photo. This had to be Fred Silverman! I flipped it over. Written in a cramped hand was "Me and SS in Reno."

SS. The same initials that were on Hannah's mysterious note. Silverman? But his first name was Fred, right?

I heard sounds coming from the direction of the staircase. I quickly tiptoed over to the door and put my ear to it. Joannie's voice wafted up to me. "Did you hear that thud? It sounded like something fell."

Ollie: "Oh, I'm sure it's nothing. You know how old houses can get. I'm really interested, though, in those antique kitchen cabinets. They could be refinished, right?"

"Oh, yes," Joannie responded. Then my heart sank as she added, "My goodness, where's Nora? Do you think that's what we heard? Is she upstairs?"

"Oh, she might have wandered around on her own," Ollie said casually. "You know Nora. I'm sure she's fine. Now, getting back to those cabinets . . ."

I was positive that Ollie wouldn't be able to buy me much more time, but I figured I'd found what I came for. I picked up the book and replaced the photo and torn bit of paper in it. The book was large but fortunately my tote bag was giant-sized. I shoved the book inside, then with Nick at my heels hurried down the staircase, being careful not to make too much noise. We reached the bottom and scurried into the parlor just as Joannie and Ollie emerged from the kitchen area.

"There you are," cried Joannie. "I wondered where you'd gone off to."

Ollie glanced at his watch. "Oh, gee, look at the time. I'm afraid we have to get going or I'll be late for another appointment."

"Oh, but you haven't even seen upstairs," Joannie cried.

"I'll call your office for another appointment."

"Well, don't wait too long. I think the state wants this sold as quickly as possible. Here's my card." Joannie pressed a square of paper into Ollie's hand as we ducked out and onto the porch. I looked over my shoulder to make sure Nick was behind us, and I saw Joannie watching us from the porch. Neither Ollie nor I said a word until we were back in his car, and then he leaned toward me and waggled his finger.

"Man, do you owe me for that one. Talk about being pushy. I think Joannie must have written the book on it."

I laughed. "I do owe you, indeed. I think it was successful, though."

"Good. Show me when we get back to Hot Bread. I think, at the very least, today's escapade deserves a Thin Man tuna melt."

"No problem."

As we pulled away, another car came down the winding road. I gasped as I recognized the occupant—Ethan Howell. Ethan pulled over and parked almost exactly in the same spot we had, and I frowned.

Either Ethan was meeting Joannie there, or he was her other prospective buyer. I couldn't help but remember our recent conversation when he'd indicated his reluctance to put down roots, all of which made that option very, very curious indeed.

• • •

We returned to Hot Bread, and I immediately started to make Ollie his tuna melt. Ollie settled himself at my back table, talking absently to Nick, who'd resumed his post in front of my refrigerator, his eye on the bowl of tuna. Once the sandwich was on the griddle, I spooned some of the tuna into Nick's bowl. He waddled over, gave a loud meow, and a few minutes later the sound of contented slurping reached my ears.

"Now, while we're waiting for my sandwich, show me what you found," Ollie said.

I needed no further urging. I reached into my tote bag and pulled out the book, then removed the photo and the slip of paper. "These fell out when I dropped the book," I said to Ollie. "I thought it might be a photo of

Lawton and his pal Fred Silverman, but see what's written on the back."

Ollie turned the photo over and read the inscription. "Maybe it's not Fred Silverman," he suggested. "Maybe it's someone else."

"I doubt that. Betty said that Lawton was pretty much of a loner. That trait must run in the family. Besides, the photo was taken in front of a casino, and Betty said they were gambling buds. That Silverman was the one who got him hooked."

"Okay, then maybe Betty was mistaken about the name? Maybe it was Sam Silverman, or Stan Silverman?"

"Both of which sound a lot like Fred," I remarked sarcastically.

"Okay, then, Lawton was getting sick, right? Maybe he just had a case of shaky hand syndrome. Maybe he just wrote the *S* twice."

"So he meant to write 'Me and S in Reno? Maybe . . .'" I stared off into space for a few seconds, then snapped my gaze back to Ollie. "What about a nickname? Maybe Silverman had a nickname that started with an S?"

"Possibly. How are you going to find that out?"

I whipped out my phone. "The same way I found out all the other details." I punched in the number of the Cruz Sweet Shoppe, and a few moments later Betty Callahan answered. "Hi, Betty, it's Nora Charles again. I'm sorry to bother you, but I was just wondering. You wouldn't happen to know if this Fred Silverman went by any other name, would you?"

"Another name? You mean like a nickname? No, I don't think—oh, wait! I remember Hannah calling him Old Slippery a few times. Lawton sometimes called him Slippery because he was such a smooth operator when they went gambling. He used to get them comps and free drinks, things like that. Does that help you?"

"Very much, thanks." I rang off and looked at Ollie. "His nickname was Slippery. He could well be the SS Hannah had that ten o'clock appointment with the night she died. And if it was him—I'll bet even money he's our murderer. He might have even murdered Manny, too."

"How do you figure that?"

"Well." I tapped the book. "I think Manny might have found something in this book that led him to connect the dots."

Ollie frowned. "The photo? Then why didn't he take it?"

"I think he found something that interested him more." I laid the yellowed edge of paper in front of Ollie. "I'm thinking that the rest of this paper is what Manny took, and what got him killed. I'm guessing that it could have been directions to where he hid the money."

Ollie's eyes widened. "You mean like a treasure map?"

"Exactly. Betty said that Lawton knew the ins and outs of that house better than anyone. He must have made a map to give his partner so he could find his share of the money, and then died before he could get it to him." I pulled out the scrap of paper Nick had been playing with and set that on the table. "Nick found that. It could be a code, or it could be something just as simple as a phone number."

Ollie's fingers closed around the scrap of paper. "How about I investigate this while you work on finding out more about Slippery Silverman?"

I grinned at him. "I was hoping you'd say that. I need to get in touch with Hal Frey, too, and find out the latest on Enola."

I took Ollie's sandwich off the griddle and set it in front of him. As he tucked into it my phone buzzed, and I saw Mollie Travis's name pop up. The minute she heard my voice the teen cried out, "Oh, Nora! I wanted to call you as soon as I found out. Remember I told you I was going to show that sketch to my friend Kara?"

My heart started to beat wildly. "Yes. She recognized him?"

"Yep. His name is Joshua Glennon."

"Great," I said. "Did Kara know where he lives, or what school he goes to?"

"Some fancy private school in Calaveras County." Mollie's voice dropped to a conspiratorial whisper. "The word is he got into a bushel of trouble and got suspended. He's staying with his aunt here in Cruz now."

"O-kay. Did your friend know the aunt's name?"

"That's the best part," Mollie said, her tone smug. "His aunt is—"

A mental picture of the dark-haired woman in the Cruz High yearbook suddenly flashed through my mind, and I let out a gasp. "It's Kay," I cried. "Kay Trilby is his aunt."

"Ah, heck, Nora," Mollie grumbled. "You're no fun."

Chapter Twenty-four

As I steered my SUV down the long graveled drive, I thought how much Kay Trilby's house reminded me of the O'Hara plantation in *Gone With the Wind*. The large, rambling home was built in the tradition of a Southern mansion. Four massive white pillars graced the sweeping porch, which was surrounded by clusters of bright purple and pink bougainvillea. The lawn was a lush green and beautifully manicured. On the whole, it gave off vibes of contentment and lazy afternoons, and as I parked I half expected to see the doors fly open and Scarlett herself race down the flight of stone steps, gathering up her crinoline skirts, her dark hair flying out behind her. Instead of Scarlett, however, I was greeted at the door by a rather dour-faced woman in a crisp black maid's uniform.

"Nora Charles to see Mrs. Trilby. I'm expected," I added.

The woman gave a soft grunt and motioned for me to follow her. As my heels sank into the plush Aubusson carpet I had to fight to keep my jaw from dropping. The Trilby mansion was certainly everything I'd ever heard about it, and then some. We walked down a long hallway to a closed set of French doors. The maid flung them open and motioned for me to go inside. "I shall tell Mrs. Trilby you are here," she said. "Please make yourself comfortable in the meantime."

She withdrew, shutting the double doors behind her. I craned my neck, taking in the plush surroundings. Exquisite oil paintings, definitely originals, covered every wall. The fireplace, located at the far end of the room, was definitely Italianate marble. A gilt chandelier dangled overhead, and the furniture—a long couch, a love seat, and two Queen Anne chairs—were all done in rich brocaded fabric. The color palette was soft and inviting: baby pink, oyster white, sky blue. I was admiring a set of carved ivory Buddhas displayed in one of the many cherrywood curio cabinets in the room and wondering just how I was going to broach the subject of her nephew when I heard the parlor door open. I turned just as the maid cleared her throat loudly and announced, "Mrs. Trilby will see you now. Follow me, please."

I followed the maid back into the hallway and up the winding staircase to the second floor. She paused before the door on my immediate left. "Go right on in," she commanded with a sweep of her arm. I pushed open the door and found myself in a large, dark-paneled room. One wall was floor-to-ceiling shelves, filled to overflowing with books of all types: leather bound, hardcover, paperbacks. Another wall was covered with more oil paintings, each depicting different animals. There was one of two playful kittens with a ball of string, another showing a hunter and his hound, and one depicting racehorses going into the stretch, so artfully done you could almost feel the breeze as the black stallion crossed the finish line. A Sheraton-styled tambour desk, inlaid with an American Eagle, sat squarely in the middle of the room, directly in front of a massive picture window through which the beautifully manicured grounds were visible. And behind the desk, in a chair that looked to be made of butter-soft tan leather, sat the woman herself.

I stepped forward and extended my hand. "Thanks so much for seeing me on such short notice, Mrs. Trilby."

Kay Trilby took my hand and gripped it firmly. The older woman wasn't what I'd label as glamorous, but there was an air about her that spelled class with a capital C. She had on a simple white shirtdress that probably cost more than a week's worth of receipts at Hot Bread. I noticed as she tipped her silver head toward me that there wasn't a hair out of place on her head. Her makeup was minimal and skillfully applied, and her eyes, behind the massive tortoiseshell glasses perched on her nose, were bright and snapping and as full of life as the woman herself. She released my hand and motioned me into one of the two straight-backed chairs, also covered in a rich brocade similar to the parlor sofa, that flanked her desk.

"Nonsense, Nora," she said. "I'm always glad to talk to you, you know that."

"Yes, well, this was rather short notice. I was in the area, and I wanted to get the catering menu finalized if I could before Detective Anderson releases Waincroft Manor to the cleanup committee."

Kay gave her silver hair a pat. "Yes, I was on the phone with her earlier. I told her that she had to release the house within forty-eight hours." Her lips twisted downward. "She wasn't too happy, although I suppose it's understandable." She let out a long drawn-out sigh. "That house stands deserted for decades, and suddenly, when we want to hold a fundraiser there, two murders occur?"

"It is strange," I agreed. I hesitated and then added, "I understand the ghostbusters have been pleading their case to you."

She barked out a short laugh. "For all the good it's done. I mean really. Who in their right mind would believe a vampire has come back?"

"Well, the first body was drained of blood."

"For which, I am sure, there is a logical explanation, and one that doesn't include a vampire. I've got people on the verge of pulling out as it is. Their type of publicity is definitely not what we need." She tapped on the desk blotter with a red-tipped fingernail. "The girl in particular seemed very determined."

I started and leaned forward in my chair. "The girl? I thought you spoke with Grant?"

"I did. She came to me afterward on her own. Actually demanded I give her the key, so she could investigate on her own, can you believe the nerve? I threw her out." Kay pushed the papers she was working on over to the side and steepled her fingers underneath her chin. "Anyway, you're here about the menu, right? I trust Cathy delivered my suggestions?"

I crossed my legs at the ankles and leaned forward slightly in my chair. "Yes, she did. They were excellent, but I already had something similar in mind. May I?"

She gave a brief nod and I opened my tote and pulled out a single sheet of paper, which I passed to her. She took it and studied it for a full five minutes before she set it in front of her and pushed her glasses down on the bridge of her nose, so she could look at me over their rims.

"This," she said, tapping at the paper with one long red-tipped nail, "sounds simply fabulous. And the titles are so creative." She picked up the paper again, scissoring it between her long fingers. "Deviled Ham Eyeball Sandwiches. Vampire Blood Tomato Soup. Mexican Pumpkin Punch. Deviled Chicken Lollipops, Mummy Franks. That's quite a list of appetizers."

"I was striving for a menu that would appeal to all ages. As far as the entrées go, I thought the Monster Meatball Subs and the Jack O'Lantern Cheeseburger Pie would appeal to the kids, and the Dr. Jekyll Tex-Mex Lasagna would be perfect for the adults."

She handed the paper back to me. "Well, it sounds good to me. You know I trust your judgment, Nora, as I did your mother's before you. You've worked on several events for me, and you haven't failed me yet."

"I'm glad to hear it. I just wanted to come in person and show you what I had planned. I hope there are no hard feelings because I'm not using your suggestions."

Kay pushed the glasses up a bit on her nose. "I have a confession to make. Those appetizer suggestions weren't exactly mine."

I raised a brow and hoped I looked properly surprised. "No?"

"No. Actually they were my nephew's."

My heart gave a little leap. This might be easier than I thought. "Oh? I didn't realize you had a nephew."

"My sister's boy. Joshua. He's a good kid, but . . ." Her lips arranged themselves into a little moue of distaste. "What can I say? He's fifteen."

"That can be an awkward age, especially for a boy." I tried to make my tone casual. "Does he live around here?"

"No, they live in Valley Springs." Kay fidgeted a bit in her chair, and one hand reached up to tug absently at a silver curl. "I can trust your discretion in this matter, Nora?" At my nod, she continued, "Joshua is staying with me temporarily There was an incident at that fancy private school he attended."

"An incident?"

"Yes." She picked up a pencil, started to tap it against the desktop. "My sister and her husband aren't what one would call good disciplinarians. They've always let that boy run free, with minimal supervision. Modern parenting, they call it. Hmpf." She gave her head a brisk shake. "Long story short, the boy got in with the wrong crowd and got caught selling test answers to some students. He and two others were put on six months' suspension."

"How awful. I'm sure his parents were very upset."

"Oh, my sister was fairly beside herself. Not because of Joshua's suspension, but because it came at an inconvenient time for her. She was fretting that she'd be unable to accompany her husband to the UK. He'd been put on special assignment for six months, and she had her wardrobe selected and her bags packed."

I raised an eyebrow. "They were going abroad and leaving their son alone?"

"It's not the first time. The last two times he stayed with a friend, if you can call him that. If you ask me, no friend teaches someone to cheat on exams and sell test answers to other students." Her fist came down hard on the desktop, and I jumped. "I told her if going to England was so all-fired important to her, she should send Joshua to me. If I can't straighten him out in the next six months, then no one can. So far everything seems to be going pretty well. I've got him private tutors, and he's doing remarkably well at his lessons. If I had a complaint . . ." Her voice trailed off for a minute, and then she snapped her gaze back to me. "If I had a complaint, it would be the boy's been too cooperative, too quiet. It's like he's a powder keg, waiting to explode."

"I imagine he probably misses his friends. A boy that age needs interaction among his peers. Surely you know some people with children his own age he could get to know?" I suggested.

Kay's lips puckered as she thought. "My assistant has a nephew almost Joshua's age," she said at last. "And I think Carly Fletcher over at the Cruz Museum has a daughter who's fourteen. Maybe I could arrange something." Her hand shot out and covered mine. "Thank you for the suggestion, Nora. You've a good head on your shoulders, just like your mama."

I grinned. "I try."

"It's hard. I never had children, never wanted them really, so I'm pretty much a fish out of water at this parenting thing, but I'll be darned if I'll let my sister's lackadaisical attitude ruin that boy. He's got a good head on his shoulders, he just needs the proper guidance."

"Well, if anyone can make him trod the straight and narrow, it's you, Kay."

"Thanks." Kay opened the middle drawer of her desk and removed a thick ledger. "I know you offered to cater the gala for free, but I just don't feel right about it, Nora. It's a lot of work."

"Don't worry about it, Kay. I'm happy to do it. I would appreciate a receipt, though, so I could put it with my others for tax time."

"No problem." Kay opened the ledger and grunted. "Damn. Seems I'm out of receipts."

"That's all right, Kay, I can come back." I started to rise but she waved me back.

"No, no. I just ordered a batch of them, I'm just not sure where Yvonne put them. Can you wait here a few minutes?" She rose smoothly from behind the desk. "I'll be right back." Kay glided from the room before I could say another word. I frowned, debating. I needed to find Joshua and make certain that he was, indeed, the lad who'd barreled into me at Waincroft Manor, but how could I find him?

Almost as if on cue, the study door opened again. "Aunt Kay, I've finished that history lesson—oh!"

I froze in my chair. I recognized the dark curly hair, the flashing eyes, the stubborn set to the chin. This was definitely the young man who'd run from Waincroft Manor, all right. We stared at each other for a few seconds and then I said, "Hello, Joshua."

His eyes narrowed slightly. "You know me? Have we met?"

"Sort of." I grinned at him. "We ran into each other—literally—at Waincroft Manor."

"Oh! That was *you?*" Two bright spots of color appeared on his cheeks. "I—I didn't hurt you, did I?"

"No, you just knocked the wind out of me."

"Sorry about that." He started to edge toward the door. "I have to go find my aunt now." He started to turn but I sprang up out of the chair and laid a hand on his arm.

"Not so fast, Joshua."

He tried to shrug my hand away but I held on fast. "Hey, I said I was sorry."

"I'm sure you are. I'm not mad about what happened, but I do need to talk to you about it. You could be in danger."

His tongue darted out, swiped across his lower lip. "Did you see him too?" he whispered.

"Who? Do you mean the body in the coffin?"

He glanced around nervously and said, "Not so loud. My aunt doesn't know I snuck out of the house that day. I was supposed to be studying, but . . . heck, I just couldn't take being cooped up here like a criminal any longer. I swiped Andy's bike—that's the kid who does the gardening—and I took off on a little tour." He rubbed at the back of his neck with his hand. "Geez, if I'd only known . . ."

"I won't tell your aunt, but it's important that you tell me everything you saw that day, Joshua," I said. When he remained silent I added, "You know there was another murder in the mansion?"

His eyes widened. "Another one! Really?"

I nodded. "Yes. A woman named Hannah Berger. She worked at Cruz High."

Joshua stumbled over to one of the Queen Anne chairs, lowered himself into it. He ran a hand through his hair. "Geez, another one?" He looked up at me. "Do they know who did it?"

I shook my head. "No, but I think you have an idea, don't you?"

He averted his gaze. "What makes you say that?"

"Because of what you said when you ran into me, do you remember? You were mumbling under your breath, but I distinctly heard you say 'before he gets us.' And just now, when you asked if I saw him, you weren't referring to the body, were you?"

"No." He slumped further down in the chair and twisted his hands in front of him. At last he said, "If I tell you, you can't tell my aunt I was anywhere near there. She'd get upset, and I'd be restricted more than I am now . . . if that's possible."

"I'll keep your name out of it as much as I can," I promised him. "So? What happened that day?"

"Like I said, I snuck out of the house. I was tired of just being inside, no interaction with anyone except my tutors and my aunt, and the gazillion people she has working for her. I heard her talking about this gala and I looked up the Waincroft mansion online. It sounded pretty cool so I thought I'd just take a quick run over there and check it out. The back door was open, so I went inside. Honest, I was just gonna take a quick look around and go back . . . and then I saw him." He put both hands up to his face, scrubbed at his eyes. "First I thought I was seeing things. I mean, the guy looked like something out of one of those old black-and-white horror movies they show late at night."

"Can you describe him?" I asked eagerly.

"Not really. I only caught a glimpse, but he seemed pretty tall. He was a good foot taller than the other one."

I stared at him. "The other one? There were two?"

He nodded. "Yeah. They both had long black capes on, so I couldn't see them really well. I know the second figure was shorter, but that's all I could make out. Anyway, I heard 'em coming and I hid in the alcove. I was sweating bullets, hoping they wouldn't see me. They left, and I probably should have too, but . . . I wanted to see what was in that room. So I went in and looked, and I saw the coffin. I thought, hey, pretty cool. Then I thought maybe I could get a piece of the coffin lining, you know, just to prove to my friends I'd really been there, but when I opened the lid and saw that guy inside . . . heck, I lost it. I bolted out of there, well, you know." He squirmed a bit in the chair. "I thought maybe they'd come back for what they dropped. At least, I think they dropped it." He thrust his hand into the back pocket of his jeans and pulled out a piece of yellowed paper. He pressed it into my hand. "I found it just inside the door of the room."

I unfolded the paper and spread it out on my knee. "It looks like a map of some sort," I said.

Joshua nodded. "Yep. It does. I figured it might be a map of that house, but it's kinda hard to tell from just half of it." He pointed at the jagged tear that ran along the paper's right side.

I held it up. "Would you mind if I kept this for a little while?"

He shook his head. "Take it. I don't want it. It's been giving me nightmares ever since I snatched it up. I keep looking over my shoulder, wondering if Baldy knows I have it, and if he'll track me down and come after me for it."

I looked at Joshua sharply. "Baldy?"

"Oh, yeah. One thing I forgot. The guy's hood slipped a little, and I got a look at his head. He had no hair. He was bald as a cue ball." He rose, wiped his hands on the sides of his jeans. "Look, I have to go. If my aunt finds me here with you . . . well, I don't want her to start asking questions."

"Of course. I understand." I touched his arm. "Just lie low for a few days, okay? I have a feeling all this is going to wrap up soon."

"I hope so," Joshua said with feeling. "I've been trying to stick close to here all week, and I'm tired of looking over my shoulder every time I go out with my aunt. Although I have to admit I wouldn't mind poking through that old mansion. It seemed pretty interesting."

"There'll be plenty of time for you to poke around in there, I'm sure. At the gala, for instance."

Joshua's nose wrinkled. "Yeah, right. With my aunt watching me like a hawk? I don't think so."

I gave his arm a quick squeeze. "Just steer clear of there for now. Promise?"

He looked at me solemnly. "Yeah. Sure. I'd better get going." He gave me a quick wave, spun on his heel, and was gone. I sank back into the chair, leaned my head back, and reviewed what I'd learned:

One: There was not one but two caped figures in Waincroft Manor, in the same room with the body in the coffin.

Two: One of them had possibly dropped what appeared to be a crude drawing of the interior of Waincroft Manor, which was most likely meant to indicate where the stolen money was hidden.

Three: Joshua had gotten a glimpse of one of the intruders. He could tell the man was tall and bald.

I considered number three to be particularly significant in light of two facts: the guard's description of one of the robbers as totally bald, and that according to the photo I'd found, Fred Silverman, aka Slippery, was also totally bald.

Coincidence? I rather thought not. It was looking more and more to me like Fred Silverman might well be the missing robber, in search of his cut of the money stolen from the armored car. It was also looking more and more as if Silverman—and his mysterious companion—might well be responsible not only for Manny's murder but Hannah's too.

I unfolded the yellowed paper again for another look. Scrawled in the upper left corner was "WC Manor." The drawing itself was crude. There were lots of slashes and lines, but if one stretched their imagination, it might resemble a floor plan. I ran my finger along the jagged edge. Had Manny known he was being followed and ripped the map in half? There was no sliver missing from this half, so I figured there was a good chance my supposition was correct. Manny had probably hidden the half showing the money's location, hoping to elude his follower and return at another time, which meant the missing half was most likely somewhere in the mansion.

But where?

I picked up my phone and punched in Al Bennett's number. When his voicemail kicked in, I asked him if he could find out if Fishbein had a list of Manny's personal effects. Knowing the coroner and his penchant for detail, I was relatively certain he had some record of whatever had been on Manny's person. I promised to extend his free lunch privileges another two weeks if he came through and then I hung up, dragged my hand through my hair.

"So," I murmured, "Manny's at this yard sale, and he stumbles upon Lawton's book. He sees the photo and the map, somehow puts two and two together, takes the map hoping to find the stolen money and claim the reward. Maybe Silverman was at that block sale too, hoping to find what Manny did. Maybe he saw Manny find the map and he followed him. But why kill him and drain the body of blood?"

I worried at my lower lip. Okay, my theory wasn't perfect. There were a few holes, but overall I still thought it made sense. The sensible thing to do, no doubt, would be to take this map straight to Anderson along with my theory, except for one tiny detail.

That's all I had. A theory. I had no proof, and without it, Anderson probably wouldn't listen to one word of it. Nor would Samms.

"If proof is what I need, then proof I shall get," I murmured. "But how?"

That was the million-dollar question.

Chapter Twenty-five

Kay returned a few minutes later, receipt in hand. I thanked her and took my leave, hoping that I didn't appear too anxious to be on my way. Once I was in my SUV, I whipped out my cell and punched in Hal Frey's number. He answered on the second ring.

"How's Enola?" I asked without preamble. "Did you manage to get her out on bail?"

"She's fine and yes I did," he answered promptly. "She was rather upset, though, so I took her to my physician and he gave her a sedative. She's most likely sleeping in her room at the Cruz Inn now."

"What did she have to say about the alleged phone calls from Manny Delgado?"

"She admits he called her but she swears she never met the man, wouldn't know what he looked like if she fell over him. She said that he called her because he had questions concerning Waincroft Manor's architecture."

"Its architecture? What sort of questions?"

"He wanted to know how the floors were laid out, and if she had any sort of floor plan of the house. Said he was studying it and someone had recommended Waincroft Manor as a good example. She said he called her two or three times, refused to take no for an answer. Said that the third time she told him to 'buzz off or he'd be sorry.'"

"Ouch."

"Yeah, it's a good thing no one heard her say that. Anyway, the phone records along with her little coffin purchase shoved her to the top of Anderson's hit list. Just between you and me, I think Anderson's feeling the pressure from Kay Trilby to get all this wrapped up before the big Halloween gala."

"Well, Kay can be a bit overbearing," I admitted.

"To say the least. Anyway, I really don't think Anderson has enough on Enola to make a definitive case. I'm hoping to get these charges dropped. You could help, you know."

"How?"

"You and that cat of yours could catch the real killer, like you usually do."

"It's not for lack of trying, believe me."

He laughed. "Oh, I do. Say, is your sister around?"

"I'm not at home right now but she should be there. Why?"

"I've left several messages but she hasn't called me back."

"I wouldn't worry about it. Lacey is notorious for not checking voicemail. Is it something important?"

"I just wanted to confirm that I'm picking her up at seven thirty Saturday for our date, so when you do see her, could you ask her to call me? Please?"

"Sure, I'll—wait! This Saturday?"

"Yes. We were going to have dinner at La Foret in San Jose—I really don't want to cancel these reservations again . . . oh, wait, I'm getting another call. I'll keep you posted on Enola."

Hal hung up, and I slid my phone back into my tote with a frown. Wasn't this Saturday the big get-together at the Poker Face with the ghostbusters, the one that Lacey was attending with Larry Bolton—or was I wrong? I turned the key in the ignition and my SUV hummed to life. I glanced at the dashboard clock. Tonight was Lance's night to work. If I timed it just right, I'd arrive at the Poker Face just as he was starting his shift. I was in the mood for a nice cold one anyway, and maybe some juicy gossip, too.

• • •

I entered the Poker Face about twenty minutes later and saw Lance behind the bar, wiping down the counter. He saw me and waved me over to the corner stool. The bar was empty but it was still pretty early. Two guys in workmen's clothes sat at the far end, their eyes glued to ESPN, frosty mugs of beer in front of them, and a man and a woman were in the middle, heads close together, their hands wrapped around the stems of two half-empty glasses of a cocktail that resembled a Margarita. I slid onto the stool and Lance immediately came over. He slung a towel carelessly over one shoulder and splayed both palms on the counter.

"Well, well, if it isn't Nora Charles! How are you doing these days?"

I made a face at him. "I'm doing well. How about yourself?"

"Can't complain. Well, I could, but who would listen?" He tossed me a boyish grin and snapped the towel. "What can I get you? The usual?"

I nodded, and a few seconds later a frosty mug of Coors Light was in front of me. I picked up the mug, took a long sip, set it down. Lance eyed me. "You look like a woman on a mission. Wait, let me guess—you're hot on the trail of another mystery, right? The body in Waincroft Manor?"

"Make that bodies, plural. You heard about Hannah, right?"

He nodded. "Yes. She was never the most pleasant person in the world, but hardly a candidate for murder."

I took another sip of beer. "Someone thought differently." I gave a casual glance around, let my gaze rest on the door to the large room that was used for private parties. "Big night Saturday, huh?"

Lance shrugged. "Saturday's always our busiest night, you know that."

I tapped at the rim of my mug. "I was talking about the private party. The one the ghostbusters are having?"

He frowned, and then his expression cleared. "Oh, that." He gave a careless wave. "That got canceled."

I scooted to the edge of my stool. "It did? When?"

He inclined his head toward a table in the rear. "Since about two hours ago."

I turned and looked in the direction of Lance's gaze. Seated at one of the rear tables were Grant, Davey and Felix. If the expressions on their faces were any indication, they weren't exactly happy campers. I noted an almost empty pitcher of beer sat in the middle of the table, and their mugs looked in desperate need of a refill.

I slid off the stool, reached in my tote for my wallet. I slid two twenties across the bar to Lance. "Send a fresh pitcher of beer over there." I indicated their table with a nod of my head. "And another mug of Coors for me in a few minutes." I paused. "Maybe a platter of nachos too."

Lance touched two fingers to his forehead. "You got it. Good luck."

I gave him a thumbs-up, grabbed my mug and walked back to the table. As I approached I heard Grant say, "Well, it's not the end of the world. From the little we got to see of the mansion, I seriously doubt there was any paranormal activity there. I just wasn't feeling the energy. The only one who's really disappointed is Tammi—" He glanced up, caught sight of me, and said, "Why, hello, Ms. Charles. Would you care to join us?"

I slid onto the bench next to Felix. "Don't mind if I do." I glanced around the table at the almost empty pitcher and mugs. "It looks as if you're having a celebration of sorts."

Grant's lips twitched. "Actually you could call it sort of a going away party."

"Going away?"

"Yes. We're hitting too many stone walls, between Detective Anderson and Mrs. Trilby. Without the support of at least one of them, we can't hope to do a proper investigation so . . . I'm pulling the plug on this project."

Davey turned to me, eyes bright. "Besides, we got wind of another great opportunity this morning. There's a mansion in Santa Ana County, New Mexico, with reported spooky goings-on. I'm willing to bet there's a lot more paranormal activity there than there ever was at Waincroft Manor."

I sincerely doubted that, but I didn't voice my opinion. Instead I said, "Really? You don't believe the spirit of Anton Bartescue inhabits Waincroft?"

Davey and Grant both snorted at the same time. "Hardly," said Davey. "When we went there the other day nothing at all registered on our meters. We felt no presence."

Felix leaned forward. "That's not to say there couldn't be one. I keep trying to tell these people that Bartescue was a vampire, so his spirit might not react the same way as other specters."

Jose approached the table, bearing a tall pitcher of beer, a heaping platter of nachos, and a fresh mug of Coors Light for me. Grant looked up as he started to set the tray down. "Hey, we didn't order this," he said.

"I know. I did," I said. "Lance told me you were leaving, and I thought this would be a nice goodbye present."

"Oh, well . . . thanks." Grant grabbed the pitcher off of the tray and immediately refilled his glass, then handed the pitcher to Davey. "That was real nice of you, Ms. Charles."

"It's a shame you had to cancel your party for Saturday," I said. As they all turned to look at me, I added, "My sister Lacey was supposed to be Larry Bolton's date."

"Oho, so that's who he was bringing." Davey grinned and raised his mug. "He said he had a hot date. To be honest, Larry was more disappointed than any of us that we're moving on."

"Oh, I don't know about that," cut in Felix. "Tammi wasn't happy."

I glanced around the table. "I thought someone was missing. Where is Tammi?"

Davey shrugged. "Who knows? That chick is unpredictable. I thought she was gonna have a stroke when Grant told her we were leaving. She said that just because we're quitters didn't mean she was."

"So she's sticking around?"

He shrugged. "Looks that way. Makes sense, I guess. After all, she was the one who wanted to come here. We were all set to check out that locale in Arizona when she called us, told us about the murder. She was really hot to come here, insisted it'd be better than the locale last year. She thought discovering a vampire would make for much bigger ratings." Grant's lips twisted into a sardonic grin. "I guess maybe I am stupid, huh? I let her talk me into it."

I leaned forward. "So Larry Bolton didn't tell Davey about the murder? You found out from Tammi?"

Davey nodded. "Yeah. I mean, it was a plus that my cousin is on the Cruz PD, and that he supplied us with some information. By the way, I've told him to never do it again, under any circumstances," Davey added quickly. "He realizes he was wrong."

Grant pulled a small bottle out of his pocket and opened it. He shook a small pill into his palm and started to put it into his mouth, but Davey reached over and slapped at his wrist. "Hey—is that your anxiety med? You can't take that with beer!"

"Oh, heck, I forgot." Grant replaced the pill in the bottle, slid it back into his pocket and grinned rather sheepishly at me. "I have bouts of severe anxiety, so my doctor recommended Paxil. I only just started taking it this month."

"Yeah, and what does he do the first night he's on it! Takes it with a chaser of Heineken. Thank God Tammi was there," Davey said.

I looked at him. "What did Tammi do?"

"She explained, in great detail, what could happen if he continued doing that." Davey gave a mock shudder. "I tell you, it was so graphic it gave me the heebie-jeebies."

"Well, it was only natural, considering her past," said Grant. "I for one was very grateful." He reached in his pocket, pulled out his cell, glanced at the screen, and then jumped up. "Hey, guys! We got the okay from that guy in New Mexico. They want us there tomorrow morning, so we'd better get packed and out of here!"

As they all clambered to their feet, I touched Felix's arm. "Just one question before you leave. What did Grant mean when he said it was only natural, considering Tammi's past?"

"Just that it wasn't out of the ordinary for her to give unsolicited medical advice. She's got a degree in pharmacology."

Chapter Twenty-six

When I let myself in the back door of Hot Bread about twenty minutes later, I found Lacey on my computer, engaging in her favorite pastime of online shopping. She glanced up as I entered.

"Hey, sis. You look beat."

"I am." I tossed my tote bag on the counter and walked over to have a look. I eyed the very pretty navy blue lace dress that was on the computer screen. "Very pretty. Another Mizrahi?"

Lacey nodded. "Yep. It's on sale, too. Only fifty dollars at the Macy's in Colombia. The blue looks better with my skin tone, don't you think? I thought I might take a drive over there later."

I raised an eyebrow. "And I suppose, since your date with Larry Bolton fell through and you won't be prodding him for information, you'll be paying for this on your own?"

Her cheeks colored. "I was going to tell you. He only called to tell me a little while ago. How did you find out?"

"The other ghostbusters were at the Poker Face." I looked her up and down. "Is that why you haven't returned Hal's phone call?"

Her cheeks were flaming now. "I made that date with him to try that restaurant three months ago. First I had to cancel, then he did, and when I accepted Larry's invite I completely forgot Hal rescheduled it to this Saturday." She brushed her hand across her forehead. "Things have a way of working out, though, don't they?" She looked longingly at the screen. "Think Hal will like me in that dress?"

"Yes, but I don't see why you need to buy another new one. You have a closet full of clothes that neither Hal nor Peter has seen you in."

Lacey shook her head. "I see why you find it hard to date much," she muttered. "Haven't you ever heard the old saying, 'I've got a closetful of clothes but nothing to wear'?"

"Yes. But you do have a closetful of clothes and plenty to wear. You're just a shopaholic."

"Merow."

Nick poked his head out from underneath the table. I laughed. "See, even Nick agrees."

Lacey stuck her tongue out at the cat. "Traitor," she hissed.

Nick hissed back and disappeared underneath the table.

"I think he's mad at you, Nors," Lacey said. "You know he likes to accompany you on your sleuthing expeditions."

"Yes, well, I went to Kay Trilby's. I'm not sure what her policy is on pets, but after getting a look at the inside of that house, I'd say not taking Nick was a pretty good call."

Lacey let out a low whistle. "Classy, eh?"

"With a capital C."

Lacey rested her chin in both hands. "So? Did you and Ollie figure out who the murderer is yet? Because I'm willing to bet it's not Enola—"

Lacey stopped speaking as we heard a scraping sound, and then three Scrabble tiles came flying out from underneath the table. I picked them up and groaned. "Not these again."

Lacey peered over my shoulder. "T.A.B. Tab?"

"A possibility, but I think it's more like this." I switched them around so they spelled out *bat*. "He's been spelling this out ever since we found that first body and people were talking about Bartescue." I knelt beside the table and lifted the tablecloth. Nick lay sprawled against the wall, one paw resting on the velvet pouch that held his favorite toy. "Nick—get it through your kitty head. There are no such things as vampires. A vampire didn't murder those people. Although from Joshua's description, the perp could be Nosferatu's double. If I recall that old movie, he was bald."

Lacey frowned. "Who's Nos-nos—what you said? And who's Joshua?"

"Nosferatu. He was a vampire in a German horror film from the 1920s. Joshua is Joshua Glennon, Kay Trilby's nephew, and the boy who ran out of the mansion that day. I was right, he did see the killer. Fortunately, it doesn't appear that the killer saw him—or should I say killers? Joshua said there were two people. It's too bad he didn't get a good look at either of them, or I'd ask you to make another sketch for Anderson. Which reminds, me, she might have a job for you."

I thought my sister was going to fall off her chair. "What! Are you serious?"

"As a heart attack. She thought your other sketches were very good, and she said I should tell you to drop off your résumé."

My sister's smile faded, replaced by a frown. "Doesn't the Cruz PD already have a sketch artist?"

I shrugged. "Considering all the changes Anderson's been making lately, who knows? Maybe she wants another one on staff, or maybe the current one is about to be history. In any event, it's something you'd like to do, right? I'm sure you'd prefer that to making sandwiches."

She grinned. "What, and give up my dream job? No offense, Nors, but you know that I'm not half the chef you are."

"I'm pleased you refer to me as a chef," I said teasingly. "Anyway, I'll miss the extra help, but you know I'll support any decision you make."

"If Anderson does hire me, it'd make more sense for me to stay in Cruz," Lacey said thoughtfully.

"You wouldn't have to, if you wanted to go back and live with Aunt Prudence. It's not that far away."

"True, but I've been thinking of getting my own apartment for a while now."

That surprised me. "Really?"

"Sure. Cruz is my hometown, after all, and besides, I like being near Hal."

"Just Hal? What about Peter?"

She blushed. "I like being near him too. Like you said, St. Leo isn't that far away." She tossed me a saucy wink and got up from the table. "I'm going to head over to Macy's. Want to come?"

I shook my head. "I've got a few things to work on. Don't forget about Hal. He told me to tell you he's waiting for your call."

"I will call him when I get back. Anticipation makes the heart grow fonder, right?" She blew me a kiss and a second later I heard her barreling up the stairs.

Actually, it was absence that made the heart grow fonder, which made me think of Daniel. Had his absence made me grow fonder of him? I couldn't say, since I'd been pretty preoccupied, not only with Samms, but with this mystery, but I'd have to give it some thought.

Then again, if I had to think about it, the answer was pretty obvious, right?

I checked my phone for messages. There were none from Hank, so I dialed his number. When his voicemail kicked in, I asked him to check out Tammi Barton. That done, I put my phone down and took out the yellow parchment paper. Nick wriggled out from underneath the table and lofted onto the chair next to me, resting his chin on the table's edge, his golden gaze fixed firmly on the map. I studied the assortment of slashes and lines and sighed.

"One really does need a floor plan of that house to figure out what all this means. There are three floors, and this could be of any one of them.

Besides, Waincroft Manor has so many narrow halls, little unexpected rooms, doors leading into goodness knows where. Without a definite location in mind, it could take weeks, months even, to find the stolen money."

Nick opened his mouth in a yawn so wide I could count the ridges in his mouth.

"Sorry to bore you," I told the cat. I turned my attention back to the map. "What I need is a schematic of Waincroft Manor." I scratched behind my ear. "Where could I possibly get that?"

Nick hopped down from the chair and out of the corner of my eye I saw his black plume of a tail vanish through the doorway that led to my upstairs apartment. A few minutes later I heard a loud *thunk!* and something that sounded like a *thwack!* I got up and hurried over to the stair door.

"Nick!" I cried.

Lying in a heap at the bottom of the staircase were two of Nick Atkins's journals. I kept the journals in a locked drawer of my desk; however, that never seemed to stop my kitty when he wanted me to see something that was in them. One of the journals had landed facedown, spread open. I picked it up and turned it over. Scrawled in Atkins's famous chicken scratch across the top of the page was the notation:

Need to locate original floor plan for historic structure.

"Merow."

I glanced up at the top of the stairs. Nick sat there, tail wrapped around his forepaws, his eyes gleaming. I scanned the page quickly. Apparently one of Nick's clients was claiming that the city had no right to put him out of his building, since it was considered a historic structure. Atkins was in search of the original floor plan that would prove there had been remodeling done, which would not only be against the law in a historic structure, but grounds for a lawsuit. At the bottom of the page he'd scrawled:

City Hall. Building Department.

I slapped my palm against my forehead, feeling more than a bit foolish since I hadn't thought of that myself. I glanced at the clock. Cruz City Hall was open late tonight. I picked up the journals and set them on the bottom stair, then hurried over and stuffed the map into my tote. I walked over to the door and paused, my hand on the knob, and looked at Nick, who'd come down the staircase and was sitting in the entrance to the kitchen, his head cocked.

"Well? Are you coming or not?"

Nick let out a joyful yelp and immediately proceeded to follow me to the SUV.

• • •

Kylie Craig, who'd clerked at City Hall for ages and was one of my loyal customers, was unfortunately not on duty tonight. Instead there was a girl I assumed was a college intern, who looked barely twenty-one, and who was as interested in this job as I was in growing turnips—which is to say, not very. Finally she directed me to an area with microfilm machines and the admonition, "If it's a really, really old building, it might be on here— might being the operative word—but don't count on it."

After an hour and a half I was forced to admit defeat. There were a few floor plans on file, but they were mostly for industrial buildings. There were no records of any residential buildings, whether they were considered of historical value or not. As I was getting ready to leave, I saw a familiar face in the lobby.

"Nan Webb!" I greeted the assistant curator of the Cruz Museum effusively. "What are you doing here?"

"I'm supposed to meet one of the museum patrons here. She's got some old family photos that will be just right for a display the museum is thinking of doing." Nan looked me up and down. "I might say the same about you, Nora. What are you, hot on the trail of another mystery?"

"You might say that. I was trying to find an old floor plan of the Waincroft mansion. I thought maybe the Building Department might have some records, but apparently they don't go back that far."

"The Waincroft mansion? Oh, that's right. The Halloween gala." Nan gave a little shudder. "I'm surprised Kay still wants to have it there, considering all that's happened the past week. I mean, two murders! Everyone's talking about that old legend again and I've got to tell you, there are some who are considering asking for a refund."

I squared my shoulders. "Trust me, a ghost or a vampire isn't responsible for those murders. It's a flesh-and-blood person."

"Regardless, people are leery of the place. Not that anyone was really fond of it to begin with. Which is probably why Kay's so fixated on it. She loves proving people wrong." She looked at me shrewdly. "So what's your interest in all this, aside from the fact it's a juicy mystery?"

"Anderson likes Enola Waincroft for the murders, and I think she's innocent."

Nan's smooth forehead creased in a frown. "Enola Waincroft? Why on earth would Anderson think she had anything to do with any of that? She hasn't lived here in years."

"It's a long story."

"Hmm, I can just imagine. The Waincroft Curse." She made little air quotes around the last two words. "Look, if you really need to get a floor plan of the place, I think I can help you out."

"You can? Don't tell me the museum has one?"

"No—but the Historical Society might. Anders Cullum is on the committee, and he's a good friend of mine. I'll call him right now." She took out her phone and punched in a number. "If I'm not mistaken, they're having a meeting tonight—oh, hello, Anders. Its Nan Webb. Fine, thank you. Yes, it's been awhile. We'll have to do lunch soon. Listen, the reason I'm calling, I've got a friend who needs to see a floor plan of Waincroft Manor, and I thought the Society might have—what's that? Yes, I'll hold." She turned away from the phone and whispered, "He said I'm the second person who called inquiring about a floor plan for Waincroft."

"Really? Who was the other person?"

Nan shrugged and then turned back to the phone. "I'll send her right over. Her name is Nora Charles. Thanks, it was great to talk to you too." Nan rang off and slid her phone back in her pocket. "He said that the meeting doesn't start till seven thirty, so if you can get over there before then, he'll be happy to show you what he has."

"Thanks a lot for this, Nan. I owe you one."

"Great." She beamed at me. "I look forward to collecting."

I hopped into my SUV and drove immediately over to the Cruz Historical Society. Their offices were in a large brick building on Fremont, a quiet street lined with graceful oak trees, enormous mulberry bushes and flowering dogwoods. I found a parking space right in front and hurried up the graveled walkway and through the massive oak double doors into a beautiful, dark-paneled lobby. A woman in a dark blue suit, her grayish frizz of hair bent over a ledger, sat at a massive wood reception desk. She glanced up as I approached. "May I help you?" Her gaze dropped to the ledger, then back to me. "If you're here for the meeting, you're early. It doesn't start until seven thirty."

"Thank you, no, I'm here to see Anders Cullum. Nora Charles."

Her gaze swept me head to toe, and then she picked up the phone and pressed a button. "Mr. Anders? There's a Miss Nora Charles to see you? Oh? Very well then." She set the phone back down and twisted her lips in what I assumed was meant to be a smile. "You can go right on back." She swung her arm in the direction of a long hallway. "Third door on the left."

Anders Cullum was a big teddy bear of a man. His countenance reminded me of a Norman Rockwell Santa Claus. He had the requisite white hair and beard, and his eyes, behind wire-rimmed glasses, twinkled like two stars. His Brooks Brothers suit was well cut, but it couldn't hide his paunch—one that I imagined might well shake like a bowlful of jelly if the man laughed. We exchanged greetings, and then he motioned me over to a beautiful Hepplewhite inlaid desk at the far corner of the room. A rolled bundle of stiff sheets lay on top of it.

"Well, here they are. The original plans for Waincroft Manor."

He picked up the bundle and painstakingly laid them out across the table. There were four sheets in all, and not even paper. They were glazed linen, and the markings on them looked to be in India ink. He caught my gaze and smiled.

"That's how they did 'em back in those days. Architects drew their designs on cartridge paper, which was then traced onto tracing paper or linen using India ink for reproduction. Blueprints weren't used until the 1890s."

"Fascinating." I leaned in for a closer look. The sheets were marked Main Floor, Second Floor, Attic and Basement. I reached into my tote and pulled out the yellowed parchment and unfolded it. I noted Cullum looking at me curiously so I said, "A friend found this at a garage sale." I pointed to the notation in the corner that clearly read "Waincroft Manor." "He was curious as to just what floor this might pertain to."

"May I?"

Cullum took the yellowed paper and held it aloft as he bent over the maps. Finally he pointed to the one in the middle. "Offhand, I'd say it's the first part of the schematic for the main floor. See here." He laid the paper down next to the floor plan and pointed. "You can see where those lines and strokes are almost identical, indicative of the main entryway and hallway leading into the main portion of the house." He leaned over, scrutinizing each paper closely. "It appears to have been cut off in the middle, before the great room and these other back rooms. I'm not an architect, of course, but comparing it to the other drawings, I'd say the main floor is your best bet."

I dipped my hand into my tote, pulled out my iPhone and switched it into camera mode. "Do you mind?" I asked. He shook his head, and I took several pictures, two of the plans for the main floor, and one of each of the others, just in case. I slid my phone back into the tote and offered Cullum my hand. "Thanks. You've been a big help."

He gave my hand a quick squeeze, released it, then cocked his head at me. "I know who you are. You own Hot Bread, true, but you also like to solve mysteries. There was no friend who found that half map was there. You found it. You're trying to solve these murders, aren't you?"

I figured there was no point in lying. "Yes."

He nodded. "Well, I hope you can. I don't have to tell you, these killings have gotten lots of people on edge. There's been talk of many of them pulling out of that benefit, and that would be a shame for the Cruz Youth Center."

"Yes, it would." He handed me back the map and I slid it into my tote. "By the way, I understand someone else was inquiring about these plans?"

Cullum's features arranged themselves into a deep scowl. "Yes. I have to say, I wasn't impressed, not at all. She said that she was a reporter, doing a story on houses with ghostly backgrounds. I'm sorry to say I didn't believe her for one second. I told her the plans had been lost when we moved from our former quarters on Spring Street to here." He scratched his head and his lips twitched. "I'm not sure she believed *me*, though."

It was my turn to frown. "A woman was inquiring? Do you remember what she looked like?"

I braced myself, fully expecting Cullum to describe Enola. Instead he said, "I sure do. Tall, pale skin, long blonde hair with streaks of red. Dressed to the nines, too, in a killer purple outfit. She said her name was Anne Bennington, and she was a reporter for *Upbeat Magazine*." He snorted. "I called and checked. They never heard of her. Like I believed her anyway. A story on ghostly houses would definitely not be *Upbeat Magazine*'s cup of tea." At my puzzled look he added, "The title is misleading, unless you've actually read it. It's a gentleman's magazine. You know, like *Playboy*."

• • •

I'd just settled myself behind the wheel of my SUV when my cell phone rang. I fished it out of my bag, saw Ollie's number and answered with a cheery, "Hey! Find out anything?"

"Oh, yes. That number's listed under Frederick Grey. He specializes in making customized wigs and toupees out of human hair. He just finished a special order for a black toupee a few weeks ago. Guess who his customer was?"

"I'm going to take a wild guess and say—Fred Silverman?"

"Well, actually it was Frederick Silverman. Grey told me they bonded over a discussion on their mutual hatred of their first names. Now, I've told you what's new on my end. How about you?"

"Lots," I replied. "Now I just have to figure out what it all means."

Chapter Twenty-seven

Before I went home, I decided to make a quick stop at the Cruz Inn and look in on Enola. She answered the door almost immediately when I knocked. The first thing I noticed was how pale and wan she looked.

"Hal told me not to worry, but how can I help it?" She sighed. "Someone is framing me, Nora. You must believe me."

I patted her arm. "I do. Try to rest, Enola. We'll get to the bottom of this. One thing I'm sure of: you didn't kill either of those people."

Enola let out a deep sigh. "I think right now you and maybe Hal are the only two in Cruz who feel that way."

"I'm sure there are others who believe in you, too. Tell me, Enola—just where did you put that bag of clothes to be cleaned?"

"Out here." She opened the door and motioned to the corner. "You just put the bag here in the hall and someone from the cleaning staff picks it up. It is supposed to be returned to you within forty-eight hours."

"Do you have another bag you can show me?"

Enola walked over to the hall closet, opened it, and pulled out a thick white bag. She handed it to me, and I looked at it speculatively. There was only a drawstring, no locks or ties to keep the contents secure. I glanced around the hall. No security cameras that I could see. There was nothing to prevent anyone from coming up and removing something from the bag, if they wanted.

"You didn't see anyone lurking around the hall when you put your other bag of cleaning out?" I asked.

Enola's brow puckered for a moment and then she said, "Just the maid."

"The maid?"

"There was a girl standing at the far end of the corridor, behind one of those pushcarts. I assumed she was one of the cleaning staff." She sighed again. "I never got my other clothes back—but what does it matter now? Soon I'll be wearing prison stripes, or do they wear orange now?" She tossed her head. "I look horrid in orange."

I laid my hand on her shoulder. "Chin up and try to stay positive. I've got a feeling this whole mess is going to get cleared up a lot sooner than you think."

• • •

I pulled into my driveway and went inside the rear entrance that led up to my apartment. Once there, I went into my den and immediately flopped into my leather recliner. I leaned back and closed my eyes.

Thwack! I grunted as a heavy weight landed square on my chest. I opened my eyes and stared into Nick's golden ones. He lay sprawled across my chest, his slightly extended claws digging into my shoulders.

"Nick, watch it. You aren't exactly a lightweight, you know."

He stared at me through unblinking golden eyes.

I reached around and grasped his middle as I lightly disengaged his claws from my shoulders. Then I snuggled him to my chest and kissed the back of his furry neck. "Oh, Nick. It's all here, I just know it, but for some reason the answer is eluding me."

Nick purred loudly, then dug his front claws into the front of my shirt. I released him and he jumped down and pranced over to the far corner of the den. He deepened his purr and curled up into a tight furry ball.

I pulled out the whiteboard that I kept next to my desk, set it on the chair, then pulled a Magic Marker from the desk drawer. I drew a square in the center of the whiteboard and labeled it "Manny Delgado." Beneath that square I drew another and labeled that one "Hannah Berger."

"Okay. Here we have the two victims. What's the common denominator?"

Over to the right I wrote "Lawton Biggs." Underneath that I wrote "Fred Silverman."

"Lawton Biggs had one half of what I'll call the treasure map, the directions to where the robbery money was hidden. Fred Silverman had the other half. I'm going to take a guess that they planned to meet after a decent interval to collect the money, but Lawton took ill and died before that could happen." I tapped the Magic Marker against my palm. "So why didn't Silverman show up sooner?" I wrote that question out next to Silverman's name. Then I moved over to the left side of the squares and wrote "Enola Waincroft."

"Enola had interaction with both victims. She spoke with Manny on the phone regarding Waincroft's architecture, or at least that's what she says. And she and Hannah flat out hated each other."

I nibbled at my lower lip. Hannah and Enola had hated each other, all right, but enough to kill? And Enola really had no motive to kill Manny, unless—and this was really stretching it—she knew the money was hidden in Waincroft Manor and wanted his half of the map.

I wrote down another name: Anne Bennington. Aka Tammi Barton? She was the one inquiring about Waincroft's floor plan. Why? And why use an alias?

Nick rotated one and a half times, settled at my feet, and started purring.

"The other ghostbusters said she had a degree in pharmacology," I muttered. "She might have enough medical knowledge to drain a body of blood, but if she's the one who did it, why?" I nibbled at my lower lip for a few minutes and then raised a finger in the air. "Maybe the exsanguination was meant to be nothing more than a ploy? I've been trying to think why the ghostbusters would turn up here so conveniently. Maybe they were supposed to be used as a diversion, to support the legend of Bartescue and keep people away from the mansion. Everyone, that is, except our killer. He wanted the mansion all to himself, to look for that missing money."

Nick sat straight up, raised one paw in the air. "Er-owl!"

I started to pace back and forth. "Silverman ordered a toupee from that wigmaker. He's probably somewhere here in Cruz, in disguise. He called Hannah at the school—I'm sure he's the SS from her note—and she probably confronted him, threatened to expose him. So he killed her with Enola's scarf, hoping to put the blame on her—wait, wait." I scrubbed my hands over my face. "Enola said she saw a young woman hanging around her floor that day. If it was Tammi, she could easily have lifted the scarf from the laundry bag to plant on Hannah's body."

I flopped back down in my recliner. I was close, I could feel it. I just had to iron out a few kinks in my theory. Well, okay, more than a few kinks. I reached over, snagged my tote, and fished out my cell phone. A few minutes later I had a nice printout of the photograph I'd taken of the first floor schematic of Waincroft Manor. I whipped out the parchment map and compared the two. I had to agree with Cullum—it certainly looked as if the first floor was where Lawton had decided to stash the loot.

Now if I could only find his half, with the directions as to just where he'd secreted it!

My phone buzzed, and I saw Al Bennett's number pop up on screen. I snatched at the phone eagerly. "Hello?"

"Good news and bad," Al said. "The good news is, of course Harvey had a comprehensive listing of the effects found on John Doe's person. The bad news is, he gave the whole bundle to the FBI when they picked up the body."

I let out a long sigh. "Great."

"However," Al continued, "my brother-in-law is nothing if not obsessive when it comes to stuff like that. He took photographs of each and every item on his digital camera." A pause. "A camera he just happened to leave here when he was over for dinner last night."

If Al had been in front of me, I would have grabbed him and kissed him right on the lips. "I don't suppose you can send me copies of those photos?"

"I could. Of course, you'd have to swear to secrecy, because if he ever finds out, he'll surely either fire me or kill me."

"Cross my heart."

"And I think this finding is worth at least another month's worth of free lunches. Maybe even two."

"Get those photos here in the next five minutes and I'll give you three."

"Hey, what about if you get them right now?"

My phone pinged. Sure enough, there was an email from Al with six attachments. "Okay, you win. Six months' worth," I cried.

A beat and then: "I was hoping for a year."

"Don't press your luck."

"Hey, a guy's gotta try."

I hung up from Al and opened the photos, one by one. After I'd opened the last one, I let out a long sigh.

No map, which pretty much confirmed my suspicion about Manny ditching it somewhere inside Waincroft Manor. I was pretty sure, though, Silverman wouldn't let that little detail deter him. He'd most likely rip the whole edifice apart until he found the money.

Which meant I had to find it first.

My phone buzzed again and this time Hal Prince's number popped up. I answered it quickly. "I hope this is good news."

"Me too. Okay, you asked for anything I could find on Fred Silverman, so here goes: He started out as Frederick E. Howell, with a nice little rap sheet starting from when he was a teen. Small robberies, then he graduated to petty larceny, did a short stretch in prison for grand larceny. Got out, changed his name to Frederick Silverman—his mother's maiden name— and managed to get himself hired as a guard at the First National Bank. Apparently at the time he was hired they were undergoing some personnel issues, so they didn't do stringent background checks. He disappeared shortly after that big armed car robbery, turned up a few months later in need of cash, so he held up a bank and got caught. Spent two years in California Department of Corrections and Rehabilitation, got out about a year ago for good behavior, but he never made his first visit with his parole officer. Dropped out of sight, and no one's seen hide nor hair of him since. Apparently Silverman's pretty good at covering his tracks." He paused. "The FBI thought of him immediately for that heist, by the way, but they couldn't turn up any concrete evidence linking him to the crime."

"Sounds like he covered his tracks pretty well there too. How about Tammi Barton?"

"No rap sheet, no record of criminal activity. She graduated USC with a degree in pharmacology, worked at a local pharmacy for a while in Santa Ana and then took a job working in the medical office at CDCR."

"The same prison where Fred Silverman was incarcerated," I cried. "An amazing coincidence, wouldn't you say?" I knew Hank felt the same way about coincidence that I did—that there were none. "What's the time frame?"

"She was employed there when he first went to CDCR, but she quit her job a few months after he was released. Apparently they were chummy during his incarceration. The police watched her for a while, but she didn't contact Silverman or vice versa. She hooked up with those ghostbusters, been working with them ever since. Quite a switch from being a pharmacology major, eh?" I could hear him shuffling papers in the background.

"By the way, any chance you know an Anne Bennington?"

"Anne Bennington? No . . . although Bennington is Tammi's mother's maiden name."

"Another coincidence," I murmured.

"Maybe. Do you want me to keep digging?"

"No, thanks, you've been a big help. I'll see you soon, right?"

"Count on it."

I hung up, more convinced than ever that Tammi Barton was a part of all this—after all, she had medical knowledge. Joshua had said he'd seen two hooded figures. I was willing to bet Tammi was the second, the one responsible for draining Manny's body of blood. I rose from my chair and stretched. The whys and wherefores of all this would have to wait for now. The most important thing was to find that money before Silverman and Tammi did. Silverman had to be around here somewhere, in disguise. If I could only figure out where . . .

I reached into my tote's zippered compartment where I'd stashed the photo of Lawton and Silverman and let out a gasp of dismay. My ballpoint pen had burst, and ink was spattered across the top of the photo. I fished it out carefully and let out a groan. A nice blob of black now covered Silverman's bald pate and the top of Lawton's curly hair. I squinted at the photo and something clicked in my brain. I pulled open the desk drawer, whipped out another pen, and worked on turning the black blob on Silverman's head into something resembling a thick mass of hair. When I'd finished I sat back to survey my handiwork. Darned if Silverman didn't look a lot like . . .

Another memory came flooding back, a memory of a chance remark that at the time hadn't registered, but had remained in my subconscious, probably because I'd known, deep down, that something wasn't quite right. My eyes flew open and I turned to look at Nick.

"Come on, buddy. We can't waste any more time. We're going on a treasure hunt."

Chapter Twenty-eight

Nick and I piled into my SUV, and I thanked Providence that few people were acquainted with the circuitous route that took me to the back door of Waincroft Manor. I cut the lights as I maneuvered the SUV down the graveled path and nodded in satisfaction as I noticed there were no other vehicles anywhere around. I parked behind a clump of bushes, in almost exactly the same spot where I'd seen Hannah's car that day. I tried not to think about it as Nick and I hurried up the back steps and tried the door that led to the kitchen.

Locked. Damn.

I tried the windows on either side of the door. They were locked too. I debated getting a rock and breaking one of the windows when I heard a sharp "Merow" from the other side of the porch. I followed the sound and saw Nick sitting on a windowsill. The window was wide open. I didn't think twice, just climbed inside, Nick beside me, and took a quick look around as I brushed myself off. I'd brought a mini-flashlight with me, and I flicked it on. The room I found myself in was small, and the floor was laid in an intricate pattern of squares of highly polished wood. I looked at the floor. "Hm, if some of these squares are loose, maybe there's a cavity or something underneath that might make a good hiding place, what do you think, Nick?"

Nick turned around twice and stretched out. I immediately dropped to my knees and started examining every inch of the space, running my fingertips along the edges of each square in the pattern and along all the cracks. I was just about to give up when one of the polished blocks suddenly moved under my touch. It lifted up easily, revealing an opening below.. I turned my head slightly and saw Nick watching me. He gave me a long, slow blink.

"Yeah, I know. It seems too easy, doesn't it?" Still, I thrust my hand into the opening. My fingers touched something stiff, and I pulled on it. It didn't budge. "Stuck," I muttered. I grasped the object harder and gave it a good yank. I landed backward right on my derriere, and I looked at what I held in my hand. A yellowed piece of paper, folded into a tight square. My heart was pounding so loudly I could barely breathe as I carefully unfolded the paper. I felt the jagged edge before I saw it, and I couldn't suppress the delighted squeal that rose to my lips as I unfolded the missing map half.

"Not the money, Nick, but the next best thing."

I scrabbled in my tote and pulled out the other half of the map, put them side by side. Sure enough there was a large X on one of the lines on Lawton's half of the map. I pulled out the printout of the schematic of the mansion's main floor and pored over it. The mark appeared to be in the main room, where both the bodies had been found.

"Figures," I said to Nick, tucking the papers under my arm. Together we moved into the hallway and walked the few steps to the great room. I spread the map out on the floor. The X appeared to be drawn across a large built-in floor-to-ceiling bookcase at the far end of the room. Leaving the map on the floor, I walked over to the bookcase and examined it closely. I'd leafed through that book on architecture, and I remembered reading that some old mansions had secret rooms built into them to hide slaves. The entrances could be hidden behind large pieces of furniture—like a bookcase. This bookcase was bare of books, which made searching it somewhat easier. I ran my fingers up and down and along the top and bottom of each shelf, pressing against the grain of the wood. Finally, on the next-to-last shelf, my questing fingers touched a hunk of metal—a button or lever of some kind. I pressed down on it and heard a sharp click, followed by a loud, grinding noise. The whole bookcase groaned and then slowly moved inward, revealing a dark hole beyond. "Wow, how do you like that, Nick? Nick?"

I glanced around the room. Nick was nowhere to be seen.

"Great. You wander off now?" I hesitated, torn between finding out what was in the dark aperture and hunting down my wayward kitty. Deciding that Nick could take care of himself, I moved forward, but I'd barely taken two steps when the toe of my shoe touched something rough and stiff. I bent over to pick it up, then slowly backed out into the main room to look at my prize. Clutched in my hand was a thick burlap bag. The words *First National Bank* were emblazoned on its side. I lay the bag down on the floor and pulled at the strings. Piles of tightly bound hundred-dollar bills spilled out. I got up, walked back to the hole and felt around again. Twenty minutes later, I had three sacks chock-full of money spread out on the floor in front of me. I had to admit, it was a pretty good hiding place. "Hey, Nick," I called. "Get in here and see what we've found." I reached over to grab my tote. "Who should I call first, Samms or Anderson?"

"Neither, Ms. Charles."

My head snapped around and I saw a dark caped figure emerge from a door all the way over on the other side of the room. I caught a flash of blue steel and knew he carried a gun. I rocked back on my heels and looked him square in the eyes as he approached me.

"Hello, Ethan. Or would you rather I call you Fred?"

Ethan let out a low chuckle and lowered his hood. Moonlight streamed in from the large picture window and highlighted his bald pate. "Either is fine," he said with a shrug. "How long have you known?"

"Not long. Today, actually," I admitted. "You see, my pen burst and covered your head in that photograph with black ink. That wigmaker did an excellent job, by the way."

Ethan's lips twisted into a sneer. "Clever girl."

"Then I remembered something else, something you said to Enola and Joannie in my shop. That they should give Hannah a break, it was tough to lose a sibling. There was no way you could have known Lawton was Hannah's brother, unless . . ."

"I knew Lawton. Ah, it's always the little slips that come back to haunt you, am I right?"

I looked at the pile of bills on the floor. "It must have been frustrating for you when you discovered Manny'd ripped the map in half."

Ethan's upper lip curled. "Frustrating doesn't even begin to cover it. He deserved to die for that alone." He bent down, picked up a packet of bills, fingered it. "All this money is quite a sight, isn't it? And since poor Lawton is no longer with us, it's all mine now."

"You mean ours."

I glanced up. Tammi had appeared, walking so softly on thick-soled sneakers I hadn't heard her. Neither had Ethan, apparently, because I saw him cringe slightly as he turned to face her. "Of course, ours, my dear," he said smoothly. "You were a big help in all this, after all. Draining that poor man of his entire blood supply, just so we might persuade people a vampire was responsible for his death." He chuckled and in the pale moonlight I had to agree with Joshua—the man looked positively sinister. "I am, of course, familiar with the legend of this house. Lawton certainly talked about it enough. I felt at times as if I actually lived here, so when Tammi suggested bringing the legend to life, so to speak, I was on board."

I slid my gaze to Tammi. "That was your idea?"

She thrust her chest out proudly. "Yep. I thought maybe people might start to think there was something to that legend and keep their distance. We didn't count on the road flooding out, or that detective being so hard-nosed, or Kay Trilby not being interested at all in hiring our paranormal services. What sort of person wants to hold a gala in a house where such a horrific murder was committed anyway? One thing she was good for, though, was getting the police out of here pretty quick." She jabbed her thumb at her companion. "And then Ethan here had to go and kill Hannah and complicate things more."

"She recognized me," Ethan muttered. "She'd only met me once, but there was something about my eyes, she said, that she always remembered. She tracked me down through that wigmaker, and she was furious with me for dragging Lawton into my scheme, as she put it. Hey, I told her no one held a gun to his head. He was more than willing to help me plan that heist. He needed his half to settle his gambling debts so he wouldn't lose the family house. She told me that I wasn't getting any money, that she was going to tear that house apart until she found it and returned it. I was going back to prison if I had anything to say about it. What else could I do but kill her?"

I looked at Tammi. "You stole Enola's scarf, didn't you?"

"Ethan wanted me to keep an eye on her. He knew she'd ordered that coffin we found, because he'd seen her come out of the funeral parlor and he recognized her from a photo Lawton had shown him. He figured we could use her as a patsy. That bloodstained scarf was a real bonus."

I glanced down at Tammi's feet and saw two red gasoline cans. "What are they for?"

Ethan laughed hollowly. "Once we found the money, we intended to make sure there could be absolutely no way it could ever be traced back to us. This building is an old eyesore anyway. We'll be doing the community a favor." He reached out to chuck me under my chin. "Unfortunately, there will be one casualty. Possibly two, if your cat is still hanging around here."

My tongue snaked out, slicked across my lower lip. "Come on now, think about what you're doing. You don't want to add arson and another murder to your list of crimes, do you?"

I heard a distinct click, like the hammer going back on a gun, and then I felt something jab into the small of my back—hard.

"In for a penny, in for a pound, I say," Tammi hissed in my ear. "Now be a good girl and throw your cell phone on the floor."

I reached into my pocket, removed my cell, laid it down on the floor. Tammi reached out and snatched it up, jammed it into the pocket of her black robe. "Now raise your hands above your head. *Do it*," she yelled as I hesitated.

I raised my hands, slowly, my eyes darting around the darkened room. Still no Nick.

Ethan pulled a length of rope out of the folds of the voluminous cape he wore. He stepped forward, jerked my hands down in front of me and started to tie them up. Tammi stood off to one side, the gun still pointed right at my chest.

"So," I croaked out. "What's your plan?"

"To tie up loose ends, and then catch a plane bound for Costa Rica." Ethan finished tying my hands and then he bent down, started scooping the money up and stuffing it back into the burlap sacks. "I'm sorry, Ms. Charles. Joannie told me you were rather a bit of a snoop that liked solving mysteries, but I confess I underestimated you. And since you are involved with not one but two FBI men, and I'm more than a blip on their radar, I can't leave you alive to start blabbing to them."

"They know I'm working on this," I said. "Samms will figure it out, and he'll come after you."

Ethan let out a deep chuckle. "The FBI has been 'working on' finding me for years now, and they've never been able to make anything stick. And even if your friend Samms does figure it out, by then I'll be far, far away, in a foreign country. Untouchable. And you, my dear, will be ashes."

Tammi glared at him over the rim of the gun. "You mean *we'll* be far away, right, Ethan?"

He finished putting the last of the money into the sacks and stood up. He crossed over to Tammi and bent down, gave her a quick peck on the cheek. "Of course, my dear." He pulled more rope out of his cape and motioned to me. "Sit."

I sat down on the floor, and Ethan bound my ankles. Then he dragged me over beneath the window. "It won't be long now. Hopefully the smoke inhalation will kill you long before the flames start to lick and tear at your flesh." He turned to Tammi and held out his hand. "Give me the gun."

She wheeled on him, fire in her eye. "Why? So you can shoot me and keep all the money for yourself? I didn't go through all this, uproot my life for the last two years, to get tossed aside like yesterday's trash."

"Would I do that to you?" Ethan said soothingly.

"In a heartbeat," snarled Tammi.

Ethan's arm snaked out, wrenched the gun from Tammi's grasp. His other arm grabbed her around the middle and spun her around. "You're right," he hissed, and then he clocked her on the side of the head with the gun. Tammi let out a low moan and slumped to the floor. Ethan quickly tied her hands and ankles and dragged her over, propped her up next to me. Then he picked up the two cans of gasoline, walked over to the far side of the room and started to spill them around. When he was finished, he stood in the doorway. "I need a bit more gasoline. But don't worry, I'll be back to say goodbye."

He kicked the gas cans out into the hall and then walked over and picked up the sacks of money. Then he walked out, leaving me and Tammi alone in the dark, the smell of gasoline permeating our nostrils.

"Nick!" I hissed into the darkness. "Nick, where are you?"

No merow answered me. I struggled with the cords that bound my wrists, but they were far too tight and threatened to cut off my circulation, although that was probably the least of my worries. I sat in silence for a few minutes, and then the quiet was shattered by a loud *bang!* I strained my ears. Was that the sound of scuffling feet?

Suddenly the door blew open and a slight figure stood framed in the doorway.

"Joshua!" I cried. "I thought I told you to stay away from here."

"I know. I just had a feeling, though, that I should come here." The boy leapt over the mass of gasoline and hurried over. He pulled a pocketknife out of his pocket and started to work on my ropes. "I saw him, outside. Baldy. He has a truck loaded with gasoline parked up the hill. I figured something was up, so the minute I saw him disappear down the trail I came right inside."

That explained why I hadn't seen another vehicle. "Hurry," I urged the teen. "We've got to get out of here before he gets back, and we've got to find my cat."

"Is he a big guy, black and white?" Joshua motioned with his chin toward the window. "He's right outside on the porch. I saw him pacing around, and when he saw me he raised his paw and pointed to the window, so I figured someone might be in here."

Joshua cut through the last bit of rope and then started to work on my ankles. My wrists were freed, but my left hand was asleep. I started to flex them and wiggle them around in an effort to get the blood flowing again. After a few seconds Joshua had my ankles free and he took my arm and helped me up. I stood, wobbled a bit, and then plunked back down on the floor.

"I'll be okay." I waved Joshua away. "Just give me a minute." I inclined my head toward Tammi. "We can't leave her here, but she's out cold."

"No problem. She doesn't look very heavy." Joshua had her up and thrown across his shoulders, fireman style, in a matter of seconds. "Let's get out of here. Oh, great."

From the expression on his face, I knew whatever he'd seen wasn't good. I peered over his shoulder out the window and saw what had captured his attention—Ethan had returned with more gas cans and was sprinkling them all around the front entrance.

"We haven't got much time," I said, and then a burst of light made me stop, peer once more out the window. The entire front entrance was a wall of flame.

"Oh, no." I hurried back over and peered out into the corridor. A cloud of thick black smoke hit me in the face. I coughed and staggered back, gasping and wheezing.

Joshua was looking around the room. "Can't make it out this window. The flames are already spreading."

Joshua set Tammi down and leaned out the window. "Looks like the flames haven't reached the left side of the house yet. If we could get out that way . . ."

"Wait!"

I crossed over to the front of the bookcase, where the maps were still spread out on the floor. I picked up the copy of the original schematic and pointed. "See this, right behind the X? Doesn't it look like a corridor?"

Joshua peered over my shoulder. "It does, but how—" His eyes lit up as he saw what was behind the bookcase. "Oh—it's got to be behind there. And from the looks of this map, it extends all the way to the outside—if it's accurate."

"At this point, it's the best chance we have. Let's go."

Flames, deep and red, were now sprouting up closer. Joshua slung Tammi over his shoulder and we moved forward into the room. My mini-flashlight cut a wide swath of light as we inched our way along a long corridor. I let out a cry as the beam of light showed what looked to be a door at the very end. We hurried over, and I held my breath and grasped the handle. It turned, and we spilled out onto the back porch. We glanced up. The entire side of Waincroft Manor was covered in flames now. I ran onto the grassy knoll, Joshua following at a slower pace with Tammi. He tossed her down like she was a sack of meal and flopped down beside me.

Together we watched as the roof of Waincroft Manor crashed inward in a mass of flames. The walls popped out next, and then the whole structure crashed inward upon itself. I watched the curling smoke, the licking flames, and let out a deep breath. The wail of a police siren could be heard in the distance, accompanied by the whine of a fire engine. And out of the darkness strode Nick, his black plume of a tail swishing to and fro. He walked calmly up to me, butted his head against my arm. I pulled him onto my lap and buried my nose in his ruff. He looked at me. "Merow."

"I'm glad you're okay too," I said.

Nick gave my head a butt, and then his pink tongue darted out, swiped against the tip of my nose.

"Aunt Kay will be a wreck," Joshua observed, in the matter-of-fact manner only a teenage boy has. "She really wanted to have that gala here."

Chapter Twenty-nine

"Here's to another close call for our Nora!"

Ollie, Chantal, Lacey, Hal Frey, Enola and I were all grouped around the table in the rear of my kitchen at Hot Bread the following afternoon. After my harrowing experience the evening before, I'd closed Hot Bread for the day and slept until noon, something I've done about twice in my life. Chantal and Lacey had both managed to put together a scrumptious lunch of chicken gumbo, lobster salad on a bed of lettuce, and spiced shrimp with beans, three of my favorite dishes. Now as we all sat back, fat, sassy and happy, as the saying goes, Chantal broke out a bottle of sparkling cider for a toast.

Ollie looked at me above the rim of his fluted glass. "You took some chance, Nora."

"If I hadn't, Ethan, or rather Silverman, might have found the money, killed Tammi and gotten away. He was determined to get it no matter what."

Hal leaned forward. "I understand they caught him running across the field. Someone took the battery out of his truck."

My lips curved into a smile. "Joshua did that. He told me he dialed 911 on his cell, too, just before he went in the house, but his battery died just as the operator answered. I'm sure he's the reason the police got there so quickly."

Ollie chuckled. "He's a rather bright boy. If Kay can put him on the straight and narrow, he'll end up being a huge success someday."

I laughed. "Oh, I have no doubt Kay will make sure her nephew gets in with a good crowd. I wouldn't be surprised if she convinces her sister to let him live with her. If she does, though, she's going to have to give him a lot more freedom than she has." I took a sip of my cider. "How did Kay take the news about Waincroft Manor?"

"A lot better than anyone thought." Chantal laughed. "She immediately called Nan Webb and booked the Museum's Red Room for the Halloween gala. Told her that it was a 'classier venue' anyway."

"Is it heartless of me to say I'm glad the family mansion is no more?" Enola asked. "It was never anything but trouble, and I hate to admit it, but Silverman was right. It was an eyesore. I thought I'd donate the insurance money to the Cruz Youth Center. I make more than enough to live on with my curio shop, after all. I'd like to know something good came out of that mansion."

I beamed at her. "I'm sure the kids will be very grateful to you. That's a wonderful idea, Enola."

There was a knock at the back door, and my sister jumped up to admit Samms. He nodded at everyone, then slid into an empty chair next to Hal. "How are you feeling today, Nora?" he asked. "All recovered from your heroics of last night?"

"I'm not the hero of this piece," I said. "It's Joshua, and Nick of course."

"All's well that ends well," Ollie quoted, raising his cider glass. He looked at Samms over the rim. "So, I imagine you got a confession out of old Fred/Ethan, right?"

Samms nodded. "Oh, yeah. He was a bit reluctant at first, but when his girlfriend woke up and started singing, he broke down." His gaze locked on mine. "It was pretty much like you figured it, Red. Silverman planned the robbery down to the last detail, but he needed some inside help at ArmLink with the driver's schedule, and it wasn't hard to make friends with Lawton. All he had to do was listen, as he put it, ad nauseum to the history of Waincroft Manor. He saw right away Lawton was interested in making a quick buck, so he introduced him to gambling, and the rest just fell into place.

"Lawton was in charge of hiding the money. He convinced Silverman that Waincroft Manor was the perfect place, and he'd hide it where no one would find it. He made the map, but before he could contact Silverman he was diagnosed with terminal cancer and died shortly thereafter. In the meantime, Silverman was getting desperate. He hadn't heard from Lawton, and he started to think he'd been double-crossed. He wanted to track Lawton down, but he needed money so he robbed a small bank, got sloppy and got caught."

"How did he hook up with Tammi?" asked Chantal.

"The pharmacy where she worked closed, so she took a job at the prison. She and Silverman got chummy there. He had a good line and she fell for it, thought it was exciting, stealing all that money. She found out Lawton died, and then the two of them started making their plans. She thought it was a good idea, right from the start, to make it seem as if the legend of Waincroft Manor was more than that. Grant's cousin also worked at the prison as a guard. She made friends with him, told him that her lifelong ambition was to hunt down ghosts. He in turn recommended her to

Grant for a job, so she left the prison and hooked up with them. It was an easy matter for her to convince Grant to put her on the team, especially once she came up with the idea of faking that ghost at the lighthouse."

"I thought that video looked faked," I said. "Did the others know?"

Samms shook his head. "Just her and Grant. According to Goodeve, they had to do something to stay in business. Anyway, while she was laying the foundation, Silverman was making sure he played the model inmate so he'd be granted parole. He got out, laid low for a while, changed his name to Ethan Howell and covered his tracks pretty darn well."

"Poor Manny," observed Ollie. "He never stood a chance."

"No," Samms agreed, "he didn't. Silverman had been watching Hannah, waiting for a chance to snoop and find the map. They'd pretty much decided they were going to get that money come hell or high water, but Silverman figured if he could find the map it'd go a lot faster. He saw Manny take it, and he followed him and heard him on the phone with me. So he made a quick call to Tammi and they put their plan into action. They followed Manny to the mansion, intending to jump him, take the map, then kill him and drain his body, but Manny figured out he was being followed and ditched the half of the map that revealed the money's location. According to Tammi, she wanted to torture the location out of Manny, but Silverman lost his temper and whacked him over the head with a poker. That coffin that Enola had delivered to the mansion fit right in with their plans. They figured worst-case scenario they'd try and pin it on her."

"As usual, the best-laid plans," I said. "I can't exactly say I feel sorry for either one of them."

Ollie scraped his chair back. "Well, we'd better let you get some rest. After all, you'll be a busy woman tomorrow, answering everyone's questions about what happened."

"Ssh, Ollie," hissed Chantal. "I haven't shown her the paper yet."

I rolled my eyes. "Swell."

Nick leapt up onto my lap and butted my chin with his head. I wrapped my arms around him as Ollie, Chantal, Lacey, Enola and Hal slowly filed out my back door, leaving me alone at the table with Samms. He leaned over and gave me a good, hard kiss on the lips.

"You sure put a scare into me," he murmured.

"I put one into myself," I admitted. "Thank God the architect who designed Waincroft Manor put that secret room behind the bookcase with an exit leading out." He grasped my hand. "Are you up to going out tomorrow night? We can always cancel."

"On *Phantom*? Not on your life. It'll put me in the mood for that Halloween gala next week—speaking of which, the committee still has to decorate the Red Room."

Samms chuckled. "Good luck with that."

A scraping sound caught my attention and I looked down. Nick squatted there, his paw over three Scrabble tiles. I chuckled, knowing full well which ones they were. I picked them up and laid them on the table. "B-A-T," I said. "I guess you really wanted a vampire to be responsible, eh, Nick?"

Samms frowned. "Are you sure that's what he means? I think if your cat was trying to tell you a vampire was responsible, he'd have spelled out vampire."

I arched my brow. "You do have a point," I admitted. "But there's not much you can spell with those letters. Bat, of course, and tab are the only ones that come to mind."

Samms reached over and moved the tiles around so they spelled out T-A-B. "TAB. Tammi Barton's middle name is Anne, so this could stand for her name—Tammi Anne Barton." He barked out a laugh. "How do you like that? Your cat knew who was guilty right along. He was spelling out the killer's initials."

I looked at Nick. Nick looked back at me.

And then he blinked. Twice.

From Nora's Recipe Book

Ollie's Honest to Goodness Hotcake Sandwich

1 tablespoon milk
2 eggs
2 slices cheese, any kind
2 slices ham, any kind
3 strips of bacon
Sausage link or patty
Frozen waffle (2) or pancakes (2)

Mix milk and eggs, pour into hot pan.

Add cheese and ham.

In separate pan, fry bacon and sausage.

Toast the defrosted waffles, then put omelet between them.

Put bacon or sausage (or both!) on side.

You can substitute pancakes for the waffles.

Serve with butter and syrup.

Nora's Coconut-Banana Delight Smoothie

1 cup of assorted frozen cut fruit: banana, mango, pineapple, peaches
1 can of coconut water
1 cup ice cubes
1 cup coconut yogurt, regular or Greek

Combine all ingredients in blender and pulse on high for 3–4 minutes or until contents liquefied.

Tip: For a dessert you can eat with a spoon, add extra ice and pulse for 1–2 minutes.

Nora's Halloween Mummy Franks

1 can crescent rolls
3 slices cheese
12 hot dogs
Mustard and/or ketchup

Preheat oven to 375.

Cut rolls into rectangles, then cut into 12 pieces lengthwise.

Cut cheese slices into quarters.

Wrap four pieces of dough and 1/3 cheese slice around hot dog to look like
a bandage.

Put on greased cookie sheet, cheese-side down.

Bake 13–15 minutes or until dough is golden brown.

Pour mustard and ketchup into ramekins and serve.

About the Author

While Toni LoTempio does not commit—or solve—murders in real life, she has no trouble doing it on paper. Her lifelong love of mysteries began early on when she was introduced to her first Nancy Drew mystery at age ten—*The Secret in the Old Attic*. She and her cat pen the Nick and Nora Mysteries, the Urban Tails Pet Shop Mysteries, and the Cat Rescue Mysteries. Catch up with them at Rocco's blog, catsbooksmorecats.blogspot.com, or her website, tclotempio.net.